The silent sister veiled in white and blue
Between the yews, behind the garden god,
Whose flute is breathless, bent her head
  and sighed but spoke no word

T. S. Eliot, ASH WEDNESDAY

BOOKS FOR YOUNG ADULTS BY RICK YANCEY

THE
EXTRAORDINARY
ADVENTURES
OF
ALFRED KROPP

RICK YANCEY

BLOOMSBURY

NEW YORK LONDON OXFORD NEW DELHI SYDNEY

To Sandy

And—naturally—for the boys,
Jonathan, Joshua & Jacob

First published in the United States of America in October 2005
by Bloomsbury Children's Books
New paperback edition published in December 2015
www.bloomsbury.com

Bloomsbury is a registered trademark of Bloomsbury Publishing Plc

For information about permission to reproduce selections from this book, write to
Permissions, Bloomsbury Children's Books, 1385 Broadway, New York, New York 10018
Bloomsbury books may be purchased for business or promotional use. For information on bulk
purchases please contact Macmillan Corporate and Premium Sales Department at
specialmarkets@macmillan.com

Excerpt from "Ash Wednesday" from COLLECTED POEMS 1909–1962 by T. S. Eliot,
copyright 1936 by Harcourt, Inc., copyright © 1930 and renewed 1958 by T. S. Eliot,
reprinted by permission of the publisher.

The Library of Congress has cataloged the hardcover edition as follows:
Yancey, Richard.
The extraordinary adventures of Alfred Kropp / by Rick Yancey. — 1st U.S. ed.
p.   cm.
Summary: Through a series of dangerous and violent misadventures, teenage loser Alfred
Kropp rescues King Arthur's legendary sword Excalibur from the forces of evil.
ISBN-13: 978-1-58234-693-9 • ISBN-10: 1-58234-693-3 (hardcover)
[1. Adventure and adventurers—Fiction. 2. Arthur, King—Fiction.
3. Orphans—Fiction.] I. Title.
PZ7.Y19197Ext 2005   [Fic]—dc22   2005013044

ISBN 978-1-61963-916-4 (new edition) • ISBN 978-1-59990-412-2 (e-book)

Printed and bound in USA by Berryville Graphics Inc., Berryville, Virginia
3 5 7 9 10 8 6 4

All papers used by Bloomsbury Publishing, Inc., are natural, recyclable products
made from wood grown in well-managed forests. The manufacturing processes
conform to the environmental regulations of the country of origin.

1

I never thought I would save the world—
or die saving it. I never believed in angels or miracles either,
and I sure didn't think of myself as a hero. Nobody would
have, including you, if you had known me before I took the
world's most powerful weapon and let it fall into the hands
of a lunatic. Maybe after you hear my story you won't think
I'm much of a hero anyway, since most of my heroics (if you
want to call them that) resulted from my being a screwup. A
lot of people died because of *me*—including *me*—but I guess
I'm getting ahead of myself and I'd better start from the
beginning.

It began with my uncle Farrell wanting to be rich. He never had much money growing up and, by the time Mr. Arthur Myers came along with his once-in-a-lifetime deal, my uncle was forty years old and sick of being poor. Being poor isn't one of those things you get used to, even if being poor is all you've ever been. So when Mr. Myers flashed the cash, all other considerations—like if any of it was legal, for instance—were forgotten. Of course, Uncle Farrell had no way of knowing who Mr. Arthur Myers actually was, or that his name wasn't even Arthur Myers.

But I'm getting ahead of myself again. Maybe I should just start with me.

I was born in Salina, Ohio, the first and last child of Annabelle Kropp. I never knew my dad. He took off before I was born.

Mom's pregnancy was difficult and very long. She was almost ten and a half months along when the doctor decided to get me the heck out of there before I exploded from her stomach like some kind of alien hatchling.

I was born big and just kept getting bigger. At birth, I weighed over twelve pounds and my head was about the size of a watermelon. Okay, maybe not the size of a watermelon, but definitely as big as a cantaloupe—one of those South American cantaloupes, which is a lot bigger than your California variety.

By the time I was five, I weighed over ninety pounds and stood four feet tall. At ten, I hit six feet and two hundred pounds. I was off the pediatrician's growth chart. Mom was pretty worried by that point. She put me on special diets and started me on an exercise program.

Because of my large head, big hands and feet, and my general shyness, a lot of people assumed I was mentally handicapped. Mom must have been worried about that too, because she had my IQ tested. She never told me the results. When I asked her, she said I most definitely was not. "You're just a big boy meant for big things," she said.

I believed her. Not the part about being meant for big things, but the part about me not being retarded, since I never saw my scores and it was one of those things where you have to believe that your parent isn't lying.

We lived in a little apartment near the supermarket where she worked as an assistant manager. Mom never got married, though occasionally a boyfriend came around. She took a second job keeping the books for a couple of mom-and-pop stores. I remember going to bed most nights with the sounds of her calculator snapping in the kitchen.

Then, when I was twelve, she died of cancer.

One morning she had found a tender spot on her left temple. Four months later, she was dead and I was alone.

I spent a couple of years shuttling between foster homes, until Mom's brother, my uncle Farrell, volunteered to take me in, to his place in Knoxville, Tennessee. I had just turned fifteen.

I didn't see much of Uncle Farrell: He worked as a night watchman at an office building in downtown Knoxville and slept most of the day. He wore a black uniform with an embroidered gold shield on the shoulder. He didn't carry a gun, but he did have a nightstick, and he thought he was very important.

I spent a lot of time in my bedroom, listening to music or reading. This bothered Uncle Farrell because he considered himself a man of action, despite the fact that he sat on his butt for eight hours every night doing nothing but staring at surveillance monitors. Finally, he asked me if I wanted to talk about my mom's death. I told him I didn't. I just wanted to be left alone.

"Alfred," he said. "Look around you. Look at the movers and shakers of this world. Do you think they got to be where they are by lying around all day reading books and listening to rap music?"

"I don't know how they got to be where they are," I said. "So I guess they could have."

He didn't like my answer, so he sent me to see the school psychologist, Dr. Francine Peddicott. She was very old and had a very long, sharp nose, and her office smelled like vanilla. Dr. Peddicott liked to ask questions. In fact, I can't remember anything she said that *wasn't* a question besides "Hello, Alfred," and "Good-bye, Alfred."

"Do you miss your mother?" she asked on my first visit, after asking me if I wanted to sit or lie on the sofa. I chose to sit.

"Sure. She was my mom."

"What do you miss most about her?"

"She was a great cook."

"Really? You miss her cooking the most?"

"Well, I don't know. You asked what I missed most and that's the first thing that popped into my head. Maybe because it's almost dinnertime. Also, Uncle Farrell can't cook. I mean, he cooks, but what he cooks I wouldn't feed to a starving dog. Mostly we have frozen dinners and stuff out of a can."

She scribbled for a minute in her little notebook.

"But your mother—she was a good cook?"

"She was a great cook."

She sighed heavily. Maybe I wasn't giving the kind of answers she was looking for. "Do you hate her sometimes?"

"Hate her for what?"

"Do you hate your mother for dying?"

"Oh, jeez, that wasn't her fault."

"But you get mad at her sometimes, right? For leaving you?"

"I get mad at the cancer for killing her. I get mad at the doctors and . . . you know, how it's been around for centuries and we still can't get rid of it. Cancer, I mean. And I think, what if we put all the money we spend on these wasteful government projects toward cancer research. You know, stuff like that."

"What about your father?"

"What about him?"

"Do you hate him?"

"I don't even know him."

"Do you hate him for leaving you and your mom?"

She was making me feel freaky, like she was trying to get me to hate my father, a guy I didn't even know, and even like she was trying to get me to hate my dead mother.

"I guess so, but I don't know all the facts," I said.

"Your mother didn't tell you?"

"She just said he couldn't commit."

"And how does that make you feel?"

"Like he didn't want a kid."

"Like he didn't want—who?"

"Me. Me, I guess. Of course me."

I wondered what the next thing I was supposed to hate was.

"How do you like school?"

"I hate it."

"Why?"

"I don't know anyone."

"You don't have any friends?"

"They call me Frankenstein."

"Who does?"

"Kids at school. You know, because of my size. My big head."

"What about girls?" she asked.

"Girls calling me Frankenstein?"

"Do you have a girlfriend?"

Well, there *was* this one girl—her name was Amy Pouchard, and she sat two seats over from me in math. She had long blond hair and very dark eyes. One day during my first week, I thought she might have smiled at me. She could have been smiling at the guy on my left, or even not smiling at all, and I just projected a smile onto a nonsmiling face.

"No. No girlfriends," I said.

Uncle Farrell talked to Dr. Peddicott for a long time afterwards. He told me she was referring me to a psychiatrist who could prescribe some antidepressants because Dr. Peddicott believed I was severely depressed and recommended I get involved with something other than TV and music, in addition to seeing a shrink and taking anti-crazy drugs. Uncle Farrell's idea was football, which wasn't too surprising given my size, but football was the last thing I wanted to do.

"Uncle Farrell," I told him, "I don't want to play football."

"You're high-risk, Al," Uncle Farrell answered. "You're running around with all the risk factors for a major psychotic episode. One, you got no dad. Two, you got no mom. Three, you're living with an absentee caretaker—me—and four, you're in a strange town with no friends.

"There was another one too . . . Oh, yeah. And five, you're fifteen."

"I want to get my license," I told him.

"Your license for what?"

"For driving. I want my learner's permit."

"I'm telling you that you're about to go off the deep end and you want to talk about getting your learner's permit?"

"That reminded me, the fact that I'm fifteen."

"Dr. Peddicott thought it was a great idea," Uncle Farrell said.

"A learner's permit?"

"No! Going out for the football team. One, you need some kind of activity. Two, it's a great way to build confidence and make friends. And three, look at you! For the love of the Blessed Virgin, you're some kinda force of nature! Any coach would love to have you on his team."

"I don't like football," I said.

"You don't like football? How can you not like football? What kind of kid are you? What kind of American kid doesn't like football? I suppose next you're going to say you want to take dancing lessons!"

"I don't want to take dancing lessons."

"That's good, Al. That's real good. Because if you said you wanted to take dancing lessons, I don't know what I'd do. Throw myself over a cliff or something."

"I don't like pain."

"Ah, come on. They'll bounce off you like—like—pygmies! Gnats! Little pygmy gnats!"

"Uncle Farrell, I cry if I get a splinter. I faint at the sight of blood. And I bruise very easily. I'm a very easy bruiser."

But Uncle Farrell wouldn't take no for an answer. He ended up bribing me. He wouldn't take me to get my learner's permit unless I tried out for the football team. And if I didn't try out for the team, he promised he would put me on so much antidepressant dope, I wouldn't remember to sit when I crapped. Uncle Farrell could be gross like that.

I really wanted my permit—I also didn't want to be so doped up, I couldn't remember how to crap—so I went out for the team.

2

I made the team as a second-string right guard, which basically meant I was a practice dummy for the first-string defense.

Coach Harvey was a short round guy with a gut that hung over his pants, and calves about the size of my head, which, as I mentioned, was large. Like a lot of coaches, Coach Harvey liked to scream. He especially liked to scream at me.

One afternoon, about a month before Uncle Farrell struck his deal with the chief Agent of Darkness, I saw how much screaming he could do. I had just let a linebacker blow by me and cream the starting quarterback, the most popular kid in school, Barry Lancaster. I didn't mean for this to happen, but I was having trouble memorizing the playbook. It seemed very complicated, especially seeing it was a document intended for big jocks, most of whom could barely read. Anyway, I thought Barry had called a Dog Right, but actually he had said "Hog Right." That one letter makes a huge difference and left Barry on the turf, writhing in agony.

Coach Harvey charged from the sidelines, silver whistle clamped between his fat lips, screaming around the hysterical screeches of the whistle as he ran.

"Kropp!" *Tweet!* "Kropp!" *Tweet!* "KROPP!"

"Sorry, Coach," I told him. "I heard 'dog,' not 'hog.' "

"Dog, not hog?" He turned his head toward Barry, still twisting on the ground. He kept his body turned toward me. "Lancaster! Are you hurt?"

"I'm okay, Coach," Barry gasped. But he didn't look okay to me. His face was as white as the hash marks on the field.

"What play was that, Kropp?" Coach Harvey snapped at me.

"Um, Dog Right?" I said.

"Dog! Dog! You thought hog was dog? How is dog like hog, Kropp? Huh? Tell me!"

The whole team had gathered around us by this point, like gawkers at the scene of a terrible accident.

Coach Harvey reached up and slapped my helmet with the palm of his hand.

"What's the matter with you, boy?" He slapped me

again. He proceeded to punctuate his questions with a hard slap against the side of my head.

"Are you stupid?" Slap.

"Are you stupid, Kropp?" Slap.

"Are you thick, is that it, Kropp?" Slap-slap.

"No, sir, I'm not."

"No, sir, I'm not *what?*"

"Stupid, sir."

"Are you sure you're not stupid, Kropp? Because you act stupid. You play stupid. You even talk stupid. So are you absolutely sure, Kropp, that you are not stupid?" *Slap-slap-slap.*

"No, sir, I know I'm not!"

He slapped me again. I yelled, "My mother had my IQ tested and I'm not stupid! Sir!"

That cracked everybody up, and they kept laughing for the next three weeks. I heard it everywhere—"My mommy had my IQ tested and I'm not stupid!"—and not just in the locker room (where I heard it plenty). It spread over the whole school. Strangers would pass me in the hallway and squeal, "My mommy had my IQ tested!" It was horrible.

That night after the practice, Uncle Farrell asked how it was going.

"I don't want to play football anymore," I said.

"You're playing football, Alfred."

"It's not just about me, Uncle Farrell. Other people can get hurt too."

"You're playing football," he said. "Or you're not getting your license."

"I don't see the point of this," I said. "What's wrong with not playing football? I think it's pretty narrow-minded to assume just because I'm big, I should be playing football."

"Okay, Alfred," he said. "Then you tell me. What do you want to do? You want to go out for the marching band?"

"I don't play an instrument."

"It's a high school band, Alfred, not the New York Philharmonic."

"Still, you probably need to have some kind of basic understanding of music, reading notes, that kind of thing."

"Well, you're not going to lie around in your room all day listening to music and daydreaming. I'm tired of coming up with suggestions, so you tell me: What are your skills? What do you like to do?"

"Lie in my room and listen to music."

"I'm talking about skills, Mr. Wisenheimer, gifts, special attributes—you know, the thing that separates you from the average Joe."

I tried to think of a skill I had. I couldn't.

"Jeez, Al, everybody has something they're good at," Uncle Farrell said.

"What's so wrong about being average? Aren't most people?"

"Is that it? Is that all you expect from yourself, Alfred?" he asked, growing red in the face. I expected him to launch into one of his lectures about the movers and shakers or how anybody could be a success with a little luck and the right mindset.

But he didn't do that. Instead he ordered me into the car and we drove downtown.

"Where are we going?" I asked.

"I'm taking you on a magical journey, Alfred."

"A magical journey? Where to?"

"The future."

We crossed a bridge and I could see a huge glass building towering over everything around it. The glass was dark tinted, and against the night sky it looked like a fat, glittering black thumb pointing up.

"Do you know what that is?" Uncle Farrell asked. "That's where I work, Alfred, Samson Towers. Thirty-three stories high and three city blocks wide. Take a good look at it, Alfred."

"Uncle Farrell, I've seen big buildings before."

He didn't say anything. There was an angry expression on his thin face. Uncle Farrell was forty and as small and scrawny as I was big and meaty, though he had a large head like me. When he put on his security guard uniform, he reminded me of Barney Fife from that old *Andy Griffith Show,* or rather of a Pez dispenser of Barney Fife, because of the oversized head and skinny body. It made me feel guilty thinking of him as a goofy screwup like Barney Fife, but I couldn't help it. He even had those wet, flappy lips like Barney.

He pulled into the entrance of the underground parking lot and slid a plastic card into a machine. The gate opened and he drove slowly into the nearly empty lot.

"Who owns Samson Towers, Alfred?" he asked.

"A guy named Samson?" I guessed.

"A guy named Bernard Samson," he said. "You don't know anything about him, but let me tell you. Bernard Samson is a self-made millionaire many times over, Alfred. Came to Knoxville at the age of sixteen with nothing in his pockets and now he's one of the richest men in America. You want to know how he got there?"

"He invented the iPod?"

"He worked hard, Alfred. Hard work and something you are sorely lacking in: fortitude, guts, vision, passion. Because let me tell you something, the world doesn't belong to the smartest or the most talented. There are plenty of smart, talented losers in this world. You wanna know who the world belongs to, Alfred?"

"Microsoft?"

"That's it, smarty-pants, make jokes. No. The world belongs to people who don't give up. Who get knocked down and keep coming back for more."

"Okay, Uncle Farrell," I said. "I get your point. But what about the future?"

"That's right," he said. "The future! Come on, Alfred. You won't find the future in this garage."

We took the elevator to the lobby. Uncle Farrell led me to his horseshoe-shaped desk that faced the two-story atrium. About halfway between the security desk and the front doors was a waterfall that fell over these huge rocks that Uncle Farrell told me had been hauled down at great expense from the Pigeon River in the Smokies.

"Funny thing about life is you never know where it's going to take you," Uncle Farrell told me. "I'm working at the auto body shop when in strolls Bernard Samson. He strikes up a conversation, and next thing I know here I am making double what I pulled in at the shop. And for sitting—for nothing! *Double* for *nothing*, just because the richest man in Knoxville decides to give *me* a job!"

Mounted on the desktop were dozens of closed-circuit monitors set up to survey every nook and cranny of Samson Towers.

"This system is state-of-the-art, Alfred. I mean, this place is tighter than Fort Knox. Laser sensors, sound detectors, you name it."

"That's pretty cool, Uncle Farrell."

"Pretty cool," he echoed. "You betcha. And this is where I sit, eight hours a day, six nights a week, in front of these monitors, staring. Watching. What do you think I'm watching, Alfred?"

"Didn't you just say you were watching the monitors?"

"I am watching nothing, Alfred. Eight hours a day, six nights a week, I sit in this little chair right here, watching nothing."

He leaned very close to me, so close, I could smell his breath, which did not smell very good.

"This is the future, Alfred. *Your* future, or something like it, if you don't find your passion. If you don't figure out what you're here for. A lifetime of watching nothing."

3

I studied hard for my driver's test, but I flunked it. So I took it a second time and flunked again, but I didn't miss as many questions, so at least I was improving as a failure. Uncle Farrell pointed to my scores as proof I lacked the guts to achieve even something as simple as a learner's permit.

Things were not much better at school. Barry Lancaster's wrist was still badly sprained, which meant he was now a bench player just like me. Barry wasn't happy about this. He went around telling everybody how he was going to "get Kropp," so I spent my days looking over my shoulder, waiting for the getting to start. I became jumpy; every loud noise, like the slamming of a locker door, was enough to make me nearly wet my pants.

One afternoon in early spring, I came home to find Uncle Farrell already out of bed.

"What is it?" I asked.

"What's what?"

"Why are you out of bed?"

"Aren't you the king of Twenty Questions."

"That was only two questions, Uncle Farrell, and they were kind of related, so that probably would only count as one and a half."

"You know, Alfred, people who think they're funny rarely really are."

"I don't think I'm funny. I think I'm too tall, too fat, too slow, and too much of a screwup, but I don't think I'm funny. Why are you out of bed, Uncle Farrell?"

"We have company coming," he said, wetting his big lips.

"We do?" We never had anyone over. "Who's coming?"

"Somebody very important, Alfred. Put on some clean clothes and come into the kitchen. We're eating early."

I changed my clothes and found my Salisbury steak frozen dinner fresh from the microwave sitting at my spot on the kitchen table. Uncle Farrell was drinking a beer, which was unusual. He never drank beer at dinner.

"Alfred, how'd you like to move out of this dump and live in one of those huge mansions in Sequoia Hills?"

"Huh?"

"You know, where all the rich people live."

I thought about it. "That'd be great, Uncle Farrell. But when did we get rich?"

"We're not rich. But we might be. Someday." He was smiling a mysterious smile while he chewed his Salisbury steak.

"And you'll be taking your driving test again next week—how'd you like a Ferrari Enzo for your first car?"

"Oh, boy, that'd be great, Uncle Farrell," I said. He got like this sometimes. It's no big secret that it's lousy being poor. But there's poor and then there's really poor, and we weren't really poor. I mean, I never went to bed hungry, and the lights always stayed on, but I guess it wasn't easy working a lonely night job for the richest man in Knoxville. He wasn't getting much sleep lately either, and that can make you a little loopy. "But I'd rather have a Hummer."

"Okay, a Hummer. Whatever. The kind of car doesn't matter, Al. This guy who's coming tonight—he's a very rich man and he's got this proposition that . . . well, if it works out the way I hope, you and me, we'll never have to worry about money again."

"Honestly, Uncle Farrell, I didn't know we worried about it now."

"His name is Arthur Myers and he owns Tintagel International. You ever hear of Tintagel International?"

"No."

"Well, it's one of the biggest international conglomerates there is, maybe bigger than Samson Industries."

"Okay."

"So here's the deal, Al. One night I'm on my shift and it's just like any other night, nobody but me at the desk, doing nothing, when all of a sudden the phone rings and guess who's on the other end."

"Mr. Myers."

"Right!"

"What's a conglomerate?"

"It's a business that owns businesses, or something like that. That really isn't the point. Alfred, you need to stop interrupting me and focus a little, okay?"

"I'll try, Uncle Farrell."

"So anyway, Mr. Arthur Myers says he's got a business proposition for me."

"The owner of one of the biggest conglomerates in the world had a business proposition for you?" I asked.

"It's crazy!"

"It sure sounds crazy."

"That's what I thought!" Uncle Farrell tapped his fork on the plate and started talking really fast. "Who am I but this lowly little night watchman? But I met with him and it turns out he's the real McCoy, and he needs my help. Our help, Alfred."

"Our help?" The more he talked about this funny deal, the funnier I felt.

"See, Myers and Bernard Samson go way back. Good buds from, I don't know, the old country or something. Anyway, Myers convinced Samson to invest in this big business deal—I'm not sure of all the ins and outs but apparently there was a lot of money involved and it went bad. It went real bad. Samson lost a lot of money and he blamed Myers for it."

"Why did he blame Myers?"

"I don't know. Now listen, and stop interrupting, Alfred. We don't have much time."

"Why don't we have much time?"

"I'm getting to that."

"To what?"

"The reason we don't have much time!"

He took a deep breath.

"Mr. Samson blamed Mr. Myers for this deal that went bad. He took it pretty hard, Samson did, and so he did a terrible thing."

"What did he do?"

"He stole something."

"From Mr. Myers?"

"No, from the Louvre in Paris. Of course from Myers! Samson stole it and locked it away in his office."

I started to get it. "His office in Samson Towers?"

"That's right. Now you're getting it. Samson Towers, the night watchman of which happens to be yours truly."

"And Myers wants you to get it back for him."

"Right. That's right, and—"

"What is it?"

"What's what?"

"The thing Samson stole."

"Oh. I don't know."

"You don't know?"

Uncle Farrell slowly shook his head. "I have no idea."

"Uncle Farrell, how are you going to get it if you don't know what it is?"

"That's a detail, Alfred. Just a detail. The point is—"

"A pretty big detail if you ask me."

"Do you want to know what the point is?"

"Sure."

His mouth was moving but no sound was coming out.

"You interrupt me and every thought in my head just flies away! Whoosh! Right out the window! Where was I?"

"You were going to tell me the point."

"The point? Oh. Yeah! The point is he's paying me one million dollars to get it."

I stared at him. "Did you say one million dollars?" I asked.

"Well, I didn't say one million pesos, that's for sure!"

I thought about it. "This is illegal."

"No, it isn't illegal."

"But if Mr. Samson stole it, why doesn't Mr. Myers go to the police?"

Uncle Farrell wet his lips. "He said he didn't want the police involved."

"How come?"

"He said he wanted to keep everything real quiet. He doesn't want to press charges because the papers and the TV would pick it up and he doesn't want that."

"Maybe this thing belongs to Mr. Samson and Mr. My-ers is lying. Maybe he's just using you because you're the guy with the keys."

"Well, I am the guy with the keys—that's why he needs me—but I'm no thief, Al. Look, I didn't bring this up to get your permission. I brought this up to ask for your help."

"My help?"

"That's right," Uncle Farrell said. "I can't do it alone, Al. And I figured who'd be better to help me than you, since you stand to gain in this operation too. One million dollars! Think about it, Al, because you're only fifteen; you haven't lived very long, not as long as me, and things like this, these kinds of opportunities, they're once-in-a-lifetime!"

"I'll have to think about it," I said.

He stopped chomping his microwave steak, his mouth hanging open a little so I could see the food.

"What do you mean you'll have to think about it? Think about what? I'm your uncle. I'm all the family you got left since your good-for-nothing father abandoned you and your mother died of cancer, God rest her soul. This could be the sweetest deal ever to come down the pike, one million smackers for an hour's work, and you're telling me you got to *think* about it?"

"It's just a lot to think about, Uncle Farrell."

He snorted. "Well, you better think quick, Alfred, be-cause—"

The doorbell rang. Uncle Farrell gave a little jump, then forced a smile. Uncle Farrell had very large teeth.

"That's him; he's here."

"Who's here?"

"Myers! I told you we didn't have much time."

"Mr. Myers is here?"

"You know something, Alfred? You would think, with a head the size of yours, you'd be able to think a little bit quicker. Clear off the plates and meet us in the living room, will ya? You don't keep a man like Arthur Myers waiting."

He hurried from the kitchen. I heard the front door open and Uncle Farrell say, "Hey, Mr. Myers! Right on time. Come on in, make yourself at home. Alfred! Alfred is the kid I told you about."

I heard the sound of a man's voice talking, but I couldn't understand the words, he was speaking so softly. I carried the plates to the sink and wiped down the kitchen table.

In the living room, I heard Uncle Farrell say, "Would you like something to drink, Mr. Myers?" And then he yelled to me, "Alfred! Make some coffee, will ya?"

So I got the coffee going, and then I stood there by the sink, chewing on a thumbnail. I knew he wanted me in there to meet this Arthur Myers, but for some reason I was scared. The whole thing struck me as some shady deal. Why would someone as rich and powerful as Arthur Myers give Uncle Farrell a million dollars to pull a "recovery" job for him? What was in Samson Towers that was so valuable?

But my biggest question was what would happen to me if Uncle Farrell got caught breaking into Bernard Samson's office. If he was in jail, it was back to the foster home for me.

I waited until the pot was finished brewing, then poured two cups and carried them into the living room.

Uncle Farrell was sitting on the edge of the sofa, leaning toward the chair in which Arthur Myers sat. I noticed a large leather satchel with gold clasps sitting on the floor beside him.

Arthur Myers was thin, with long brown hair pulled into a ponytail hanging halfway down his back. His silk suit was a funny color, almost multicolored, and when he moved, the light played off the material and made it shimmer, first blue, then white, then red. But the most noticeable thing about him were his eyes, set very deep into his head under a jutting brow. They were so brown, they almost looked black. And when he turned those eyes toward me for the first time, I shivered, as if I'd walked over a grave.

"Alfred!" Uncle Farrell said. "Coffee! Great! How do you like your coffee, Mr. Myers?"

"Black, thank you," Mr. Myers said. He took the cup from me. He had an accent that sounded kind of French but kind of not; I don't know, I'm no good with accents.

"So you are Alfred Kropp," he said. "Your uncle thinks a great deal of you."

"He does?" I turned to Uncle Farrell. "Cream and two scoops of sugar," I said, and handed him his cup.

"Indeed he does," Mr. Myers said. "But he failed to mention your impressive . . . proportions. Tell me, do you play football in your school?"

"I went out for the team," I said. "I made second-string

right guard. Coach wouldn't put me in much because I couldn't remember the plays. But if we got ahead by twenty points he put me in. I blew a play in practice and our star quarterback got hurt. I may have ruined his only chance to get into college and I think he's going to kill me for it."

"Come here, Al, and take a load off," Uncle Farrell said, patting the couch. He was wetting his lips. He turned to Mr. Myers. "I've filled Al in on most of the details of the operation."

"I had my reservations, as I told you," Mr. Myers answered. "But I understand the necessity for an accomplice. As long as he can be trusted."

"Oh," Uncle Farrell said. "You bet."

"I'm not sure I can," I said. Both men stared at me. "I mean, I'm not too quick on the uptake—I can't even memorize a football playbook—and this whole thing smells fishy to me."

Arthur Myers crossed his long legs, rested his elbows on the armrests, steepled his thin fingers together, and said, "In what way does it 'smell fishy' to you, Mr. Kropp?"

"Well, Mr. Myers, for one thing you just used the word 'accomplice.' That kind of implies you're putting Uncle Farrell up to no good."

"An unfortunate choice of words, then. How is 'partner'? Would you prefer that word?"

"Hey, I think that's a great word," Uncle Farrell said.

"The other thing is," I said, "how do we know this whatchamacallit in Mr. Samson's office is really yours?

Maybe it belongs to Mr. Samson and you're making this story up to get us to steal it for you."

"Alfred!" Uncle Farrell cried. He mouthed to me, "Ix-nay on the ealing-stay."

Mr. Myers raised his hand. "That is quite all right, Mr. Kropp. The boy has a sense of honor. All in all, not a bad thing, particularly in one so young." Then he turned those dark eyes right on me and I felt a pressure in my chest, as if a huge fist was squeezing me. "What would you like, Alfred Kropp? Testimonials? Eyewitness accounts? A certificate of authenticity or proof of purchase, as from a cereal box? It is a family heirloom, a treasure that has been handed down from generation to generation. Bernard Samson took it from me in retaliation for a business deal gone awry, an unfortunate occurrence that was nevertheless not my fault. If you know anything about the man, you understand why he took it."

"I don't know anything about him," I said. "I've never even met him. Why did he take it?"

"For revenge."

"Have you asked him to give it back, whatever it is?"

Mr. Myers stared at me for a second before Uncle Farrell said, "Yeah, that's a good point, Mr. Myers. I mean, what exactly *is* it you need recovered?"

"This," Mr. Myers said, pulling a long manila envelope from his pocket and handing it to Uncle Farrell. He was still looking at me.

"I was just thinking maybe you don't need to shell out a

27

million dollars to get it back," I said. "Maybe you and Mr. Samson should just make up and then he'll give it back."

"Really, Mr. Kropp?" He was smiling at me. My face felt hot, but I barreled on.

"Well, I'm not pretending to know how things work in the world of big business and conglomerations, but if I had a fight with a friend or he borrowed something and wouldn't give it back, I'd invite him over to hang out, maybe play some video games, or you would probably have martinis, and I'd schmooze a little and then I'd ask for whatever it was back. I'd say, 'Hey, Bernie (or Bernard or whatever you call him), I know you're pretty sore, but that thing you took means a lot to me, been in my family for generations, and maybe we could work something out, because I'd hate to get the cops involved,' or something along those lines. Have you thought about doing that?"

"You're correct, Mr. Kropp," Mr. Myers said, the same stiff smile frozen on his lips. "You do not know how 'conglomerations' work. Are you and your uncle turning down the job? Time is of the essence."

"How come?" I asked.

"My, Mr. Kropp," Arthur Myers said to Uncle Farrell. "How proud you must be of this boy. So direct! So thoughtful. So . . . inquisitive."

"I'm all the family he's got left," Uncle Farrell said. "Plus he spends a lot of time alone, you know, because I'm sleeping during the day and away all night. It's a miracle he isn't in juvie hall, if you ask me."

Uncle Farrell had opened the envelope and pulled out an eight-by-ten glossy photograph that he now held out to me.

I looked at the picture.

"It's a sword," I said.

"Yes." Mr. Myers laughed for some reason. "And the Great Pyramid is just a headstone."

It was mounted in a glass case, like a museum piece. A dull silvery color with a fancy handle. But "handle" wasn't the right word. There was a word for the handle of a sword. I bit my lip, trying to think of the word. There was some kind of writing on the flat part of the blade, or maybe just a fancy design, I couldn't tell.

"I took that picture years ago," Mr. Myers was saying as I stared at the picture. "For insurance purposes. Samson was fascinated by our family heirloom from the moment he saw it. He offered to buy it from me at a fantastic price, but of course I refused. It is hardly worth what he offered, but its sentimental value is astronomical."

"I know how that is," Uncle Farrell said. "I've got a baseball from the 1932 Cubs that—"

"I *have* asked for it back," Mr. Myers said. "I have even offered him money, all to no avail. I do not see that I have any recourse now but to seize it."

"I say the old so-and-so has it coming," Uncle Farrell said.

"I cannot do it myself, of course. And I understand I am putting your uncle's very job in jeopardy. That is why I'm offering this bounty. Speaking of which . . ." He slid the leather case toward Uncle Farrell. "The down payment. I will pay the balance upon delivery of the sword."

Uncle Farrell's fingers were shaking as he undid the gold clasps. Inside were bundles of twenty-dollar bills.

"Oh, my sweet aunt Matilda!" Uncle Farrell whispered.

"Five hundred thousand dollars," Mr. Myers said softly. "You may count it if you wish."

"Oh, I trust you, Mr. Myers," Uncle Farrell said. "You bet I do! Look at this, Alfred!"

But I wasn't looking at the money. I was looking at the picture of the sword in its glass case. I had a hundred questions racing through my mind, but they were whirling so fast, I couldn't get a grip on one.

Then Mr. Myers said, "As I told your uncle, Mr. Kropp, I need someone to retrieve the sword for me. A man of consummate skill and discretion. A man who is incorruptible, untouched by the temptations of evil men. I need someone who is indefatigable, Mr. Kropp. A man who will not give up or falter when all odds are against him. In short, I need someone who will lay down his life to recover a treasure that is beyond any value mortal men may place on it."

" 'Lay down his life'?" I asked. "Uncle Farrell, he's saying you might have to lay down your life."

"He's just trying to make a point, Alfred. Some people exaggerate to get across what they're saying. You know, to get your attention. He doesn't mean literally lay down your life. Right, Mr. Myers? Huh? Not literally lay down our lives." Mr. Myers didn't say anything. Uncle Farrell wet his big lips and said to me, "You should listen to Mr. Myers. You can learn a lot from a guy like him."

Mr. Myers said, "I could turn to more . . . ruthless men for my purpose. I know such men, but I do not trust them. For the very quality that makes them ruthless makes them untrustworthy. I need someone I can trust. Someone who will not betray me."

"Well, you've come to the right place, Mr. Myers!" Uncle Farrell said. "You can trust us. You can consider your fancy sword as good as returned."

"Excellent," Mr. Myers said. "As I mentioned, time is of the essence. Samson leaves for Europe tonight and will return in two days."

"We're going in tonight," Uncle Farrell said firmly. "Or tomorrow night. Tonight or tomorrow, either one, but maybe Al has homework, I don't know." He looked at me. "Anyway, very soon, one of the two nights. Tonight or tomorrow night, right, Al?"

"How do you know the sword's in his office?" I asked Mr. Myers.

"I don't know for certain, but I do know for certain it isn't in his home."

"We don't need to know how you know that," Uncle Farrell said. "Right, Alfred?"

"What happens if it isn't there?" I asked. "Do we have to give back the five hundred thousand?"

"Hey," Uncle Farrell said. "That's a pretty good question!" He was clutching the satchel to his chest as if he were afraid Mr. Myers might reach over and yank it away.

"Of course you may keep it," Mr. Myers said. "That money is for your trouble. The rest is for the sword."

We had a big fight after Mr. Myers left. Despite the money sitting there on the sofa that was ours to keep whether we found the sword or not, I still felt really weird about doing this. It just felt wrong. Maybe Mr. Samson really did take the sword and hide it in his office, but that didn't make stealing it back the right thing to do.

"It's not like he's asking us to knock somebody off or do something really evil. And it's a million dollars, Alfred. We could do anything we wanted, live anywhere we wanted, have anything we wanted!"

It didn't matter how many objections I raised. To Uncle Farrell, money trumped everything.

He even said, "You do what you want, Al, but maybe I need to rethink this whole arrangement of ours—I mean, maybe you're too much for me to handle . . . Maybe I should send you back to the foster care . . ."

That ended the fight. He knew I didn't want to go back to foster care.

4

The very next day my math teacher informed me I was flunking. That was bad enough, but not as bad as being assigned a tutor to save my grade, because my tutor turned out to be Amy Pouchard.

We met for thirty minutes after school, just me—Alfred Kropp—and Amy Pouchard, she of the long golden hair and dark eyes. Sitting right next to her I could smell her perfume.

"Where are you from?" she asked me in that twangy east Tennessee accent. "You talk funny."

"Ohio," I said.

"Are you a resource student?" Resource students were

either mentally challenged or from a really bad background, or both. I guess some people would say I was both.

"No, I just suck at math."

"Hey," she said. "Kropp! You're the guy who had his IQ tested!"

"Something like that."

"And you broke Barry Lancaster's wrist."

"It isn't broken and I didn't actually do it. Somebody else did, but it was my fault, which I guess is practically the same thing."

"I hate tutoring," she said.

"Then why do you do it?"

"Because I get extra credit."

"Well," I said, "I really appreciate it. It's hard for me—math, I mean—and it's been hard too getting used to a new place, a new school, and things like that."

She put a piece of gum in her mouth and the spearmint warred with the musk of her perfume.

"I'm going to a shrink," I admitted, at the same time not really sure why I was admitting it. "Not that I want to go, but my uncle is making me. She's about a thousand years old and she wanted to know if I had a girlfriend."

She smacked her gum and stared at me. She couldn't have cared less. She was tapping the end of her pencil on the desktop, and her whole being was in a state of couldn't-care-less-ness.

"So I told her I didn't . . . have a girlfriend. Because a new school is hard, um, in terms of meeting them. Girls. Plus the fact that I'm shy and I'm pretty self-conscious of my size."

"You are pretty big," she said around her wad of gum. "Maybe we better work on some problems."

"Like, I was wondering," I said, my mouth now so bone-dry, I would have mugged her for a stick of her gum. "About your ideas on dating somebody my size."

"I have a boyfriend."

"I was just searching out your ideas, really."

"Barry Lancaster."

"Barry Lancaster is your boyfriend?"

She flipped her hair over her right shoulder and nodded, and the gum went click-click-click in her mouth.

"Some guys have all the luck," I said, meaning Barry Lancaster and in a funny way, me too.

Uncle Farrell had to pick me up that afternoon, since I missed the bus. We drove straight to the driver's license place and I took my test for the third time. This time I passed, missing four questions, one less than the maximum allowable. To celebrate, I drove us to IHOP for dinner. I ordered the Rooty Tooty Fresh and Fruity. Uncle Farrell had the patty melt. He was wearing his black uniform and wetting his lips more than usual.

"So, what have you decided, Alfred?"

"About what?"

"About this operation for Mr. Myers."

"I think it's incredibly unfair of you to threaten me with a foster home to make me do it."

"Forget unfair. Is it fair that you won't help your only flesh and blood?"

"You just told me to forget fair and then you ask me if something's fair."

"So?"

"That isn't fair."

"Sometimes I think you're toying with me, Alfred, which is incredibly cheeky for a kid in your position. Final time, last chance, do-or-die: Are you going to help me tonight?"

"Tonight? You're doing it tonight?"

He nodded. He was on about his third cup of coffee and his nod was quick and sharp, like a bobble-head's. "I have to. Samson is out of town and Myers wants his sword back ASAP. It's now-or-never time. Fourth quarter, ten seconds left."

"So you're going to do it whether I help you or not?"

"I gave my word, Alfred. I made a promise," he said pointedly, as if reminding me I should keep mine, although I couldn't remember actually making any promises. "So the only question left is . . . are you going to help me?"

When I didn't answer right away, he leaned in close and whispered, "You think I won't do it? You think I won't send you back to foster care?"

I wiped my cheek with my napkin, which was sticky with syrup, and I felt the stickiness on my cheek.

"Maybe if you try, I'll tell the police you stole the sword."

"Keep your voice down, will ya? I'm not stealing anything.

I'm recovering it for the victim. I'm doing a good deed, Al. Now, last time I'm going to ask. Are you going to help me?"

I dabbed my cheeks again with my sticky napkin, and for some reason I thought about Amy Pouchard and the fact that Barry Lancaster was probably going to kill me when he found out she was tutoring me in math, and then I thought about my mom who died and the dad I never knew. The only person I had left was sitting across the table from me, slugging down coffee, nervously wetting his lips and drumming his fingers on the table.

"Okay," I said. "But I'm a minor, so whatever happens up there they'll blame you for it."

"Whatever happens up there," he said, "it's gonna change both our lives forever."

I would remember those words when Uncle Farrell turned to me and whispered my name, *Alfred,* right before he died.

5

In the car on the way to the Towers, I asked him, "Uncle Farrell, have you thought about how you're gonna do this?"

"Do what?"

"Get the sword. What about all the security cameras?"

"We're going to cut the power."

"To the whole building?"

"No, just the power to the security system. Power goes out every now and then."

"There's no backup?"

"You can override it. If it stays down over ten minutes, though, a call automatically goes to police headquarters."

I thought about it. "Okay, so we have ten minutes from the time you cut the power till the cops know."

"Yeah. But it's maybe another five, ten minutes before a cop gets there."

"How do you know?"

"We've run drills before, Alfred." He sighed, and his head went shake-shake-shake again.

"Okay. Let's say a terminal window of no more than fifteen minutes."

" 'Terminal window'? You've been watching too many movies, Alfred."

"What if someone shows up downstairs while we're in Mr. Samson's office?"

"While *you're* in Samson's office."

"Me?"

"Well, I can't do it, Alfred. Why do you think you're here? I've got to provide cover downstairs. I'll get you in, you get the sword, and then we get out. Then I call Myers and we swap the sword for another cool half-mil."

We drove in silence for a while. Samson Towers loomed ahead, silhouetted against the night sky.

Uncle Farrell said, "Now, stay right here in the car, Alfred." He pulled into the underground parking lot. "I'll come back and get you once the shift's changed."

So he left me there, hunkered in the front seat. My watch read 10:45. I have to admit, even though this deal seemed awfully fishy to me, I was excited. It was kind of like a spy movie, only we weren't spies and this wasn't a movie. So maybe it wasn't like a spy movie but more like a fifteen-year-old kid and his uncle trying to steal a sword that may or may not belong to a guy who was paying them a truckload of money to steal it.

Uncle Farrell came back downstairs and I got out of the car.

"All clear," he whispered. "I've already cut the power to the system. Hurry, Alfred!"

He popped the trunk and pulled out a beat-up old duffel bag.

"What's that for?" I whispered. The garage was empty and I wasn't sure why we were whispering.

"You want to be seen lugging a big sword into our apartment building, do you? Here." He handed the bag to me.

We took the elevator from the garage to the main floor, where the fountain spattered and gurgled and our footfalls echoed eerily in the great empty space.

I followed him to the guard station with the bank of surveillance monitors. They were all dark. I noticed tiny dots of sweat beaded on his forehead.

"Okay, Alfred, let's go."

We got into the elevator and Uncle Farrell pulled out the key for the executive suite. He was sweating pretty bad by that point. I was sweating too, and my tongue felt very thick in my mouth. We didn't say anything. Secretly I was hoping our quest would come up a big fat zero. That way we could tell Mr. Myers we couldn't find it and be half a million dollars richer without actually taking anything that wasn't ours and that might not even be his.

The elevator doors opened and we stepped out. I could feel my heart slamming in my chest and it actually hurt to breathe. I inhaled shallower and shallower, to lessen the pain.

The double doors leading into Mr. Samson's office suite were directly ahead of us. Uncle Farrell looked at his watch. I had already checked mine.

"Okay, four minutes down; we're fine," he said.

He slipped the key into the lock and the doors opened silently. I felt for the light switch.

"No lights," Uncle Farrell hissed. He pulled the flashlight from his belt.

"Somebody could see that too," I said.

"Well, gee, Alfred, I left my infrared night-vision goggles at home, so I guess we don't have much choice."

He clicked on the flashlight and the beam of light glanced off the dark mahogany of the secretary's desk.

"Where is it?" I asked.

"I don't know."

"You don't know?"

"But I don't think it would be out here."

He pulled a pair of rubber gloves from his pocket.

"Aren't those for washing dishes?" I asked.

"I got 'em from the janitor's closet. Here, put them on."

"Where are yours?" I asked.

"I work here, Al," he reminded me. "My fingerprints won't mean anything."

"But won't the cops wonder why your fingerprints are all over Mr. Samson's things?"

He stared at me for a second. "We only got one pair."

I pulled off the left glove and handed it to him.

"I'm right-handed," he said.

"So am I," I said.

We stared at each other for a second.

"What?" he asked. "I can't be expected to think of *everything*."

I sighed, and put the glove back on. He swung his flashlight toward the left, where it glinted on the gold-plated doorknob of the door leading to Samson's office.

"If it's anywhere in this place," he breathed, "it would be in there. Hold the light, Al."

I shone the flashlight on Uncle Farrell's key ring as his shaking fingers searched for the right key. I tried to check my watch, but it was too dark and Uncle Farrell needed the light.

He found a key he thought was the right one, but it wasn't. He cursed and started over.

He tried another key. This one slid right in and we stepped into Mr. Samson's inner office. There was a massive desk facing the door, a leather sofa along the wall beside it, and bookcases lining three sides of the room. The place was huge, about twice the size of Uncle Farrell's apartment. Against the far wall, to the left of the desk, was another door.

"Okay," Farrell said. "Where would it be?"

I thought about it. "Well, it's a sword, and it must be pretty big. He can't just hide it anywhere."

"Maybe those bookcases open to a secret chamber or somethin'," Uncle Farrell said. "Saw that on *Scooby-Doo*."

"You watch *Scooby-Doo?*"

"When I was a kid. Al, that show's been around forever."

"If this was *Scooby-Doo*, you'd be the bad guy," I said. "The bad guy was always the janitor or the night watchman."

"What a relief it is, Al, that it's not."

The far wall was one big window, all glass, commanding a view of the downtown below. Just enough light came through that Uncle Farrell could switch off the flashlight and still see. He went to the other door and disappeared inside. I heard him gasp. "Jeez Louise!" He stepped back into the room.

"Bathroom. I think the faucet's made of solid gold."

I looked at my watch. "Nine minutes into the window. We got to hurry."

I didn't know where to look in the big, sparse office. All I could see were bookcases, filled mostly with knickknacks and pictures, a potted palm tree, a sofa, a coffee table, the desk and chair, and that was about it. I pulled on a drawer handle in the desk, but it was locked. Of course, he couldn't fit a full-length sword into a desk drawer. Maybe Uncle Farrell was right, and we should look for a secret hiding place somewhere. Maybe a safe behind that big watercolor over the sofa. You saw that all the time in the movies. Uncle Farrell stood by the door leading to the reception area, his cool completely gone.

"Why are you just standing there?" Uncle Farrell snapped at me.

"I don't know where to look," I admitted. "Maybe Mr. Myers was wrong. Maybe it isn't here."

"It's here," he insisted.

"How do you know?"

"I don't know. I just know."

"You don't know but you just know?"

"Shut up, Alfred. I'm trying to think."

I sat down in Mr. Samson's leather chair. I had never sat in a more comfortable chair in my whole life. It felt like the chair was hugging me. I wondered how much a chair like this cost.

"What are you doing now?"

"I'm thinking," I said.

"Alfred, we don't got that kinda time."

Bernard Samson kept a clean desk. His blotter was bare. On one corner sat a framed photograph of a man with a big white dog that looked like a cross between a wolf and a Saint Bernard. I wondered if the man was Mr. Samson—maybe he got that kind of dog because his name was Bernard too. Other than the picture, there was a penholder and a nameplate, in case somebody forgot when they walked in who was sitting in the big fat hugging chair. I looked at the picture again. The man was broad-shouldered, with a large head and a mass of golden brown hair that he wore swept back from his high forehead, like a lion's mane.

I lifted the blotter an inch or two, which isn't an easy thing to do when you're wearing Playtex rubber gloves; sometimes guys hid things under their blotters.

"Uncle Farrell, if you had a priceless sword, where would you hide it?"

"In my priceless patooty." He peeked into the other office, as if he was waiting for the cops to storm in any second. Uncle Farrell had gone twitchy all over.

"Maybe it's behind that picture over the sofa," I said.

"'Maybe it's behind that picture over the sofa,'" he mocked me, but he kneeled on the center cushion and gingerly lifted the bottom of the frame. I knew the answer before he said it.

"Nothing." He flopped onto the sofa and rubbed his forehead.

I pulled the chair closer to the desk and rested my elbows on the blotter.

"I don't think it's here," I said.

"Shut up. I'm trying to think, Al."

"Or maybe it was here and Mr. Samson moved it."

"Why would he move it?"

"Maybe somebody told him what Mr. Myers was up to."

"Maybe, maybe, maybe," Uncle Farrell said. "If maybes were pickles we could have a picnic."

"Maybe he's too smart for us," I said, meaning Mr. Samson.

"Smart?" Uncle Farrell raised his head and glared at me from across the room.

"What did I tell you about that?" he asked. "Being smart doesn't matter as much as people think. You want to know what matters more than smarts? Stubbornness. Stubbornness and *energy*, Alfred. *That's* what gets you ahead in this world."

He dropped to his knees and shone his flashlight under the sofa. I looked at my watch. The terminal window had passed.

"Uncle Farrell, we have to go."

"I'm not going."

"We're going to get caught."

"I'm not walking out on half a million dollars!"

I pushed myself up, and somehow my belt buckle caught under the edge of the desk. It got stuck there, so when I stood, it pulled up, and the top of the desk hitched about half an inch. My buckle slipped free and the desktop smacked back down.

From across the room, Uncle Farrell was still on his knees, staring at me. "Well, I'll be jiggered," he whispered.

6

"It's heavy," I told him. "Take that side." I had cleared everything off, putting it all on the bookshelves behind me.

"Jeez Louise, I guess it is heavy." He puffed out his cheeks as we lifted. "Quick now, Alfred. I got to get downstairs to meet the cops. You stay up here till they're gone."

That made me nervous. I didn't want to be alone in the dark, but I couldn't think of any way around it.

The desktop was hinged on the front side, like the lid to the biggest music box ever made. Uncle Farrell took a deep breath as we both leaned over to peer inside.

"Holy nut-buckets!" he breathed. "Wouldn't you know?"

Inside the hidden cavity was a silver keyboard, like the pad of an ATM or calculator, built into the desk itself.

"There's a code," I said. "You punch in a code and that opens something."

"What's the code?" he asked. He looked like he was about to cry.

"I don't know," I answered.

"Well, of course you don't know, Alfred! I wasn't asking the question because I thought you knew!" He looked at his watch and chewed on his big bottom lip.

"Okay, Al, this is okay," he said in that false-positive tone adults sometimes take with kids. "I'll get on downstairs to meet the cops and you stay up here."

"Stay up here and what?"

"Break the code."

He gave me an encouraging pat on the back and headed for the door.

"Uncle Farrell!" I called after him, but he ignored me. I heard the elevator bell go *ding*, and then there was the loudest silence I had ever heard.

I stared at the pad. The PIN was probably Mr. Samson's birthday, or the year he founded the company, or maybe just some random number that had nothing to do with anything. Since I didn't know any of those numbers, I just started punching digits at random. Nothing happened, and it occurred to me I could punch numbers from now until doomsday and nothing might work.

I gave up, lowered myself back into the chair, and looked

at my watch. What if the cops demanded to see the suite and he was leading them up here right now? Part of the plan should have included walkie-talkies.

Being nervous and bored at the same time is an odd combination; I couldn't sit still, so I leaned forward and peered into the interior of the secret compartment. A little voice inside my head whispered *"telephone,"* then whispered it again, *"telephone,"* and I wondered why my little voice was whispering *"telephone"* like that.

Then it hit me. "Letters," I whispered.

Mr. Samson's phone sat on the floor beside the desk. I picked it up and set it on my lap. Like most phones, each key had three letters that corresponded to each number, like ABC was the number 2.

So I started punching in some numbers.

7-2-6-7-6-6 = SAMSON. Nothing. 2-3-7-6-2-7-3 = BERNARD. Nothing. What was the name of the dog in the picture? I punched in 9-6-5-3 (WOLF) on a hunch.

Nothing happened.

I sighed and looked at my watch. Uncle Farrell had been gone for five minutes. He had said being smart didn't matter so much, but right then it sure would have helped. More out of desperation than anything else, I punched in the first thing that popped into my head: 2-5-3-7-3-3.

From beneath my feet came a whining sound, like a motor revving up, and the floor began to shake. I pushed back from the desk with a little yelp as the desk itself began to rise, like an invisible magician was levitating it.

A huge silver metal pole rose slowly from the carpeting, until the top of the desk was about two inches from the ceiling.

The pole had an opening on the side facing me, and inside the hollow space, hung on two silver spikes, blade facing down, was the sword.

I had brought the picture, just to make sure I got the right sword, but I didn't need the picture to know this was the one. In the bluish glow from the city lights outside the window, it seemed to shimmer, like the surface of a lake on a cloudy day.

I took a deep breath and grasped the sword handle. It practically flew out of the column; I didn't expect it to feel so light. I thought it would weigh a ton, but it felt no heavier than a ballpoint pen. It sounds funny, but right away it felt like a part of me, a five-foot extension of my right arm. Grinning like a kid playing pirate, I swung it around a few times. It hissed as it cut the empty air. I held it up to the streetlights, turning it so the ambient light glittered off the edges.

I ran my left thumb along the blade. Immediately, a thin line of blood began to seep out of the wound. I hadn't even felt it. The blood brought me to my senses, though. I stuffed the sword into the duffel bag. Then I stuck my thumb in my mouth: I didn't want to drip my DNA all over Mr. Samson's office during my getaway.

I trotted to the door and stopped—what if the cops demanded to see Mr. Samson's office for some reason? Should I hide somewhere till Uncle Farrell came back up? I hesitated in the doorway, hugging the duffel against my chest while I sucked nervously on my thumb, the taste of blood in my mouth. I didn't know how to lower the desk, so I left it and stepped out into the hallway.

I closed the door, checked the lock, and headed straight for the elevator to wait for Uncle Farrell.

I leaned against the wall, my heart still pounding hard, sweat trickling down the middle of my back and my chest. The duffel bag felt very heavy all of a sudden. I pulled my thumb out of my mouth. The bleeding had stopped, but my thumb tingled, like it had fallen asleep. I panicked for a second, thinking maybe the blade was poisoned and I would die in this semidark hallway.

Then I heard the elevator coming. It must have taken a long time for Uncle Farrell to get rid of the cops, I thought as I pushed myself away from the wall. I still felt a little dizzy, but the duffel didn't feel as heavy.

The doors slid open and I was saying, "What took so long, Uncle Farrell?" when two big brown shapes stepped out. I backed down the hall, toward the emergency exit door that opened onto the stairwell. Two big men dressed in flowing brown robes, like monks, stepped out of the elevator, their hoods pulled low to cover their faces.

One stepped ahead of the other and said softly, so softly, I could barely hear him, "We don't want to hurt you. We just want the sword." He held out his hand.

His tone was so nice and reasonable, I almost handed him the sword. I might have too, but at that moment, the one behind him made a snarling sound and rushed me, his right hand coming out of the folds of his robe, and in that hand was a long saber, thin as a pool cue, black and double-bladed.

The first monk made a move to hold him back, but he was too late. Before I even had a chance to think, I jammed my hand into the duffel bag and whipped out the sword. My attacker hesitated, but only for a split second. He was nearly on top of me when I felt the sword in my hand whistle over my head—I don't even remember lifting my arm—and then I watched as my arm brought it down, aimed right at the guy's forehead.

He cried out and brought his sword up at the last second. The sound of the swords smashing into each other reverberated like thunder in the tiny hallway. He fell back a little, stunned by the blow.

The tingling in my thumb had spread to my arm, and I brought the sword around again as the first monk gave up trying to negotiate and rushed me.

His partner fell back, gripping the wrist of his blade hand. I fell back too. This taller monk moved more slowly than his buddy, but it was a thoughtful kind of slowness. I backpedaled until I bumped the stairwell door.

"Surrender the sword," came the voice beneath the brown hood. A pale hand reached for me as another raised the black tapered blade.

I reached for the handle of the door with my left hand, shoved it down, then kicked at it with my foot. At the same time, my sword was whistling toward his left ear. He blocked the swing with the black-bladed sword. I grabbed his left wrist and yanked hard, stepping to my right at the same instant, and that sent him flying past me into the stairwell. I heard him cry out in pain as he tumbled down the stairs.

The smaller monk had recovered and now he rushed me, swinging his weapon so fast, it was just a dark blur in front of my eyes—but my sword was blocking every thrust, parrying every blow, like it had a mind of its own. I didn't know how I was fighting this guy, who obviously knew what *he* was doing when it came to swordplay.

The sword in my hand seemed to weigh nothing at all, and everything started to slow down to a dreamlike dance: I could see his sword coming from a mile away.

He made one more desperate lunge at me. I turned his blade easily and brought my left fist down hard against the side of his head. He sank to his knees.

"Sorry," I said. "I don't want to hurt anybody. I'm just trying to help my uncle so he won't send me to a foster home. Who are you?"

Before he could answer, a hand grabbed me from behind and yanked me into the stairwell. It was the bigger man, the one who had first spoken. He swung me around and slammed his body hard into mine, forcing me back against the wall. He clutched my right wrist and held it against the concrete; the blade of my sword clinked against it. He took the tip of that black-bladed sword and pressed it against my Adam's apple.

"Drop the sword if you want to live," he whispered.

"Okay."

I dropped the sword. For a second neither one of us moved; I think we were both surprised I dropped it. Then, without even thinking about it, I brought my knee up as hard as I could into his crotch. He fell straight down and didn't move.

I hopped over his body, grabbed the sword, and met the other one coming through the door. He saw his fallen companion and gave a little cry. I grabbed him by the front of the robe and flung him behind me.

"Stop him!" the leader choked out from the floor.

I sprinted down the hall, the tip of the sword tapping against the carpeting as I ran. I punched the down button at the elevator. If no one had hit the call button since my attackers came out, it should be waiting for me.

The doors slid open, and Uncle Farrell was standing inside with a third monk in a brown robe, also holding a black-bladed sword, which was pressed across Uncle Farrell's neck.

7

"Alfred!" Uncle Farrell squeaked at me.

"Throw down the sword," the new monk said. "Throw it down or he dies."

"Uh, Alfred," Uncle Farrell gasped. "I think you better do what he says."

I heard the stairway door open behind me. I glanced over my shoulder and saw the first two monks coming toward me, the taller one—the one I had kneed—limping a few steps behind his partner.

"There is no escape," the tall monk said. "If you give us the sword now, you still may live."

"If you kill my uncle," I said to the monk in the elevator,

"I'll kill all of you." I sounded a lot braver than I felt. There was no way I could kill anyone, but these monks didn't know that.

"We don't want to hurt anyone," the tall monk said. "We want only the sword."

"So give it to them, Al," Farrell said. "Stop screwin' around!"

Right then the smaller monk behind me lost patience, I guess, because he leaped forward with a cry, bringing his black blade over his head. The tall monk cried, "*No!*" as he came for me. I blocked his downward thrust with an upper-cut (if that's the word for it; I don't know fencing talk) of my bigger sword. I heard a loud screech of metal hitting metal. It sounded just like a car wreck.

His smaller blade shattered on impact. I grabbed his wrist and swung him into the elevator, pieces of glittering black metal raining down on us.

He fell into Uncle Farrell and the third monk, knocking both off balance. I reached into the elevator, grabbed Uncle Farrell by the hand, and pulled him out. I dragged him a couple of steps toward the stairs, but there was still the tall monk standing between us and the exit.

"Upon my honor," he said. "All we want is the sword. Please. You know not what you are doing."

He held out his hand. "Give me the sword and you will not be harmed. You have my word."

I walked toward him, dragging Uncle Farrell with me, the tip of the sword pointed at the tall monk's stomach. I didn't know what I was doing, but I was doing it pretty well up to this point.

"Step out of the way," I told him. "We're leaving."

"You will not get far," he promised.

From beneath the hood, I swear I could see his eyes glowing, not red, like a demon or something, but a gentle bluish light, like the glow of a night-light.

"You cannot keep it long," he said. "We know who you are."

Then the tall monk did something that took me totally by surprise: He stepped out of the way.

Behind me, one of the other monks cried out, and the head monk raised his hand. His hand was very pale and his fingers long and delicate, almost like a woman's.

"No," he said quietly. Then he said to me, "We will meet again."

We hit the stairs, and the large door slammed shut behind us, echoing like a gunshot.

8

I took the steps two at a time, dragging Uncle Farrell behind me. I went down two flights, then paused at the landing, listening, but heard nothing.

"Twenty-seven floors to go," I said. "Can you make it?"

"The freight elevator—we can take that," Uncle Farrell gasped.

I pushed open the stairway door and pushed Uncle Farrell too, down the dark hall to the freight elevator. He fumbled with his keys, fussing at me the whole time. What was the matter with me, taking on a bunch of saber-shaking monks? He said I had screwed up everything, particularly his life. I was thinking about the duffel bag I had left in the hall outside Samson's office. I think I read somewhere that the cops can pull fingerprints off fabric.

Uncle Farrell was right: I had screwed up everything, his life and mine too.

He finally found the right key and when the elevator doors opened, we fell inside and he hit the lobby button. We leaned against the back wall of the elevator and tried to catch our breaths.

The doors opened onto the lobby. "Mr. Myers was right," I said. "This isn't your ordinary sword."

We stepped into the lobby.

"Where'd you learn to swing a sword like that?" he asked. He didn't wait for an answer, which was a good thing, because I didn't have one.

"You broke the code?" he asked.

I nodded.

"Well, you're just a young man of many hidden talents, aren't you? What was the code?"

"Two-five-three-seven-three-three."

"What's that?"

"That," I said, "is my name."

He stared at me. I said, "It also could be 'Alepee,' but that doesn't make much sense."

"Neither do you. Somebody ratted us out, Alfred."

"Or maybe the desktop was wired," I said.

"Right. Alarm goes off in the monastery and the monks break from vespers and scramble for battle."

The lobby was eerily quiet, except for the splashing of the water in the fountain.

"What happened to the cops?" I asked.

"That's what I'd like to know," he growled. "It's true. Never one around when you need one." He told me the third monk was waiting for him in the lobby when he stepped out of the elevator. He put a sword to his throat and took Uncle Farrell straight back to the penthouse.

Uncle Farrell stopped at his desk and hit the switches. The monitors flickered back to life. The hall on the top floor was empty. I looked at the wall behind the desk where the red indicator lights showed the location of all six elevators. The express elevator was still on the top floor.

"They took the stairs," I said.

"What do we do now?" Uncle Farrell asked. It was as if holding the sword put me in charge.

I thought about it. "Call the cops."

"Huh?"

"Maybe the monks or whoever they are intercepted the automatic emergency call. Call the cops, Uncle Farrell."

"And tell them *what*?"

"Tell them you've got three guys, maybe more, running around with swords." I reached around him again and hit a button that was labeled "Alarm." A red light began to flash on the panel.

"Okay, and while I'm waiting for the cops I think I'll whip up a snack for me and the monks when they get here. What are you talking about, Alfred?"

"They don't want you," I said, meaning the brown-robed monk men. "They want the sword, and the sword isn't going to be here."

"You're leaving? Al, you can't leave."

"Sure I can, Uncle Farrell. Give me your car keys."

"You can't have my car!"

"You'll get fired if you leave."

"Alfred, I'm about to be a millionaire—do you really think I care if they fire me? We're getting outta here!"

We took the access stairs to the underground lot. Uncle Farrell drove while I sat in the backseat, the sword across my lap. Three cop cars roared past us in the direction of Samson Towers, sirens wailing.

Once we were safely away, my own panic and fear started to set in. I broke out in a cold sweat and fought back tears. "Okay, Uncle Farrell, you've got to tell me what's really going on here."

"I don't know."

"Where'd those guys come from?"

"I don't know."

"How'd they get into the building?"

"I don't know."

"Why is my name the code to the secret chamber?"

"I don't know."

Apparently, there wasn't much Uncle Farrell did know. That made it even worse, the thought that I was the real brains of the operation.

He drove straight to our apartment. He doubled-parked

on the street. It was almost three a.m.; we didn't see anybody going up the stairs. Uncle Farrell went in first so I could check out the hall one last time.

Then I stepped into the dark room and asked, "Uncle Farrell, is everything all right?"

I flipped the switch and heard Uncle Farrell gasp. He was standing about ten feet away, by the sofa. Behind him stood Arthur Myers, his forearm across Uncle Farrell's throat.

"Of course it's all right, Mr. Kropp," Arthur Myers said.

9

"Alfred," Uncle Farrell wheezed. "I can't breathe."

"He's having some difficulty breathing, Mr. Kropp," Mr. Myers said. "Drop the sword and step away, please."

I dropped the sword. It made a dull clang as it hit the floor.

"Very good. Step away, toward the window, please."

I sidestepped to the window, keeping my eye on them.

Mr. Myers let Uncle Farrell go, stepped around him as he fell back onto the sofa, and strode quickly to the sword. He picked it up and turned it from side to side.

"All right," I said. "You have the sword. You can go now, Mr. Myers."

"Wait a minute," Uncle Farrell said, rubbing his throat. "I want some answers first. What in the name of Jehoshaphat is this sword and who were those guys in the funny robes trying to take it?"

"They weren't trying to take it," Mr. Myers said. He was staring at the sword with a weird expression. "They were trying to stop you from taking it." He leveled his eyes at me and something dark passed over his face.

"You have done me a great service, Mr. Kropp," he said to Uncle Farrell, but he was still staring at me. "So I will pay you in kind."

"That's good," Uncle Farrell said. "We had a deal, and I almost got killed getting it."

"Oh, yes. They certainly would have killed you for the sword. They are sworn to protect it at all costs. They are ruthless men of iron will, Mr. Kropp. Ruthlessness has gotten a bad reputation over the years, but there is honor in ruthlessness, a purity to it, would you not agree?"

Mr. Myers had the sword now, but he was getting at something important, something he wanted us to understand before he left.

"They are my enemies, in a way, since we work at cross-purposes, but I admire them," Mr. Myers said. "They have much to teach us about the importance of the will." He turned to me. He was smiling. It was the kind of smile that could give smiling a bad name.

"You see, Alfred Kropp, the will of most men is weak. It buckles at the slightest challenge. It crumbles at the first sign of resistance. It does not listen to the dictates of necessity. Are you following me, Mr. Kropp?"

"Not really," I said. "You've got the sword, Mr. Myers. Can we have the money now?"

"I'm going to give you something much more valuable than money, Mr. Kropp. I am going to give you an important life lesson. I am going to teach you what happens when your will conflicts with one that is stronger."

In two strides, he was in front of the sofa, and I could do nothing but watch as he drove the sword into my uncle's chest, burying the blade into the cushions behind him. Uncle Farrell's eyes slid in my direction and he whispered, "*Alfred*," before he died.

10

Myers came toward me. I froze, waiting for him to slam the sword into my chest, but instead he put a finger to my lips and whispered, "Shhhhh." Then he left without another word.

I realized right away that this was the time to get some adults involved and, since Uncle Farrell was the only adult in the room and he happened to be dead, I dialed 911.

The police came. First a couple in uniforms, then the detectives, who wore rumpled jackets and crooked ties. A photographer came to snap pictures of my dead uncle, and a lady from the coroner's office. Then another lady showed up who said she was a counselor from social services. I told her instead of some counseling I could really use a glass of water. One of the policemen brought me a glass of water.

I told them everything, from the night Mr. Myers gave Uncle Farrell the down payment to get the sword, to my fight with the brown-robed sword-fighting monks, to Mr. Myers stabbing Uncle Farrell and how he promised to kill me too if I didn't keep my mouth shut.

Nobody acted like they believed me.

Then they put Uncle Farrell in a black plastic bag and carried him into the hall, where all the neighbors were standing around, gawking. One of the detectives asked me to describe Mr. Myers, so I did. I told him about the long hair drawn back in a ponytail and the shimmering suit.

One of the detectives took a call on his cell phone and he talked in a whisper for a long time. I don't know what time it was, but it must have been close to dawn when the door opened and a big man with a lion's mane of golden blond hair stepped into the room, followed by two tall men in dark suits.

"Are you done?" one of the men in dark suits asked a detective.

"We're done."

They left us alone, and the two guys in dark suits took positions on either side of the door and stared at nothing.

The big man with the golden hair sat beside me by the window. The rising sun shone through the window, glinting off the ends of his hair. He put a hand on my forearm.

"Do you know who I am?" His voice was kind and very deep.

"Are you Bernard Samson? You look like the guy in the picture."

"Yes, I am Bernard Samson, Alfred," he said softly.

"How do you know my name?" I asked.

He smiled. "What I know might surprise you."

"Are you going to explain what's going on, Mr. Samson?"

"Yes, Alfred, I am," he said in that same soft voice. "Would you like anything?"

"One of the cops gave me a glass of water," I said. "So that's taken care of. I could use some sleep. I haven't slept in twenty-four hours. Plus I'm hungry, but I'm afraid if I eat anything, I'll puke. Mostly what I'd like, though, is some answers."

He smiled. "Ask."

"Who are those guys?" I asked, nodding toward the men by the door.

"They are agents."

"Agents of what?"

"Agents of an organization that you have never heard of, that very few people have heard of, actually. They belong to an agency specifically trained to deal with emergencies such as this one."

"This is an emergency?"

"More of a crisis. You see, Alfred, what has been lost is very important."

"You mean the sword?"

He nodded.

"It doesn't really belong to Arthur Myers, does it?" I asked.

"No."

"I knew it," I said. "I tried to tell Uncle Farrell that, but he wouldn't listen."

"Yes," was all he said.

"Who is Arthur Myers?" I asked.

"He is many things."

"You're answering my questions, but you're not giving me any answers, Mr. Samson. I thought you were in Europe."

"My flight just got in."

He patted my arm again and stood up. He began to pace around the living room, his hands behind his back.

"Who is Arthur Myers?" he said. "I had never heard that name before today. But I know the man. He has gone by many names and many guises in many lands. Bartholomew in England. Vandenburg in Germany. Lutsky in Russia. Who knows what his true name is? To my friends here"—he nodded toward the men by the door—"he is known by his code name, *Dragon*. The name he used when I first met him, though, years ago, in Paris, was Mogart, so to me he has been and always will be Mogart."

Mr. Samson gave a little shake of his enormous head and laughed bitterly.

"Mogart! What can I tell you about Mogart? He is many things, and yet nothing. Mercenary, provocateur, assassin, a destroyer and murderer, but I don't need to tell you that. A lover of darkness. Yes! Of darkness. For if a man may be defined by what he does, you may think of him as simply an agent, Alfred. An agent of darkness."

His cell phone rang. I jumped a little. I don't know if it was my jumping or the ringing of the phone, but one of the men by the door jammed his hand inside his coat pocket, then slowly took it out again when Mr. Samson began to talk.

"Yes. . . . When? . . . Are you certain?" He listened for a long time. In the early-morning light his face looked old, with deep shadow-filled creases. I wondered how old Bernard Samson was. I wondered if he was telling me the truth. I wondered what exactly he was telling me.

"Very well," he said into the phone, and flipped it closed. He sat next to me again.

"I'm afraid I haven't much time, Alfred. Things are moving very quickly and time is our enemy now. We've tapped every resource at our disposal, but he has had time, too much time, to slip through the net. The rest of your questions, quickly."

"I just want to know what's so special about this sword; why three guys dressed like monks with black swords tried to kill me for it; and most of all I want to know why my uncle is dead."

"Your uncle died to send a message, Alfred. To me. To you. To those men you met last night. He died as a warning and a promise that more will die should we oppose Mogart.

I'm afraid we can fully trust that message, Alfred: More people *will* die before this is over."

"Before *what* is over? Why don't you just talk plain to me, Mr. Samson? I'm really tired and I feel really bad. I felt bad from the first about this deal and I tried to talk Uncle Farrell out of it, but he wouldn't listen, and now I feel really bad."

He patted my hand, looked at his watch, and then said, "The sword you took from my office, did you notice anything unusual about it?"

I didn't say anything.

"You fought those men with it. Have you ever fought with a sword, Alfred?"

"Not a real one. A play one, when I was a kid."

"Yet, despite your total lack of expertise, you were able to best three very accomplished swordsmen, were you not?"

"Yes. Who were they? They don't work for Mr. Myers— or Mogart, or whatever his name is, do they?"

"No."

"So they work for you."

"They work for no man, Alfred. They are part of an ancient and secret order, bound by a sacred vow to keep safe the sword until its master comes to claim it. Yes, they should have killed you for refusing to give it to them, but they are not murderers or thieves."

"No, I guess that would be Mr. Mogart and me."

"They are knights, Alfred, or at least that's what we would call them, if there were such things in this dark age."

"Mr. Samson, are you ever going to tell me what this is all about? I thought you had to go." I felt like I was shrinking to the size of a pencil lead, which wasn't a very comfortable feeling for someone my size.

"Long ago, Alfred," Mr. Samson said. "Long ago there was a man who united the greatest kingdom the world had ever known. This kingdom was not great in lands or armies, but great in the vision it gave humankind, that justice, honor, and truth were within our grasp, not in some world to come, but here, in the world of mortal men. That king departed, but his vision remained. We are the guardians of that vision, for what we guard is the last physical embodiment of it."

"You mean the sword?"

"The sword is *in* this world, Alfred, but it is not *of* this world. Forged before the foundations of the earth, not by mortal hands, it is the True Sword, Alfred, the Sword of Kings. In another time it was known as Caliburn. You may know it by its other name, the sword Excalibur."

"You're talking about King Arthur, right?"

"Yes, King Arthur."

"That's just a legend, a story, Mr. Samson."

"I don't have the time to convince you of anything, Alfred. You held it tonight. In your inexperienced hands, the Sword bested three of the finest swordsmen in the world. Yet that is only a fraction of its power. The Sword of Kings contains the power of heaven itself, Alfred, the power to create as well as to destroy. All the mortal arts of weaponry are powerless against it, but more than this, the *will* of ordinary men cannot withstand its might."

I thought of the tall monk stepping aside to let me and Uncle Farrell pass, as I held the Sword, telling him to move. *The will of ordinary men cannot withstand its might.*

Mr. Samson's eyes were shining with a faraway look, as if he was seeing things I could not see, great battles and men in gleaming armor on horseback, thundering across rolling fields.

"You asked who those men in the Towers were. Only twelve of us are left now, but they—and I—are the descendents of King Arthur's Knights of the Round Table. The Sword has been in our care for centuries and, as far as I know, this is the first time we have failed to keep it from the hands of evil men."

"You're a knight," I said, slowly shaking my head. "You're telling me you guys are knights like King Arthur–type knights?"

"Not those men, no," Mr. Samson said, gesturing toward the two gray suits still at attention by the door. "Their organization did not even know of the Sword's existence before tonight. Circumstances now demand the use of every tool at our disposal. You see, Monsieur Mogart has many powerful friends, Alfred, friends who would pay any price for a weapon against which there is no defense. And Mogart's friends are no friends of humanity. They are despots and dictators who would pay anything to possess the Sword. Do you begin to understand? There is no weapon devised by man, no army or combination of armies, no nation or alliance of nations on earth that can resist the power of the Sword."

"Mr. Myers paid my uncle to steal the Sword so he could sell it to somebody?"

"To the highest bidder, and you can guess how high those bids will go."

He touched my arm again, and I was surprised to see tears shining in his hazel eyes.

"And what kinds of men will bid on it. Alfred," he said, "an army with the Sword at its head would be invincible."

11

"It is a prize beyond any price, Alfred," Mr. Samson said. "But Mogart can expect billions for it. Tens of billions. And if we do not find him before the Sword passes into the hands of evil men, the world will plunge into an age of unimaginable cruelty and terror. Envision the horrors of Nazi Germany or the Russia of the Stalinists, multiply them tenfold, and then you will begin to understand the magnitude of this loss."

The rising sun was shining now through the window on his sharp features.

"We must retrieve the Sword before this can happen. He

may yet decide to keep it for his own use, but that result would not be much better."

"You know where he is?" I asked.

"I know where he is going. He has been preparing a long time for this day. Right now he is crossing the Atlantic, making for his keep in Játiva." He saw my confused expression and gave a little laugh. "In Spain, Alfred." He smiled at me again. "You have a thousand more questions, but I've stayed too long; I must go."

"Don't go yet," I begged. "Don't leave me alone."

He patted my hand and his smile faded. "That seems to be my doom—and yours, Alfred."

He turned and went to the door. I jumped up and followed him.

"There's gotta be something I can do," I said. "Take me with you; I could help. I'm the one who lost it; I should help get it back."

I expected him to say something like "I think you've done quite enough already." Instead, he leaned toward me and whispered, "Pray."

He started down the hall and I called out after him, "Just one more question, Mr. Samson! Why didn't he kill me too?"

He paused, then turned back to me, smiling that same sad smile. "Two reasons, I think. First, it is crueler to kill your uncle and let you live. Second, there is such a thing as honor among thieves."

He disappeared into the stairwell, followed by the two agents. Nothing he could have said would have made me feel worse than calling me a thief. I don't think he meant to hurt my feelings, though. My feelings were the least of his worries.

12

With Uncle Farrell gone, I was now a ward of the state. A couple named Horace and Betty Tuttle volunteered to take me in, pending the unlikely event of somebody adopting me.

The Tuttles lived in a tiny house on the near north side of Knoxville. Five other foster kids lived crammed into that little house. I never saw Horace Tuttle go to work, and I knew they received all sorts of checks from the state and the federal government for each kid, so I think we were how he made a living.

Horace Tuttle was a short, round little guy, always making remarks about my size, particularly my head. I think I scared him or he resented how big I was, I mean, because he was awfully small. Betty, his wife, was short and round like him, with the same conical-shaped head. They reminded me of turtles, kind of like their name, Tuttle. Maybe some people come to resemble their names, the way some people come to resemble their dogs.

I shared a bedroom with two of the other foster kids. The very first night the older one threatened to kill me in my sleep. I was feeling so low and lousy, I told him that would be fine with me.

I usually had trouble concentrating in school, but try concentrating when your uncle has just been murdered right before your eyes and you know the world is about to end. Try studying when you know World War III is about to start and it's all your fault.

I still met with Amy Pouchard twice a week. She asked why I had missed the past couple of weeks and I told her.

"My uncle was murdered."

"Oh, my God!" she exclaimed. "Who killed him?"

I thought about my answer. "An agent of darkness."

"So they caught him?"

"They're trying."

"Hey, isn't your mom dead too?"

"She died of cancer."

"You must be the unluckiest person on earth," she said, and scooted away from me a little, probably without realizing she was doing it. "I mean, your mom and now your uncle and what you did to Barry and everything."

"I've been trying to tell myself all those things had nothing to do with me, that I'm okay and everything," I said. "But it's getting harder and harder."

I was Uncle Farrell's sole heir, so I got all his things, but I only kept his TV and VCR, which I set up in my bedroom. The main thing I didn't get was the $500,000. I didn't remember Mogart leaving with the brown leather satchel, but it wasn't under Uncle Farrell's bed where he stashed it, and the police never found it, probably because I didn't tell them about it. That cash would be hard to explain and would probably get me in more trouble than I already was in, but I started wishing I still had that money. If I did, I would have taken it and run. I didn't know where I'd run, but anywhere seemed better than the Tuttles and the delinquents who lived with them.

Over the next couple of days, I would grab Horace's newspaper and take it to school and, instead of studying, I read the newspaper from front page to last, looking for anything that might give me a clue as to what was happening with Mr. Samson's quest. I wondered what good a billion dollars was in a world of unimaginable cruelty and terror, but men like Mogart have imaginations different than mine. For example, if I had been Mogart, it would have never occurred to me to hire somebody like my uncle Farrell to steal the most powerful weapon that ever existed.

I missed Uncle Farrell. I missed the little apartment and the frozen dinners. I missed the way he wet his big lips and even all his lectures about getting ahead in the world. He was just trying to help me, to show me I didn't have to end up like him. It hit me that he loved me, and I was the only family *he* had left.

To take my mind off things, I checked out a book from the library called *The Once and Future King,* about King Arthur and the Knights of the Round Table. I couldn't get through it, so I rented this old movie called *Excalibur* with a bunch of English actors I had never heard of.

Arthur was this kind of goofy kid, actually, a squire to his brother Fey, toting around his sword and taking care of Fey's horse and his armor, kind of his lackey, not even a knight. Nobody believed this kid could actually pull the Sword from the Stone, until Arthur did it and told them, "If you would be knights and follow a king, then follow me!"

Then he became king, built Camelot, and gathered his knights around the Round Table. Everything was great until his best knight, Lancelot, got together with his queen, Guinevere, and Arthur's bastard son, Mordred, came to take everything over.

There's a big, bloody battle at the end. Arthur kills Mordred, who sort of kills Arthur too, but it's confusing because they show Arthur being taken over the sea by three angel-looking women in white robes. One of the knights picks up Excalibur and throws it into this big lake, where the Lady of the Lake kind of floats up to grab it.

That last part confused me. I wondered how Mr. Samson and his knights ended up with the sword if the Lady took it after Arthur left. If I ever saw Mr. Samson again, I was going to ask him about that.

I don't know if it was that movie, which I saw about forty-nine times, that made me have the dreams. I always fell asleep while the credits rolled, and I would dream of a gleaming white castle on a mountainside, and from its rampart flew triangular flags of black and gold, and inside its outer wall a thousand knights were mustered in full armor. They carried long black swords and their faces were painted black and their expressions were terrible as they fought some guys who had breached the outer wall, men with flowing hair in brown robes, and their faces were covered with mud and grimly set. The men in robes followed a man with golden hair and somehow I knew this man was Mr. Samson, though in my dream he looked different than I remembered him. They were about ten against a thousand, they had no hope, but they fought until the last man fell, and this last man was the knight with the golden hair.

I woke after that dream with the word "Játiva" on my lips. I went to the school library and found Játiva in the atlas. It was a town in Spain, like Mr. Samson said, right at this mountain called Monte Bernisa.

I had another dream too, a terrible dream, the kind that makes you wish you could wake up. I was far above a great plain or field and saw a vast army, row upon row of blank-faced soldiers marching, stretching as far as I could see, a million or more men, and the tramp of their feet was like thunder. Warplanes screamed overhead, lines of tanks rumbled over the field, and the night sky was lit up from the concussions of long-range missiles. Before this army, on a dark horse, rode a big man holding Excalibur, his face hidden in shadow, and as the jets screamed overhead, he raised the Sword in defiance, and from the army behind him came a cry that drowned out the sound of the bombs.

The man leaped from the horse, brought the Sword high over his head, and slammed it into the ground. Brilliant white light exploded from that spot and planes fell burning from the sky, tanks erupted into flame, and whole divisions of his foes were consumed in fire or fled screaming from the flood of light.

The light slowly died away, and then I was walking in a wasteland of broken concrete, uprooted, leafless trees, crushed and twisted cars with their hazard lights blinking. Ash floated everywhere, clinging to my hair and making me cough. I was looking for someone, calling a name, but I couldn't hear who I was calling for. I was desperate to find whoever it was; if I could just find them, everything would be all right. But I always woke up without finding them.

13

After Mogart took the Sword, my life
followed the same pattern. I would stay up late watching the
news or *Excalibur*, stumble off to school after two or three
hours of sleep filled with bad dreams, read the newspaper in
class, then come home and go straight to my room to wait
for the beginning of the end of the world.

At supper, the Tuttles would start in on me.

"Look at you!" Horace shouted one night. "You don't
sleep, you don't eat, you mope around all day with your nose
glued to the television screen or the newspaper—what's the
matter with you, you big-headed palooka?"

"Oh, I don't know," I said. "Maybe it has something to do with my uncle dying."

"Dear," Betty said to Horace. "Maybe you shouldn't bring up little Alfred's uncle."

"First of all, this kid is anything but little, and second of all, I didn't bring up his uncle, he did!"

And he yelled, his pinched face puckered with rage: "Your problem is self-pity! You think you're the only person on earth who's ever lost somebody? The world is full of pain, Alfred, pain and big losers, and you've got to make up your mind to be a winner!"

"Like you?" I asked.

"Oh," Betty gasped. "Oh, oh, oh!"

"That's your other problem!" Horace screamed. "No gratitude! At least you've got a roof over your head and food for your big self! A lot of people in this world don't even have that!"

And I couldn't take any more. I left him sitting there, his thin lips moving silently, and locked myself in the bedroom. This got my roomies going, a thirteen-year-old greasy-haired thug named Dexter and his ten-year-old brother, Lester, who was also a thug, only not registering as high as Dexter on the thug-o-meter. They pounded on the door and yelled that it was their room too. I just turned the volume up on the news and pretended I didn't hear them. Then Dexter began to shout he was going to cut me; he was going to cut me bad; and that reminded me of the scar on my thumb, which was an inch long and white as dental floss. Sometimes it ached and sometimes it burned and sometimes it just throbbed and tingled. I developed this nervous habit of running my index finger along it, feeling the little indent in my flesh, especially when I was nervous or thought I was going crazy.

I started skipping school. I didn't see much point in an education when the world was about to end. I left in the mornings as if I was going to the bus stop, then cut through a side street to Broadway and walked all the way to the Old City, the historic section of downtown Knoxville. I hung out in the coffeehouses and used-book shops or paced up and down Jackson Street, looking at the homeless people or the long-haired college kids lounging in the sidewalk cafés.

Then, late one afternoon, I decided I just couldn't go back and face the Tuttles, so I ate an early dinner at a place called McCallister's. It was about five o'clock and the dinner crowd hadn't arrived yet, so I had the place mostly to myself.

Mostly, but not all. Across the room sat a tall man with long snow-white hair. He ate very slowly, carving his steak into razor-thin slices and chewing real slow. Every once in a while he lifted his eyes toward me. He looked familiar, but I couldn't remember where I had seen him before. His fingers wrapped around his wineglass were long and delicate. He had big hands, like a basketball player or a pianist.

He stood up and that's when I saw how tall he was. He pulled a white handkerchief from his breast pocket as he sneezed loudly. Then he walked out of the room without looking in my direction, and I wondered why some old guy having dinner was making me so paranoid.

I was feeling guilty at about this point because now it was past six and the Tuttles were probably sitting down to dinner and Horace was probably shouting, "Where is that Kropp? Where is that big-headed palooka?" So I called their house from a pay phone.

Betty answered. "Oh, Alfred, where have you been? Where are you now? We've been worried sick! We were about to call the police or 911, though Horace has been telling me we shouldn't call 911 except in the case of an emergency and he doesn't feel this qualifies since you're nearly sixteen and old enough to look after yourself, but I told him you're just a boy despite your larger-than-normal size, but we have been worried *sick*."

"Don't be worried, Betty," I said. "I'm okay."

"Where are you?"

"I'm going to be a while longer. I just wanted to tell you I was okay."

"Oh, Alfred," she said. "Alfred, please come home." She was crying.

"I don't have a home anymore," I said, and I hung up.

There was somebody else I wanted to call, but it took me a long time to work up the nerve to do it. I got her number from the operator and almost hung up when a guy who sounded like he might be her dad answered the phone. But I didn't.

"Is Amy there?" I asked.

After what seemed like a couple of years, I heard her twangy voice.

"Who is this?" she asked.

"Me. Alfred. Alfred Kropp."

"Who?"

"The guy you're tutoring in math."

"Oh! The dead-uncle guy," she said.

"Yeah," I said. "The dead-uncle guy. Look, I just wanted to say—"

"I knew it wasn't somebody I know," she said. "Because you called this number. People I know call me on my cell phone."

"Right," I said. "Look, the reason I called. I—I don't think I'll be at tutoring tomorrow. Or ever. I don't think I'm coming back."

There was silence. I said, to break it, "I said I don't think I'm coming back."

"I heard you. Look, I know you must be really messed up right now. I know what that's like. When I was twelve my big brother ran over my dog. I couldn't get out of bed for a *week*."

Why did I think she cared? Why was I thinking anybody cared? My own father hadn't even cared. I was an accident everybody had to suffer from, like Barry with his sprained wrist.

I said good-bye to Amy Pouchard and started to walk. It was getting dark now, and there were a lot of people about, couples mostly, walking arm in arm, and I watched them as I walked. Something made me turn around at one point and I saw him, the tall guy with the white hair, about half a block down. He was standing by a newspaper rack, pretending to read. I walked to the intersection of Western and Central, turned left, and walked half a block to Ye Olde Coffee House, right next to the old JFG coffee plant.

I went in and ordered a grande with extra cream and sugar, and sat at the long counter against the window, watching the couples pass outside.

Halfway through my grande I saw him sit down at the very end of the bar, next to the bathroom. I picked up my coffee and walked over to sit down next to him.

We drank our coffee in silence for a moment. The end of his nose was red and runny; he had a cold. He pulled out the white handkerchief. It had a design of a horse and rider on it. The rider was a knight carrying a red banner. That clinched it for me.

"How is Mr. Samson?" I asked him.

"Dead."

I thought about my dream and asked, "When did that happen?"

"Two days ago."

"Mr. Mogart—he killed him?"

"Do not say that name." He folded the handkerchief into a perfect square and tucked it back into his breast pocket.

"Who're you?" I asked.

"Call me Bennacio."

"I'm Alfred Kropp."

"I know who you are."

"We've met before," I said. "At Samson Towers. I didn't

recognize you at first without your robe. But I recognize your hands. And your voice."

He nodded. "The man you know as Bernard Samson was killed two nights ago in Játiva, on the slopes of Monte Bernisa in Spain." He sipped his coffee. He had taken off the lid and I could see he drank it black. "I was given instructions to find you in the event of his fall."

I thought about that. It didn't make much sense to me, but, since Mom died and I went to live with Uncle Farrell, almost everything had stopped making sense. "Why?"

"To tell you of his fate."

"That's important—telling me?"

He shrugged, like he really couldn't make a judgment on the importance of keeping Alfred Kropp in the loop.

"What happened in Spain?"

Bennacio kept looking out the window. "He fell. Four of our Order fell with him. I alone have escaped to bring this news to you, Kropp. It was his dying wish that you should know."

He sipped his coffee. He had a sharp nose and dark, deep-set eyes beneath thick salt-and-pepper brows. His white hair was swept back from his high forehead.

"Two of the Order fell in Toronto," Bennacio said. "They were the first, dispatched by Samson to stop the enemy before he could flee North America. Another in London. Two in Pau, before the rest of us arrived."

I did the math. Mr. Samson had told me there were twelve knights left. "That leaves just two of you."

Bennacio shook his head. "Windimar fell near Bayonne, the night before we discovered the enemy in Játiva. I am the last of my Order."

He didn't say anything for a while. We finished our coffee. Finally, I said, "I'm sorry, Mr. Bennacio."

"Just Bennacio," he said. I don't think it really mattered to him if I was sorry.

I went on. "But there's a lot of other people in on this, right? Mr. Samson brought in this secret agency, some kind of spies, I guess, or mercenaries; I don't know what you'd call them . . ."

"You are speaking of oy-pep."

"I am?"

He nodded. "O-I-P-E-P. Oy-pep." He made a face like saying the word left a bad taste in his mouth.

"What's OIPEP?"

"Did you not just say Samson told you?"

"Well, like a lot of things he told me, he kind of did but he kind of didn't. But I'm not exactly what you might call quick on the uptake. What exactly *is* OIPEP?"

He glanced around the coffee shop. "We should not talk about OIPEP here, Kropp."

He stood up. I don't know why, but I stood up too. I followed him to the door and into the night. The late-spring air was soft and warm. He took out his white handkerchief again and blew his nose.

"It is a fool's hope," he said with a little laugh.

"What is?" I asked.

He didn't give me a direct answer, sort of like Mr. Samson never gave direct answers. Maybe that was part of being a knight. "For Mogart cannot be stopped, not while he wields the Sword. Yet while I live, I must try to stop him." He turned and looked right at me for the first time. His dark eyes were sad.

"Now is the hour," he said softly. "Our doom is upon us."

He walked away without saying anything else and I watched him cross the street. Then I saw two big men step out of the doorway of an antique store and follow him. Both wore long gray cloaks that were too heavy for the warm weather.

Bennacio didn't seem to notice them; he walked with his head bowed, like he was deep in thought. A little voice inside my head said, "*Go home, Alfred.*" But I didn't have a home anymore. Now Mr. Samson was dead and all the other knights except this Bennacio guy, and it was all my fault. I could have—*should have*—told Uncle Farrell no, I wasn't going to help him get the Sword. I knew it was wrong at the time, and if I had stood my ground everybody would still be alive and I would have a home. I had hated that little apartment with the worn-out furniture and its old fishy smell. I had wished every day that my mom hadn't died and my uncle was somebody more like Donald Trump than Farrell Kropp, but now that sounded like heaven to me. I would have given anything to have it back.

Bennacio was walking north on Central, the men keeping pace a few feet behind him.

And for some reason I have never understood, I followed them.

When I turned the corner, they had Bennacio against the wall and were taking turns slugging him, one guy holding him up while the other one slammed his big fists into his gut. They were too busy pounding the crap out of him to notice me.

One of them turned to his buddy and said with a foreign accent, "Finish him." The second man pulled something long and black from the folds of his gray cloak.

"Hey!" I shouted.

They looked over at me. None of us moved for a second; then the guy holding the dagger jammed it into Bennacio's side, the other one let him go and, as Bennacio slid slowly down the brick wall, they took off east along the railroad tracks.

I ran over to Bennacio. His eyes were open and he was breathing. He was clutching that white handkerchief in both hands. I put my hand on his side and it came away covered in his blood.

"Leave me," he said.

I hauled him up, pulling his arm over my shoulder, and kind of dragged him back to Central.

"You're hurt," I said. "I'm taking you to the hospital."

"No hospital. No hospital," he gasped.

I spotted a Yellow Cab parked on the corner. I shoved Bennacio into the backseat.

"Where to?" the driver asked.

"Where to?" I asked Bennacio.

"The Marriott . . ." Bennacio gasped.

"Take us to the Marriott," I told the driver.

Bennacio leaned against me, and I tugged the handkerchief from his hands and pressed it against the badly bleeding wound in his side.

"Oh, boy," I whispered. "Oh, jeez, you're bleeding pretty bad, Bennacio."

"Hey," the cabbie said, staring at us in his rearview mirror. "Your friend okay, kid?"

"No hospital, no hospital," Bennacio kept whispering. His face was very pale and his eyes were rolling in his head as he leaned against me. I guessed he was dying.

14

I managed to get Bennacio out of the cab and into the lobby of the hotel, with him leaning against me. The clerk behind the desk gave me a look.

"My uncle," I told the clerk. "Little too much wine."

Bennacio told me his room number and somehow I got him into the elevator, up to the sixth floor, and into his room. I laid him on the bed.

His eyes were closed and he was breathing in short, hard gasps. I opened his jacket and unbuttoned his white shirt to expose the wound, a gash just below his ribs on the left side. I got some towels from the bathroom and pressed one into his side, watching the blood soak into it. I threw that towel on the floor and replaced it with another. He wouldn't stop bleeding.

"I don't know what I'm doing," I told him. "You're gonna bleed to death if we don't get you to a doctor."

He opened his eyes and looked at me. "The blade was poisoned," he said. "The bleeding will not stop." Then he raised his head a little and looked at my hand holding the towel against his side.

He must have seen the scar on my thumb, because he whispered, "You have been wounded by the Sword."

"Yeah."

"In the bathroom," he gasped. "My straight razor. Bring it to me."

I found it in a little black leather bag on the vanity. The razor had a long retractable blade that slipped into the handle. I didn't think anybody used a straight razor anymore. How did I know this Bennacio wasn't lying—that he wasn't really a goon for Mogart, come to kill me? But even if he was lying, even if he was a bad guy, who was I to let him slowly bleed to death?

I brought the razor back to him. He sat forward a little, groaning with the effort, grabbed my wrist, and held it tight.

"Hey," I said. "What are you doing?"

He grabbed the razor, placing the edge along my scar, and made a shallow cut just shallow enough to draw blood.

"Oh, my God!" I yelped, trying to pull my hand away.

He tossed the towel aside with his other hand, then

brought my bleeding thumb to his side and pressed it into the wound.

"What are you doing?" I asked.

"The Sword has the power to heal as well as to rend," he said. After a few minutes he let go of my wrist. I picked up the towel and put it back on the wound, but already the bleeding had slowed.

Bennacio closed his eyes. His breathing became easier, and for a second I thought he had fallen asleep.

"Who were those men, Bennacio?" I asked, clutching my throbbing thumb.

"Servants of the enemy . . . following me since my return to America."

Which meant he got stabbed because of me. Why had Mr. Samson sent him to me? Like telling Alfred Kropp about it was going to help them get the Sword back.

I sat beside him and felt like crying, but I didn't want to cry in front of Bennacio. Everybody around me lately was dying. All because I took something I shouldn't have. I was like some lumbering, awkward, big-headed Angel of Death.

"You want anything, Bennacio?" I asked. He didn't answer. "I don't know what to do. I mean, I'm really scared right now. Why did Mr. Samson send you here? What's going to happen now that all the knights are dead? I'm not going to live, am I? None of us are. You said our doom was upon us. I'm thirsty. You want a drink of water?"

He didn't answer. This time he had really fallen asleep.

15

I watched him sleep for a long time, un-til I started feeling sleepy myself. There was sofa in the outer room, and I lay on that for a while, but it made me nervous because I couldn't keep an eye on him.

So I went back into his room and sat on the bed. I must have finally passed out, because I woke up at dawn curled at the foot of the bed, like a big, faithful dog.

When I woke up he was still asleep, so I ordered room service, a plain bagel (since I didn't know how he liked them), a bagel with everything, a pot of coffee, and an or-ange juice.

I answered the door to get the food. When I came back,

he was awake. I helped him sit up so he could eat. He took the bagel with everything, the one I wanted, but he was the guy with the stab wound, so I didn't say anything.

"What happened in Játiva?" I asked.

"Samson believed our only hope lay in attacking the enemy in force. I argued against it, but he was the head of our Order, and in the end I acquiesced. We had tracked Mogart to his keep in Játiva, an ancient castle overlooking the city, rebuilt and refortified in preparation for this day. Samson planted a story in one of the British dailies that he was actually in London, attending a conference of foreign business leaders. He had hoped this would lull Mogart into relaxing his vigilance."

"I guess it didn't."

"They waited until we had reached the inner courtyard of Mogart's castle—and then ambushed us. Fifty men at least. Bellot fell, then Cambon, yet even so we might have succeeded. We bested the front guard and had taken the grounds, when fate turned against us and Mogart appeared with the Sword."

He took a deep breath. "And, as we fell, one by one, the angels themselves wailed and beat upon their breasts. The Sword was not meant for such work, was never forged to spill the blood of its protectors. We fell back, our hearts filled with dread, but another contingent of the enemy had formed behind us, cutting off our escape."

"He killed—he killed everyone?"

"It was a slaughter, Kropp. I fell by the gate, wounded,

though not mortally, and thus became the sole surviving witness to Mogart's ultimate treachery, the killing of our captain, the man you call Bernard Samson. What Mogart did to him I will not say here—but it was terrible, Kropp. Terrible! Yet still Samson found strength before he died to tell me to take the message to you, that he had fallen and the Sword is still not safe. In short, that the Knights of the Order of the Sacred Sword are no more."

I set down my half-eaten bagel. All of a sudden, I wasn't hungry anymore. I remembered my dream, of the brave men outnumbered in a gray castle, and the man with the golden hair falling.

"For hours I lay half dead in the blood-soaked mud of Mogart's keep," Bennacio went on. "Finally darkness fell and I deemed it safe to slip away. I was spotted, of course, and pursued here to America, though I thought I had lost my pursuers. Apparently, I have not."

He set down his cup and put his plate with the uneaten bagel on the bedside table.

"Nor will they stop until I am dead. For I am the last knight, the sole hope for the Sword's retrieval. These others, the outsiders Samson enlisted to our cause, this . . . OIPEP cannot prevail against Mogart. Only a Knight of the Order has any prayer of retrieving the Sword. And Mogart knows this."

He rolled to the edge of the bed, holding his side, wincing from the pain.

"What are you doing?" I asked.

"Leaving."

"You can't leave, Bennacio. You lost a lot of blood. You gotta rest for a couple—"

"Listen!" he said sharply. "They will not stop hunting me, Kropp. Even as we speak, they may be in this building. Now that my final oath to Samson is fulfilled, I must return to Europe and pick up Mogart's trail before the calamity strikes, before he or anyone else can use the Sword to an evil end."

He pushed himself from the bed, swayed a second on his feet, and fell back. I caught him and eased him back down as he gulped in air.

"I am the last knight," he gasped. "I am bound by my sacred oath to recover what should never have been lost."

I don't know if those words were aimed at me, *what should never have been lost,* but I took it like they were.

"What can I do?" I asked.

He cocked one of those thick eyebrows in my direction and I felt about the size of pencil lead again.

"Please, Bennacio, let me do something. Let me help. I didn't realize I was doing it until now, but I've run away. I'm not going back to the Tuttles' ever again. So if I'm not going back, then I've got nowhere to go and I can't go nowhere, I've got to go somewhere. All this—it's my fault. Well, it's also my uncle's fault, but if I had said no then none of this would have happened. He couldn't have done it without me. But he's dead now, so I'm the only one who can do anything about it, about letting Mogart get his hands on the Sword. I don't know what I can do, but you're in pretty rough shape; maybe you could use me. Please. Please, use me, Bennacio."

He almost smiled. Almost. He held on to his side, wincing. "Can you drive a car, Kropp?"

16

I told him, you bet, I could drive a car, but I had just started and didn't have much experience. That didn't seem to bother him. I helped him get dressed and he leaned on me as we walked to the parking lot. He directed me to a brand-new silver Mercedes parked near the exit.

"This is your car?" I asked.

"Yes."

"Cool car."

I helped him into the passenger seat. After I slid behind the wheel, he handed me the keys.

"This is a really nice car, Bennacio," I said. "You sure it's okay if I drive it?"

"Did you not say in the room you could drive?"

"Sure, but I only got my learner's permit six months ago and I don't have that much experience behind the wheel."

He gave a little wave of his hand, a gesture that struck me as very European. "We must use the instruments given us, Kropp."

"Oh," I said. "You bet."

The engine purred to life and I felt my scalp tingle. If things weren't so serious, I would have been thrilled.

Bennacio directed me to the interstate. I asked him where we were going, thinking I was just giving him a quick lift to the airport, but all he said was "North," which was the opposite direction of Knoxville's airport. I didn't know where we were going, only that somehow I was along for the ride. I kept checking the rearview mirror, but didn't see anything suspicious, just cars and big semis. What would a suspicious car look like anyway? Since I didn't know, *all* the cars around us started to look suspicious. It's hard enough being a novice driver tooling down the interstate in heavy traffic; try adding covert pursuit by quasi-medieval bad guys to the list.

I was about an hour out of the city when Bennacio asked, "Why did you take the Sword?"

"That was my uncle's idea," I said. "Well, I guess it was his idea by way of Mr. Myers's—I mean Mogart's idea."

"And why did your uncle take it?"

"Mogart gave him five hundred thousand dollars."

"So you took it for money." He said the word "money" like it was dirty.

"No. Not the money, really. I'm not greedy, if that's what you're thinking."

"Then why?"

"Look, Bennacio, I didn't know who Mr. Samson really was or what the Sword really was. How could I? I was just helping out Uncle Farrell. Plus he threatened to send me back to foster care if I said no. I told him we shouldn't. I told him I had a bad feeling about it and it was wrong, but he's my uncle. I'm a kid. And I ended up in foster care anyway."

But I was just making excuses. Once you're about ten, maybe eleven tops, "I'm just a kid" doesn't cut it when it comes to your core ideas like the difference between right and wrong.

We didn't say anything for a while. He was staring at the road, not looking at me.

"Where am I taking you, Bennacio?" I asked.

He didn't answer. I glanced over at him. He was still staring at the road.

"How are you going to find Mogart and the Sword once you get to Europe?"

He didn't answer. I took a deep breath and let it out very slowly. Then I tried again.

"Mr. Samson told me you guys were all descended from the original Knights of the Round Table," I said. "Which one did you come from?"

He waited before answering. Maybe he wasn't allowed to tell.

"Bedivere," he said finally.

"Hey, wasn't he the one who found the Holy Grail?"

"No, Galahad found the Grail."

"Oh. I've been watching this movie, *Excalibur*. You ever seen it?"

He didn't answer.

"I've seen it about fifty times. But a couple of parts have been confusing me. Like at the end Percival takes the Sword and throws it into this big lake and the Lady grabs it."

"Arthur did not give the Sword to Percival. The Sword was given to Bedivere."

"Well, in the movie it's Percival."

He cocked an eyebrow at me. I cleared my throat.

"So . . . the Sword belongs to you?" I asked.

"The Sword *belongs* to no man." He sighed. "Upon the fields of Salisbury Plain, Arthur fell, mortally wounded, in the last battle against the armies of Mordred. Before he drew his last breath, Arthur entrusted the Sword to my forebear, Bedivere, who was meant to return it to the waters from which it came, lest the very calamity which has now happened should befall it."

"Well, in the movie it was Percival and he *did* throw it into the lake. So if that's true, how did Samson end up with it?"

He said, "It is a movie, Kropp."

"Did Arthur really die?"

"All men die."

"Mr. Samson said you guys were keeping the Sword until its master comes to claim it. Who's the master if Arthur's dead?"

"The master is the one who claims it," Bennacio said.

"And who would that be?" I asked.

"The master of the Sword," he said

"Do you know who that is?" I asked.

"I do not need to know."

"How come?"

"The Sword knows," he said. "The Sword chose Arthur."

"How does a sword choose somebody?"

He didn't say anything.

"How do you know the Sword didn't choose Mogart?" I asked.

He leaned his head back and closed his eyes, I guess to let me know he was still angry at me or he didn't feel like talking or his side still hurt.

I pulled off the interstate around noon to get some gas and something to eat. All I'd had that day was half a bagel, and Bennacio hadn't even touched his breakfast.

I paid for my gas and bought two corn dogs, a bag of chips, and a couple of fountain drinks. Back in the car, I handed one of the corn dogs to Bennacio.

"What is this?" he asked.

"A corn dog."

"A corn dog?"

"It's a wiener wrapped in corn bread."

"Why is it skewered?"

"It's a kind of handle."

He looked at the corn dog suspiciously. I pulled to the far side of the building and parked near the air hose.

"What are you doing, Kropp?"

"I need to check your side. Pull up your shirt, Bennacio."

"My side is fine. We need to keep driving."

I just looked at him. He sighed, laid the corn dog still in its yellow wrapping on his lap, and lifted up his shirt. I pulled the dressing aside and saw the wound had already closed. I'm no doctor, but it looked almost healed.

"Let's go, Kropp," Bennacio said crisply, pulling down his shirt.

I got back on the interstate. Bennacio didn't eat his corn dog; it lay on his lap for another twenty miles as he stared out his window.

"Your corn dog's getting cold," I told him. He ignored me. I reached over, took it off his lap, pulled off the wrapping, and ate it. It occurred to me I hadn't seen Bennacio eat since the restaurant the night before.

"Maybe I should have asked before I bought you the corn dog," I said. "But I figured, who doesn't like corn dogs?"

"I am not hungry."

"You gotta eat, Bennacio. Tell me what you want and I'll stop again."

"No, no. Keep driving."

"Where am I going, exactly?"

"Canada."

I looked over at him. "Canada?"

He sighed. "To Halifax, in Nova Scotia. I have friends there."

"Jeez, Bennacio, I had no idea I was driving you all the way to Canada! Wouldn't it have been easier just to fly to Spain?"

"The airports will be watched."

"Won't they be in Halifax too? I mean, wouldn't they think of that?"

I wondered where exactly Halifax was in Nova Scotia. I wondered where Nova Scotia was. I didn't ask him, though. He had a way of talking to me that sounded like he didn't want to talk to me, like he was just being polite.

"Who are these friends in Halifax? The what-do-ya-call-'ems, OIPEP guys?"

"OIPEP is not my friend," he said.

"Then what is it? What does OIPEP stand for, anyway?" He didn't say anything, so my mind tried to fill in the blanks: *Organization of Interested Parties in Evolutionary Psychiatry.* But that didn't make any sense.

"The knights were not the only ones who knew of the Sword's existence," Bennacio said. "We were its protectors, Kropp, but the Sword itself has many friends."

"Oh. Well, that's good. It's good to have friends. I left my best friend behind in Salina, where I grew up. His name is Nick. So what happens once we get to Halifax? Are you crossing the Atlantic by boat?"

He didn't say anything.

"What?" I asked. "Too slow? You guys probably have supersonic jets or something at your disposal."

After driving in silence a while—that seemed to be the method Bennacio preferred—we hit some rain. Bennacio sipped his fountain drink, holding the tip of the straw against his lower lip with his upper, the straw pressing against his chin, not sucking but delicately drawing up the soda into his mouth. There was the gentle hissing of the rain and Bennacio slurping his drink, and those were the only two sounds for miles. It started to get to me.

"I was wondering," I said, "who Mr. Samson was descended from."

Bennacio sighed. "Lancelot," he said wearily.

I decided not to worry if I was bugging him. I was getting tired of his Old World superior act and the way he talked to me like I was a little kid or somebody with a mental condition. And I was getting sleepy. And though it was a truly awesome car, I wasn't used to driving long distances. I wasn't used to driving, period.

"That's the guy who stole Guinevere from King Arthur," I said, like Bennacio might not know that little detail. "I guess none of this would have happened if he had controlled himself. Are you married, Bennacio?"

"No. Many of us marry in secret or not at all, thus our numbers have dwindled over the years."

"How come?"

"Remember, Kropp, we are sworn to protect the Sword.

To love another, to be bound by blood to another, that is to invite blackmail—or worse, betrayal. You mention Lancelot. Samson himself never wed because he could not bear the thought of endangering another human being."

"There was something else I was wondering," I said. "How did Mogart know about the Sword in the first place?"

"All Knights of the Sacred Order know."

I looked over at him. He was staring at the rain smacking against the glass and his face was expressionless.

"Mogart was a knight?"

"Once."

"What happened?"

"Samson expelled him." He sighed. "Mogart did not take banishment well, as one might imagine."

"Then why did Mr. Samson expel him?"

Bennacio hesitated before answering. "That was between Samson and Mogart." He glanced over at me and then looked away. "It was only a matter of time until a man like Mogart appeared among us. We were fortunate over the centuries, but the ancient bloodlines became diluted over time. Our blood intermingled with that of lesser men, our valor has been tarnished by the desires of this world. The voices of the angels have faded and into the void the voice of corruption rushes."

"What angels?"

"There were some in my Order, Kropp, who believed the Sword is actually the blade of the Archangel Michael, given to Arthur to unite mankind."

I remembered Mr. Samson telling me that the Sword was not made by human hands.

"That didn't turn out too good, did it?" I asked.

"It is certainly not the first time we have disappointed heaven," Bennacio answered.

17

I stopped just outside of a little town in the Shenandoah Valley called Edinburg to pee and to find Bennacio something other than a corn dog to eat. The rain had slackened to a gray mist and the temperature had dropped at least ten degrees. I had left Knoxville with just the clothes on my back, no jacket, no umbrella, and both would probably come in handy, especially in Nova Scotia, which I pictured as rainy and windswept and desolate.

I wondered if the Tuttles were looking for me back in Knoxville or if they even cared to look for me. I thought about missing school and about Amy Pouchard, and all of that—the Tuttles and Amy and school—felt to me like it had happened to somebody else, like the memories weren't my memories but the hijacked memories of another kid. It was as if I left more than the little I had back in Knoxville. Somehow, I had left the me that made me *me*.

We ducked into a McDonald's and Bennacio ordered a Big Mac and a Coke. He asked for some plasticware, and I wondered how he planned to eat a Big Mac with a plastic fork. I ordered a large Coke to keep me awake on the road and a fish sandwich. I waited in the car with the food while Bennacio used the pay phone outside the restaurant. He talked for about five minutes. His gait was thrown off by his wound and he moved slowly, as if each step cost him something.

He sat down, closed the door, and said, "Lock the doors, Kropp."

I was about to ask him why, when the back doors opened and two big men slid into the backseat.

"Too late," Bennacio said.

Something sharp pressed into the side of my neck. A voice behind me whispered, "Drive."

I backed out of the space using the rearview, where I could see the side of someone's square-shaped head and the large hand pressing the black dagger against my neck. The skin over every inch of my body was tingling. The other guy was sitting back in his seat, looking like he didn't have a care in the world.

"Turn right."

I pulled out of the parking lot and turned right, away from the on-ramp.

"Where am I going?" I asked.

"Where do you think?" the guy behind me cracked. I guessed he was saying I was going to my grave or to hell, probably to hell for all the people dead because of me.

Bennacio said, "Think carefully about what you are doing. I do not wish to kill you."

"Shut up," the man sitting behind him said.

"There is still time," Bennacio said. "If you repent now, heaven may still receive you."

The guy holding the dagger to my throat laughed.

"Whatever Mogart has offered you—is it worth the price of your immortal soul?" Bennacio asked calmly. He might have been talking about the weather.

The guy behind me said something to his buddy. It sounded like French. His buddy grunted and said, *"Repos!"*

"Think of your wives, your children," Bennacio said. "Would you have them widowed, fatherless? If you do not value your own lives, can you not consider theirs?"

"Speak again and the fat kid dies," the guy behind me said. I glanced into the rearview mirror and saw his hand was shaking slightly. Bennacio was getting to him. I thought about what Mogart told me, about the will of most men being weak. I also was thinking that just because a guy has an oversized head and a big body, you shouldn't call him fat.

We drove a few miles until we passed a sign that said "George Washington National Forest." I was directed onto this access road marked "Rangers Only" that narrowed to a skinny one-lane, winding deep into the woods.

"Here," the guy with the dagger to my throat said. "Stop here."

"I will kill you both," Bennacio said, still in that weird, calm voice. "First you with the knife. I will turn your own hand upon your throat and use it to sever your head from your body." He nodded to the guy behind him. "Then you I shall gut as a hog in a slaughterhouse, and I shall spread your steaming entrails on the ground for the carrion to feast upon."

This guy said something to the guy behind me. I don't know what he said, but it sounded pretty urgent. *"Fou!"* the guy with the dagger hissed back.

"You guys oughtta listen to Bennacio," I said. "He's a knight and those guys never lie."

"Get out," the guy with the dagger said.

"Ave Maria, gratia plena . . ." Bennacio began to pray. The guy behind him got out of the car, opened Bennacio's door, and yanked him out.

"Get out," the man behind me said. I got out. They dragged us into the trees. *Dominus tecum. Bendicta tu in milieribus. . . .* The ground was carpeted with pine needles and dead leaves, and there was a mist in the air and no sound, not even a bird singing. I looked over to Bennacio, now on his knees, with his arms hanging loosely at his sides. *Et benedictus fructus ventris tui, Iesus.* His eyes were half closed. The man standing before the kneeling Bennacio was heavy and broad-shouldered, with short-cropped black hair and a jutting brow. My guy was slighter and shorter, though

I probably had at least ten pounds on him. He had shaggy blond hair and an ugly scar running from beneath his right eye, down his cheek, to his jawline.

I got a good look at the dagger too. It was about two feet long, black, double-bladed, with the image of a dragon's head carved into its hilt. It looked like a miniature version of the swords Bennacio and the other knights used in Samson Towers. All these guys must go the same outfitters.

Santa Maria, Mater Dei, ora pro nobis peccatoribus, nunc, et in hora mortis nostrae.

"I want to pray too," I said. I don't know why I said that, but Bennacio was praying and he seemed like the kind of guy who always did just the right thing in a crisis. I went to my knees, bowed my head, and started the Hail Mary, only in English, but when I got to the "pray for us sinners" part I stopped because I heard a scream and a loud snap like the sound of a branch breaking. That's it, I thought. Bennacio's bought it.

Then I looked to my right and saw Bennacio coming in a blur for the guy in front of me. The man raised his dagger.

He was moving in slow motion, though. Bennacio wasn't.

Bennacio grabbed his wrist and I heard another snapping sound, not quite as loud as the first, and with his other hand Bennacio grabbed the guy by his shaggy hair while he forced the dagger back toward his throat. I didn't want to see what was going to happen next, so I stood up and kind of stumbled through the trees and undergrowth, passing the bigger man, who lay twisting on the ground. I heard a soft thud behind me and I knew without looking that Bennacio had kept the first part of the promise he made in the car. Then I heard the pleading tone in the bigger man's voice as Bennacio walked back to him, and I knew he was going to keep the second part too.

I went behind a tree and threw up. I was still bent over when I heard Bennacio call softly behind me.

"Kropp! Alfred! Come!"

Don't look; don't look, just keep your head up and your eyes on Bennacio, I told myself as I walked back to the car. He was already sitting in the passenger seat. He had taken the Big Mac apart and was eating the patty, holding it in the palm of his large hand, using a napkin as a plate, cutting the meat with the side of his plastic fork. *Don't look, don't look,* I told myself, but I had to look because I didn't want to trip on any body parts on the way to the car. So I looked and saw Bennacio had kept both his promises.

18

I drove toward the interstate. Bennacio told me to turn into the McDonald's parking lot. At first I thought he wanted to wash up, but I couldn't see any blood on his clothes, not a speck anywhere. He had me cruise around the building once, then pull onto the road again and turn left into the parking lot of the gas station on the interstate side of the McDonald's.

"There it is. Stop, Kropp."

I pulled beside a car parked behind the station. Bennacio dabbed both corners of his mouth with a napkin and got out while I sat there and watched him through his open door. He pulled a set of keys from his pocket and pressed the remote button, unlocking the other car. I got out then and joined him.

"Hey," I said. "This is a Ferrari Enzo."

Bennacio didn't answer. He was searching the car. He checked the center console, over the visors, under the seats and floor mats. He opened the glove box and pulled out a sleek black cell phone.

I said, "You know, it's funny. Somebody once promised I would have one of these cars." All of a sudden I felt like crying.

"Park the car, Kropp," he said, with a little jerk of his head toward the Mercedes. "Over there." He pointed to the far corner of the lot. I parked, walked back to the Ferrari, and when I got there, Bennacio was going through the trunk. He threw the keys to the Ferrari at me.

"What, we're taking this?" I asked.

"Hurry, Kropp," he said. "They know where we are now and where we're going. There will be more."

I slid into the driver's seat of the Ferrari and said to Bennacio, "You knights sure like to travel in style."

Bennacio said, "Drive, Kropp."

I got back on the highway and the Ferrari sped up to seventy-five like it was cruising a neighborhood street. Bennacio told me to go faster. At ninety he told me to go faster again. At 110 I told him I wasn't going any faster because if I drove any faster, my stomach would come out of my mouth. He didn't say anything after that.

I wished I could put the top down. I had always wanted a

convertible and to take it onto the open road like in a commercial and go a hundred miles an hour with the top down.

After an hour, the black cell phone rang. Bennacio flipped it open, listened for a second, then said, "It is too late. They are dead." He snapped it closed and tossed it out the window.

He leaned back in his seat, closed his eyes, and said, "I must rest now. Wake me when you are tired and I will drive."

"I don't get it," I said. I was pretty upset. There had been more blood flying around than in a horror movie. I had somehow found myself in an R-rated movie when all I wanted was PG-13. "There's a whole lot I don't get, Bennacio, like why we're driving in a hot car to Nova Scotia; why people are trying to kill us; what the heck OIPEP is and how it fits into all this; how Mogart or anybody else could use a sword no matter how powerful to take over the whole world; and why any of this had to happen to me in the first place. But what I *really* don't get is why you had to slaughter those guys like that."

"They would have slaughtered us."

"But how's that make you any different from them?"

"They are servants of the enemy—"

"So?"

"—thralls of the Dragon. Would you have them live to pursue us to our end?"

"I just don't get it, that's all. Chopping off people's heads and cutting out their guts . . ."

"You would not pity them if you knew them as I do."

"I don't know anybody who deserves something like that."

"You are afraid. I understand." His eyes were still closed. He spoke kindly to me, like a father would, or how I imagined a father would, since I never knew my father.

"You may pull off and find the nearest bus terminal if you wish, Kropp. I will give you the money for a ticket. I am well enough now to drive the rest of the way."

I thought about it. I thought about it hard. His offer was tempting, but really, where would I go? I didn't want to live with the Tuttles, and if I went back to Knoxville I wouldn't have a choice. Then all of a sudden I thought about that little beach town in Florida where Mom used to take me every summer. Maybe I could go there and get a job and live on the beach until the world ended. There were a lot worse places you could wait for the end of the world.

And, really, what did I think I was doing—me, Alfred Kropp of all people—driving a hundred miles an hour in a Ferrari Enzo with a modern-day knight by my side? Who the heck did I think I was?

"It was because of what Mogart did to Mr. Samson, wasn't it?" I asked finally. "The reason you mutilated those guys."

"Samson was my captain, Kropp," Bennacio said. "And there are some debts that cry to heaven to be repaid."

19

We were about twenty-five miles north of Harrisburg, Pennsylvania, when Bennacio told me to take the next exit. We had been on the road for over sixteen hours and maybe he noticed how much I was yawning and rubbing my eyes. We hadn't stopped since Edinburg except to fill up on gas and use the john.

I started to turn into a Super 8 just off the exit, but Bennacio told me to keep driving. I drove west on Highway 501, which hugged the edge of Swatara State Park. Trees crowded both sides of the road and there were no streetlights; it felt as if we were driving through a tunnel. I thought maybe the idea was to park somewhere in the woods and sleep in the car. We passed a sign that said "Suedberg 2 mi."

About a mile past the sign, Bennacio told me to turn onto a little dirt lane that wound up a hill, then through a dense group of trees. On the other side of the trees was a bridge that spanned a little creek, and after the bridge the road narrowed until it ended at a house set back in the woods. It reminded me of the houses from those old scary children's stories, like the witch's house in *Hansel and Gretel*.

Maybe this was like a safe house for the knights, a refuge for when they were in the area, cavorting about on an adventure.

I stopped the car and Bennacio said, "Kropp, you must stay here for a moment."

He got out of the car and I called to him before he shut the door. "How come?"

"I don't know how you will be received."

He mounted the steps. The front door opened, and a dark shape was silhouetted in the light from inside. This person wore a dress, so I figured it was a woman. She hugged Bennacio, rising on her toes to kiss both his cheeks. She bent her head while he whispered in her ear. Then her head came up and she looked at me.

Maybe she said something to Bennacio, because he waved his hand toward me, and the two of them disappeared inside.

I got out and locked the car: The place was isolated and

you never know what might be lurking in the woods. I was still pretty shaken up by our encounter with Mogart's henchmen back in Edinburg, and every shadow seemed to be holding a two-foot-long black dagger. I was finding out the hard way that the world is always more dangerous than you think it is.

They had closed the door behind them and I hesitated for a second before going in. Was I supposed to knock? Maybe Bennacio's wave didn't mean *Come on in, Kropp*. Maybe it meant *Stay in the car or forfeit your life!* Then I smelled bread fresh from the oven and my stomach decided for me; I hadn't eaten anything since the corn dog.

I opened the door after a quick little knock, a sort of compromise between knocking and not knocking, and stepped inside.

The front parlor was empty, but I could hear voices coming from down the hall, which also seemed to be where the bread smell was coming from. I stepped into the parlor. A small fire was going in here, and in one corner was a little wooden stand where a candle was burning. There was a picture displayed there of a guy about my age, with long blond hair and large, bright blue eyes, wearing a purple tunic and looking grimly at the camera, a silver headband across his forehead. A single white rose lay in front of the picture. It was some kind of shrine, I guessed, and I was sure without knowing exactly *how* I was sure that I was looking at a picture of one of Mr. Samson's knights.

"Kropp."

Bennacio was standing in the entry. I pointed at the picture.

"A knight?" I asked.

He nodded. "Windimar."

"This is his house?"

"This is the house of his mother. We shall stay here for the night."

"I thought we were in a hurry."

"We are, but even knights must eat and rest, and I desire her counsel. Miriam is a soothsayer, Kropp."

"Really? Wow. What's a soothsayer?"

"She has the gift of sight."

"You mean she can see the future?"

He didn't answer. I followed him down the hall to the kitchen, where a large oak table took up most of the space. The table was one of those sturdy, rough-hewn jobs, with thick legs and a top about five inches thick. It was covered with steaming dishes: a stew in an earthenware bowl, pots of potatoes and vegetables, fruit in a big wooden bowl, and five loaves of freshly baked bread on a cutting board in the shape of a fish.

Windimar's mother moved around the table, setting out the plates and these huge mugs that reminded me of pirate movies and grog. I stood there because Bennacio was standing, feeling big and awkward, like I was taking up too much space, light-headed from hunger, and nervous for some reason. Maybe it was because nobody was talking and she had a grim look on her face as she set out the plates. She was wearing a black full-length dress and her steel gray hair was pulled into a bun so tight, it looked painful. Her eyes were the same bright sky blue as her son's, her nose perfectly straight, her lips slightly oversized for someone her age, and the only wrinkles I saw were around the corners of her eyes, which were swollen slightly, I guessed from crying.

She set places for two, one on either side of the table. Bennacio sat down at one and, relieved, I sat at the other. He muttered something that sounded like Latin over the food and we set in while she stood at the sink washing up the cookery.

It was one of the best meals I ever had. The stew was beef-based, very thick and hot, the bread so buttery, it practically dissolved on my tongue, and even my drink had substance to it, kind of sweet-tasting, like honey, warm like hot apple cider, but not apple-based . . . I don't know what the heck it was, but it was good.

Miriam stacked the pots in the drainer to dry and sat down next to Bennacio. They spoke in low voices in a language I didn't understand. It sounded not quite French and not quite Spanish and it definitely wasn't German. Maybe it was Latin or whatever language they spoke in Arthur's day, like Celtic.

I was on my third helping of stew and second loaf of bread when their conversation got intense; I guessed they were having an argument about something and I guessed too that the something was me, because she kept glancing at me and at one point jabbed a finger in my direction. I was pretty uncomfortable, them talking about me while I sat right in front of them, and I think Bennacio knew that, because he switched to English.

"Do not forget," he said to her. "Without him I would not be here."

She answered in a thick accent, "And you forget, Lord Bennacio, without him my son would be here."

So it was about me taking the Sword, which got the knights, including her son, killed. I dropped my spoon into the bowl. I wasn't hungry anymore.

"Windimar did not die for anything Kropp did; he perished keeping a vow he made to heaven, Miriam."

"Yet his vow would not have been put to the test if not for him." Again she jabbed her finger at me.

"Perhaps. At last to our generation the test has come, whether born of the divine or the diabolical who can say? Yet we must take comfort, Miriam, in the fact that heaven has used odder instruments."

"He is an instrument of destruction," she spat back at him. "At the critical hour he will fail you, Bennacio. He will stand aside while you fall."

"Now that just isn't true!" I said. "Ma'am." I couldn't keep quiet anymore. "I screwed up, big time, but ever since I've been trying to do the right thing. Maybe you don't know this, but Mogart killed my uncle. Maybe it's true I'm partly responsible for all this mess, for the Sword being lost and all the knights . . . and what happened to the knights. So that's, um, true, and the only way I can make up for it is by helping Bennacio here."

"No," she said. "I have seen it. You will fail him, and the last knight will fall." Her eyes narrowed and somehow the room narrowed too. She was staring at me at the other end of a long, darkening tunnel, her crooked finger pointed at my nose. "And you too shall perish, Alfred Kropp, alone in the dark, where neither day breaks nor night falls. The Dark One will pierce your heart and—upon his command—you will die."

20

Bennacio and I sat in the parlor after dinner. It was half past one in the morning and Bennacio said we had to leave at dawn, but neither of us felt sleepy. My seat was right next to Windimar's shrine, and his big blue eyes stared at me like a rebuke.

Bennacio wasn't in a talkative mood. He sat with his elbows on the armrests, his long fingers laced together, staring at the fire.

Miriam's words were still echoing in my head, and his silence wasn't helping my creepy mood any. So I asked, "How do you become a knight? I mean, I know you have to come from one of the original knights, but you guys aren't born knowing how to handle a sword and all that stuff. What do you do, go to knight school?"

If he got the joke, he didn't let on. "We are trained by our fathers. In some cases, we apprentice under another knight, if the father is unable."

"What about Windimar's dad?" He was young enough for his father to still be alive, judging by his picture in the gilded frame beside me.

"His father died before he could complete the training."

"You completed Windimar's training, didn't you, Bennacio?"

He didn't say anything. Miriam came into the room with a big brandy snifter for Bennacio. She asked me if I wanted anything and I could tell that took a lot out of her, being gracious to me, but I told her no.

She said something in that funny-sounding language and Bennacio shook his head, but she came back at him pretty insistently, and he finally shrugged and shook his head, waving his hand at her as if to say, *Whatever, I'm too tired to argue.* She left the room.

"How'd his father die?" I asked, expecting to hear a story about a jousting tournament gone bad.

"His riding lawn mower flipped over on him."

"You're kidding."

"Even knights are not immune to absurd ends, Kropp."

Miriam came into the room again, this time carrying a long black case that looked like a musical instrument carrier.

Maybe she expected Bennacio to play a dirge on an oboe or something. She laid it at his feet, fussing at him in that strange tongue, until he finally said, in English, "Very well, Miriam."

"He would want you to have it." She couldn't seem to let the argument go.

"And I shall take it, in his memory. I pray I will not have to use it."

"You *will* use it, Lord Bennacio, before the sun sets on the morrow."

She left us alone. I cleared my throat. "Do her visions always come true?" I asked, because who wants to die alone in the dark, where no days break or nights fall, pierced in the heart by the Dark One?

He said, "I have never questioned her gift. But you must understand, Kropp, she is nearly overcome by grief, and grief always clouds our insight, even the insight of the gifted. From his birth, Miriam has known Windimar would die a bloody death. Imagine that if you can."

"I guess it could mess you up. I remember when my mom first told me she was dying from cancer . . ." I couldn't go on. Bennacio nodded as if he understood I couldn't, and patted my arm.

After he finished his brandy, Bennacio announced it was time we got some sleep because he planned to drive straight through to Canada. There was another long discussion or argument with Miriam about sleeping arrangements, I guess, and I wasn't sure who won, but I figured it was Bennacio by her fierce expression and the way she stomped down the hall, leading me to a room.

It was Windimar's old room. There was no bathroom, but there was an antique washstand with a bowl set in a hollowed-out shelf and a pitcher of steaming water. I washed my face and brushed my teeth in the warm water from the pitcher, and then I looked around the room.

A rocking chair sat beside a small fireplace on the wall opposite the bed, where a silver and gold crucifix was hung over the headboard. On that side was a tapestry that looked very old but couldn't have been that old, because there was Mr. Samson mounted on a great white horse in full armor and around him eleven men dressed in purple and holding shields painted with a horse and rider. At least it looked like Mr. Samson—there was the same large head and flowing golden hair, and I picked out a tall knight that could have been Bennacio and a knight with bright blue thread for eyes, Windimar, I guessed, staring right at me, and he was one good-looking guy; he looked a little like Brad Pitt, except for those bright blue eyes. Jealousy never did anybody any good and I wasn't really the jealous type, but this guy was learning swordplay and how to ride a horse and pledging his sacred honor to die for a noble cause when I was sitting by my mom's hospital bed watching her die and getting the stuffing beaten out of me at football practice.

I opened the closet door and inside was a full suit of armor, shined to a mirror finish, with a six-foot lance leaning against the wall beside it. It was fully assembled and I gave a little yelp when I opened the door, thinking I was the victim of a medieval ambush.

I stared at that suit of armor for a long time. It was polished so bright, I could see little shards of myself reflected in the metal, twenty-five Kropps at least, distorted like funhouse images. Shaggy brown hair, brown eyes, average-sized nose, chin, ears, teeth. If there was one trait these knights in the tapestry shared, it was that none of them looked average. Not all were as pretty as Windimar, as noble-looking as Samson, or as intense as Bennacio, but there was a set to their jaw, a certain look in the eyes they all had in common. I wondered if I put on the armor in the closet something like that might happen to me, the way even the geekiest guy in school looked macho in his ROTC uniform. I had this nutty urge to pull the armor off its stand and put it on. Then I thought that would be the ultimate gesture of disrespect, donning the armor of the knight who died because of me. I closed the closet door.

I turned out the light and crawled into the bed fully dressed and it bothered me, Christ hanging right over me, looking down like, *What the heck are* you *doing here?* that it took a long time for me to fall asleep. It didn't help that I could hear Miriam crying down the hallway, a low moaning sort of weeping. For a crazy second I thought about finding her and telling her I was sorry, which I kind of did already but not really in the kitchen. But Miriam didn't want to hear about me being sorry; she wanted her son back. Probably if I went in there she'd find the nearest heavy object and bash me over the head with it.

Her crying went on for a long time. I had cried for my mom when she died, but not the way Miriam was crying for Windimar. It was while I listened to her cry that I realized what I did went beyond Uncle Farrell, Mr. Samson and the knights, Bennacio and Windimar. What I did was slamming people I didn't even know about, like Miriam, the shock waves of my boneheadedness spreading out in ever widening circles, like a boulder the size of Montana landing in the ocean or that huge asteroid that hit the earth millions of years ago, wiping out the dinosaurs.

I finally fell asleep and dreamed I was scrambling up this rocky slope, not exactly a mountain, more like a slag heap of broken rock and tiny glittering shards of quartz or maybe those crystals you see growing inside of caves, sparkling like big wet teeth in the moonlight. I kept slipping and sliding as I tried to reach the top. The palms of my hands and my knees were all cut up and bleeding. Every time I gained a couple feet, I lost one, but it seemed very important I get to the top. I caught ahold of a big boulder near the summit and pulled myself up.

I rested awhile, looking at the shimmering shards littering the hill beneath me, feeling kind of proud of myself that I made it at least this far.

Finally I stood up, turned, and jumped the rest of the way. The top was perfectly flat and covered with long grasses whose tips reached up and caressed my aching legs as I walked toward this yew tree.

Under the tree sat a lady wearing a white robe, and her hair was long and dark, and her face almost as pale as her dress.

I don't know why, but she seemed familiar to me, and when I got close she lifted her head and smiled.

She looked at me with her sad, dark eyes, as if she knew me, and something I had done or failed to do had disappointed her. Then she asked me a question and I woke up.

"You have been dreaming," a voice said.

I scooted up in the bed and saw Bennacio sitting in the rocker by the fireplace.

I brought my hand to my face and it came away wet. I'd been crying.

"There was this . . . lady," I said. I cleared my throat. "All in white, with dark hair."

"Did she speak to you?"

"Yes."

"What did she say?"

"She asked me a question." I didn't want to talk about it. Bennacio had a bemused expression on his face, as if he knew what I'd been dreaming.

"What was the question?" he asked.

"She asked me . . . she asked me where the master of the Sword was."

"And what was your answer?"

"I didn't have an answer."

"Hmmm." He was smiling at me. Not a big, wide smile, but a secret little smile, like he knew what my answer should have been and that maybe I knew it too, and all that was holding me back was my reluctance to think things through.

"Who was she, Bennacio?"

"That is not for me to say."

"How come?"

"She came to your dream, Alfred."

I remembered him talking about angels as if they were real and wondered if the Lady in White was one. But why would an angel talk to me?

"I never believed in angels and saints or even God, much," I told Bennacio.

"That hardly matters," he said. "Fortunately for us, the angels do not require our consent in order to exist."

Everything about this Bennacio guy reminded me of my own insignificance. I didn't think he was trying to put me down, though. He had stepped up to a different level long before he met me. It wasn't his fault I was still scrubbing around at the bottom of the slag heap.

"I never really gave much thought to stuff like that," I said. "I guess one of my biggest problems is I don't take the time to think things through. If I did, the Sword would still be under Mr. Samson's desk and Uncle Farrell would be alive. Everybody would be alive and Miriam wouldn't be crying but maybe sewing on a tapestry. Did she make that? It must have taken her a very long time. What happened to Windimar, Bennacio?"

"I have told you. He fell near Bayonne."

"No, I mean, what happened to him?"

"Do you really wish to know?" He studied me for a minute, and I wondered why he had come in here while I slept. It was like he knew I would be waking up and he wanted to be there when I did.

"Very well. He was traveling by rail to Barcelona, the rendezvous point for our assault upon Mogart in Játiva, when he was set upon by seven of the Dragon's thralls. He might have escaped, but he chose to fight.

"He was the youngest of our Order, impetuous, idealistic—and vain. He never believed that our cause might fail. His pride undid him, Alfred. For though he fought well and bravely, besting five before he was overcome, in the end the two that remained mutilated him while he still drew breath."

His voice had dropped to a whisper. He wasn't looking at me anymore, but at some point over my head.

"He was found with no eyes, Alfred. They killed him, and then they cut out his eyes."

His gray eyes turned to me then, and they were hard. "The enemy has been gathering such men to himself for two years now, Alfred, since Samson expelled him from our Order. You have not lived very long, but surely you have heard of such men. Alas, the world is full of them. Men without conscience, their hearts corrupted by greed and the lust for power, their minds twisted past all human recognition. They have forgotten love, pity, remorse, honor, dignity, grace. They have fallen, mere shadows of men, their humanity a distant memory. Mogart has promised them riches beyond human imagining, and in their lust they have descended to barbarity beyond divine imagining. Remember that before you judge me for what I did in Edinburg. Remember Játiva. Remember Windimar's eyes, and then you may judge me."

21

At sunrise the next morning I stumbled into the kitchen, where Miriam had laid out blueberry muffins and these little buttery rolls that melted in my mouth like cotton candy. I wouldn't have stayed to eat—Bennacio was nowhere to be seen and Miriam acted as if I were this large empty space, like a bubble, floating around her kitchen—but those rolls were delicious and the muffins were about the size of my fist. Finally I couldn't stand it any longer and I said, "Where's Bennacio?" because he had made such a big deal about getting an early start. Loudly too because I was nervous around her and she wasn't too good with English and, like a lot of people, I spoke louder to people who did not share my native tongue. She jerked her head toward the little window over the sink, so I figured he had gone outside and in another instant I leaped to the conclusion he wasn't out on his morning constitutional but had actually taken off without me. I ran out the front door and was relieved to see the Ferrari still parked outside.

A heavy fog had rolled in during the night, and the early-morning sunlight was red and ghostly in the wispy moisture around the dark tree trunks of the woods around Miriam's house. I heard a thudding sound in the trees off to my right, and I turned toward it as it became louder. I think I knew what was coming before it came bursting through the trees, and I fought the impulse to dash back inside.

Bennacio exploded from the woods astride a huge white horse, bending low over its massive neck, both hands gripping its halter because there were no reins or bit.

They drew up beside me. The horse's dark nostrils flared and its tail slapped its flanks as Bennacio smiled down at me.

"We're riding horses to Canada?" I asked.

"Wouldn't that be grand?" he laughed. "The hour darkens, and we must make haste now, but I could not resist one last ride." He held out his hand.

"I'm scared of horses," I told him.

"Fortunately, I am not," he said, and he grabbed me by the forearm and swung my big self onto that horse's broad back as easily as if he were throwing a coat over his shoulder. Then he leaned over and whispered something into the horse's ear and we were off.

Just a few hours before, I had been racing down the interstate at a hundred miles an hour, but that seemed like crawling next to that horse ride through the Pennsylvania countryside. The trees whistled by my ears as I wrapped my arms around Bennacio's chest, my face pressed against his back, my eyes clenched shut. I slipped right and left on the horse's back, and I pressed my teeth together because I was terrified I might bite my tongue in two.

I don't know how long we rode before I felt this lessening of pressure in my chest and a light-headedness that made me crack my eyes open and sit back a little, my death grip loosening around Bennacio's middle—maybe fifteen minutes, but it seemed like an hour or two. I leaned farther back and opened my eyes wide, and the spring air was sweet and swift against my face, the trees blurs of brown and bright green, and the sound of this steed's hooves was like muffled thunder in my ears. I actually started to laugh out loud, whooping it up like a kid on a carnival ride, while Bennacio spurred on our mount. Bennacio, the Last Knight of the Round Table, astride a white stallion, riding to the rescue of the whole darn world, with Alfred Kropp hanging on for dear life behind him, shouting and crying at the same time, glad just to be along for the ride.

22

After we returned to the house, I waited by the Ferrari while Miriam said good-bye to Bennacio on the front steps. Her hair was down and she looked even younger that way. She took Bennacio's hands in hers and was talking urgently, and whatever she was saying was getting to him. He kept shaking his head, *No, no,* and I could tell, despite not spending a lot of time around the two of them, that they had a complicated relationship. She stood on her tiptoes and kissed both his cheeks, then took his head in both hands and looked at him without saying anything for a long time.

Bennacio came down the steps, holding out his hand.

"The keys, Kropp. I shall drive now. We must reach the border at Saint Stephen before dark."

I handed the keys to him and slid into the passenger seat.
Bennacio tossed the black case Miriam had given him into
the backseat and slid behind the wheel. About the only thing
I was looking forward to was driving that Ferrari, but I
didn't argue with him about it.

"Don't you think this car's been reported stolen and we'll
be arrested?" I asked after we reached the interstate.

"I had not considered it."

"Maybe you should."

"We shall see."

I had lost track of the days, but I think it was Saturday.
The interstate was practically deserted, except for a few big
semis that Bennacio sailed past as if they were standing still.

We were somewhere between Hazelton and Scranton in
Pennsylvania.

"Was that Windimar's horse?" I asked. He didn't answer,
I guess because it was a stupid question. If you acknowledge
a stupid question, you're just encouraging more of them. I
made a resolution to evaluate the quality of my questions before I asked.

"Do you travel a lot in the knight business, Bennacio?" I
asked.

"At times."

"That's something I've been wondering. I mean, I know
your main job is to protect the Sword, but is that all you do?
Do you have adventures?"

"Probably not in the sense that you mean. But we are knights nevertheless, sworn to protect the weak and defend the innocent."

"So that's a yes, right?"

"Is it so important, Kropp? For me, it has always been enough, that I should be charged with the protection of the Holy Sword."

"So I guess you're saying it's mostly just a lot of sitting around."

He didn't answer. I went on. "Sounds like my life. Only I wasn't protecting anything holy. Just sitting around eating Bugles, drinking Coke, and listening to music. I bet this baby's got a heck of a sound system. Want to try it out? What kind of music do you like? I bet it's Gregorian chants or something like that. Sinatra maybe. Though Sinatra was no monk. I thought you were a monk in the Towers the night I stole the Sword. My mom loved Sinatra. Am I talking too much? I think my brain is on overload, trying to process everything. You know, it's a lot to process. Sacred swords and modern-day knights and the world teetering on the brink of total annihilation. I think I'm doing pretty good, considering.

"I don't travel much either, not since my mom died, anyway. Every summer she took me to the beach in Florida and we wouldn't be four miles down the road before I had to eat something. What's in the case back there, by the way?"

"A gift."

"Oh, I was hoping maybe that Miriam lady packed us a

couple of sandwiches for the road. Anyway, I always got these cravings for some pecan logs or those bags of boiled peanuts they sell from the roadside stands."

"What is a pecan log?"

"You know, pecan-encrusted nuggety things. On our Florida trips Mom would stop at these stores along the highway called Stuckey's. Stuckey's pecan logs and also turtles—not real turtles, but that's the name for this chocolate candy with pecans. I really don't know what that nugget in a pecan roll was made out of; it's sort of like candy or maybe like congealed pie filling. Sort of vanilla-y, but real sweet. When you put the crunchy pecans with it, it's really good."

"One might have it with a bread-wrapped wiener."

"Corn dog."

"Corn dog, yes."

His eyes had been flicking between the road, the rearview mirrors, and me.

Suddenly he slammed the accelerator to the floor and my head popped back against the seat. A few seconds later, when we reached 120, he hit the cruise-control button and said, "Take the wheel, Alfred."

"Huh?"

"Drive for a moment."

He let go of the wheel and I grabbed it with my left hand as he twisted around to fumble with the latches of the black carrying case.

"Bennacio . . . !"

158

He sat back down and said, "Keep your hand on the wheel. If we run off the road at this speed we will not survive."

He pulled two curved pieces of wood from the black case, fitting one piece into the other, the curves going in the same direction. He was having some trouble with it because together they were about five feet long. I glanced in the rearview mirror and saw sunlight sparking off a mass of black metal and chrome that took up both lanes, coming up fast.

"What are those things behind us, Bennacio?"

"Suzuki Hayabusas."

"They're gaining on us."

"I have no doubt," he said. "They are the fastest motorcycles in the world."

He had pulled a long white cord from the case. The cord had a hook on each end. He threw one hook over the little metal eye at one end of the stick, flipped the staff around, and his neck muscles stood out as he pressed on the curved part of the other end, bending the whole thing so he could hook the cord.

"What you are doing?" I asked.

He answered in that same calm voice, "I am stringing my bow, Kropp." He rolled down the window and wind tore into the car, whipping his hair into a white tornado.

I looked in the rearview mirror again and saw that the riders—*dragon thralls,* Bennacio had called them—had separated and were gaining fast. I counted six, but I had to count quickly or risk running off the road.

"Keep us in the lane, Alfred!" Bennacio shouted. "Steer with your right hand and hold on to me with your left!" He reached back and pulled a quiver full of arrows from the case.

"I don't think I can do that!"

"You have no choice!"

He threw the quiver over his back and scooted backwards through the open window until he was sitting on the door, leaving only half his butt and his long legs inside the car. I grabbed a fistful of his pants leg with my left hand.

Now I could hear the harsh, throaty screaming of the motorcycles' engines as five of them swarmed past the car like enraged wasps. The sixth stayed a few car-lengths behind us.

The riders were dressed all in black. Even the visors on the helmets were black. As they roared past, Bennacio let fly the arrows. I heard the shhh-*phut* of the arrow leaving the bow and saw the lead bike spin out of control: Bennacio had shot the arrow into the right side of the rider's neck, a nice shot, considering he was firing against the wind in a Ferrari Enzo going 120 miles an hour. Two of the bikes couldn't avoid hitting the leader as he went down. Both struck him with their front tires and both bikes jackknifed, throwing the thralls forward, their bodies already limp as rag dolls when they hit the pavement.

That left two plus the one behind us, and now I could hear explosions coming from our left. The guns they fired at us were pretty big, but I couldn't see what kind because

Bennacio was blocking my line of vision and besides, I had to watch the road.

We took a hit near the left bumper and I figured they were aiming for the tires or the gas tank or maybe both. The impact slung us to the right and I nearly lost control, but I overcompensated for the skid and now we were straddling the centerline.

That gave me an idea and I gently eased the wheel to the left as Bennacio let fly the arrows, one after the other, shhh-*phut*-shhh-*phut*-shhh-*phut*, shooting, reloading (or whatever archers call it), and firing faster than you could blink. I kept edging into the left lane; the riders had to choose now between dropping back and passing us before I forced them into the median.

Out of the corner of my eye I saw one of the Suzukis leap ten feet into the air with a terrific explosion—Bennacio probably got his tire. You puncture a tire with an arrow at 120 miles an hour and that's what will happen.

One rider remained on our left, and he accelerated till he was even with the front bumper, and then I could see they had been shooting at us with sawed-off shotguns. As Bennacio twisted around, I wondered why we were using a bunch of arrows against six shotgun-toting madmen on Suzuki Hayabusas.

I glanced in the rearview mirror and saw the last rider coming up with the butt of a sawed-off shotgun resting in his lap, the black barrel pointing up and gleaming in the rising sun.

The guy pacing us managed to hold his course while he twisted to his right to fire. I saw an orange flash of light and the windshield exploded, showering us with glass. I think I might have screamed, but any sound I made was drowned out by the wind howling through the busted windshield.

Suddenly I was in a very small, very powerful wind tunnel, and tears rolled straight back from the corners of my eyes and ran into my ears.

The rider to our left eased off the gas and drifted toward us. Before I could react he leaped from the bike onto the hood of the Ferrari, his abandoned bike careening to the left and into the median strip. His black outfit whipped and snapped around his body. He still held the shotgun in his right hand.

Bennacio's thigh tensed below my fist as he leaned over the hood to get off a shot before the rider blew my head off. He was too late. I saw another dull orange flash, and the rear window exploded.

I whipped the wheel hard to the right, catching the rider off guard—he flew off the hood and his scream was abruptly cut off as he hit the pavement.

Bennacio fell back into the driver's seat, his hands empty; he must have tossed his bow onto the road. Maybe his quiver was empty or maybe bows and arrows against guns just wasn't quite challenging enough for him. I fell back into my seat and tried to catch my breath, but there was no catching it and I wondered if I had wet my pants. There were shards of glass everywhere, in my lap, down my shirt, in my hair. I twisted to my left and looked behind us.

"What happened to him?" I shouted in Bennacio's ear.

"Duck, Kropp."

I just stared stupidly at him, not moving until his hand shot out and pushed my head down. The window beside me exploded inward, raining glass on my back and legs, and I sat back up without thinking, turned, and saw the end of the shotgun about a foot away.

I grabbed it with both hands and screamed out the broken window at the guy on the bike, "Let go!" like he would if only I told him to. He didn't let go.

I yanked as hard as I could before he could fire a second time and he had to choose between losing control and letting go of the shotgun. He let go and faded toward the emergency lane.

"Lean back, Kropp," Bennacio said. His voice was loud but calm, as if we were still discussing corn dogs. He picked up the gun from my lap and pointed it at the biker out my window. I yelped and threw myself back against the seat as the gun exploded practically beside my nose.

The shell went through the window and landed in the gas tank of the Suzuki Hayabusa. I felt the heat of the fireball against my face, and the concussion from the blast shook the Ferrari so hard, Bennacio had to drop the shotgun onto my lap and grab the steering wheel with both hands to keep us from spinning out of control.

"I think I'm going to be sick!" I shouted against the howling wind.

He didn't say anything. He was smiling, and I don't think it was because I told him I was going to be sick.

23

Bennacio slowed to a more comfortable eighty, but the wind was still blowing fiercely in my face, so I scrunched down in the seat. I covered my eyes and wondered when the reinforcements would arrive.

I don't know how long I sat there like that, shivering in the cold blasts of air, my knees actually knocking together and my teeth chattering in my head, but it seemed like a very long time. Then I heard the motor winding down and the wind dwindling. I took my hand away and saw Bennacio was pulling into the emergency lane. A tractor-trailer was coming up fast behind us, laying on its horn, and Bennacio gave the trucker a friendly little wave as he rumbled past.

"What's the matter?" I asked.

"We're out of gasoline," he answered as the car slowly rolled to a stop.

"You're kidding, right?"

"I am not. Come, Kropp, we must walk now."

"Walk?"

"We have no choice."

"You keep saying that. How come we never have a choice?"

"Sometimes it is easier not to have one."

We got out of the car and stood for a moment looking at it. It didn't look cool anymore. I reached through the window and grabbed the shotgun.

"No, leave it, Kropp."

I sighed and dropped it back onto the seat.

"Lemme ask you something, Bennacio. What's with the swords and daggers and bows and arrows and medieval stuff like that? Aren't you knights allowed to carry guns?"

"There's nothing that prohibits us."

"Then why don't you?"

"It is mostly a matter of pride. You may think otherwise, but guns are far more barbaric than swords. There is no elegance to a firearm, Alfred."

He smiled. "Besides, our way is more fun."

We started to walk. We hadn't gone very far, maybe a quarter of a mile, when I stopped walking. Bennacio, his head bowed, deep in thought, kept walking for several yards before noticing I wasn't beside him. He stopped and watched as I sat down and wrapped my arms around my knees.

It had turned into a nice day, with just a few wisps of cloud and a light breeze from the south. I lifted my face to the sun. Bennacio came back to me and sat down.

"I'll be honest with you, Bennacio. I'm pretty shaken up right now. I know this sort of thing must be normal for a knight, but what happened back there freaked me out a little. No. Not a little. A lot. You go to the movies and you watch these guys in car chases and shoot-outs and you think, hey, I could do that. I mean, you sit there in the dark theater and you kind of wish it was you up there taking out the bad guys. But it isn't like that in real life, though this whole thing is starting to feel more like a movie than real life—which is weird, because I'm starting to miss my real life, even though it sucked. I'm not sure how much farther I can go."

"I see." He sighed. There was a sad look in his eyes. "Unfortunately, we cannot stay here long, Alfred. The police will be here soon—and perhaps worse."

"More AODs?"

"AODs?"

"Agents of darkness."

He smiled. "Yes. AODs. Quite so."

"I don't want to hold you up, Bennacio. You've got an important job to do—saving the world and everything, and it's kind of selfish of me to tag along. Especially when I'm not even sure I *want* to be tagging along."

"You do not give yourself enough credit, Alfred. Without you, I would not have survived this morning."

He obviously said it to make me feel better, but I didn't think he didn't believe it.

"Broadway," he said suddenly.

"Huh?"

He was smiling. "You asked what kind of music I like. I love show tunes."

I don't know why, but I laughed out loud.

"I am particularly fond of Lerner and Loewe. *Camelot.* Have you heard of it?" He sang softly. " 'In short there's simply not/A more congenial spot/For happy-ever-aftering than here in/Camelot!' Predictable, I know."

I cracked up. It helped. "We gotta get a ride somehow, Bennacio," I said after I caught my breath. "We can't walk the whole way to Halifax."

Bennacio stood up. "No, we cannot. Get up, Kropp, and stand with your hands by your sides."

He was staring down the road, and I stood up and looked with him. I heard the siren before I saw the car and the flashing lights.

"Great," I said. "Cops."

The patrol car pulled into the emergency lane, cut the siren, but left the blue-and-reds spinning. The patrolman stepped out of the car, his hand on the butt of his pistol.

"Get on your knees with your hands behind your head!" he shouted at us. "Now!"

"Do as he says," Bennacio said quietly, and we kneeled

on the pavement and I laced my fingers behind my head. The patrolman's shoes went *scrape-scrape* against the concrete as he came toward us.

"You fellows know anything about what happened back there?" he asked.

"We ran out of gas," Bennacio said.

"Looks like you did more than that," the cop said. He stopped a couple of feet from Bennacio, his gun drawn now and aimed at Bennacio's high forehead.

"I have a gun," Bennacio said calmly, as if he were remarking on the weather. "Behind my back."

"Don't move!" the cop said, and he wet his lips. He wasn't much older than me, maybe nineteen or twenty, looking kind of silly in his tall brown hat, like a kid playing dress-up. He crouched down, the gun's muzzle about four inches from Bennacio's nose, and reached around his back to find the weapon that wasn't there.

Bennacio's right hand shot straight up, his index and middle finger extended from his fist, into the kid's neck. He fell straight down and lay still.

"You killed him," I said. "Jeez, Bennacio!"

"He is not dead," Bennacio said. "Come, Alfred."

He was already on his feet and walking rapidly toward the patrol car.

"We're taking his car?"

"Yes."

"Because we've got no choice."

"Yes."

"I want to go home, Bennacio."

He turned at the door. "What home, Alfred?"

He wasn't trying to be mean. He just didn't know what I meant by "home." What did I mean by "home"? The Tuttles'? Knoxville? He didn't know and I sure didn't know. I had no real home anymore.

I got in the car.

24

He cut the spinning red and blue lights, hit the gas pedal, and the Crown Victoria was soon up to 105. Cars pulled out of our way as we approached because we were obviously on some pretty important police business. I rode shotgun, next to the cop's actual shotgun, and thought if we were attacked again it was all up to me because we were out of arrows and something like a shotgun wasn't elegant enough for Bennacio.

We were in the Wyoming Valley, and to my right I could see the Poconos rising. I had never been on a road trip before, if you didn't count the trips to Florida with my mom, which you couldn't count, since that was a family thing. But you really couldn't count this as a road trip either, since the one thing all road trips have in common is they're supposed to be fun.

Bennacio turned on the scanner and listened to the chatter, but there wasn't anything about a stolen cruiser—not yet, anyway, though we both knew it wouldn't be long.

"What now?" I asked.

"We must find another means of transportation."

"Lemme guess," I said. "White stallions?"

"I was thinking more along the lines of a very fast cat," he said. He turned on the flashing red-and-blues. The car directly in front of us changed into the right lane and Bennacio followed it, coming up close on his bumper.

"A Jaguar," I said. "Fast cat, I get it, very funny, but how is carjacking part of the code of chivalry?"

He didn't answer, but reached for the button that operated the siren.

"Hey, can I?" I asked.

"If you wish."

I hit the button, the siren wailed, and Bennacio proceeded to flash his headlights at the Jaguar. It eased into the emergency lane. Bennacio stopped about ten yards behind it. Then he unhooked the shotgun from its holder and pressed it into my hand.

"I thought these were barbaric."

"Just so, but you are not a knight."

"I'm not shooting anyone, Bennacio."

"I don't think that will be necessary."

172

He reached into his breast pocket and pulled out a long, thin leather-bound folder. A checkbook. On the face of the top check, embossed in gold letters, were the words "Samson Industries." He flipped it open and signed a blank check.

"To answer your question: No, we do not steal; we do not 'jack cars,' but sometimes there are those who refuse to sell. Come, Kropp."

He was outside the car and walking up to the Jag before I could say anything. I heaved myself out of the cop car and followed him, holding the gun across my body. A big guy in a tan overcoat was stuffed behind the wheel of the little sports car. It was pretty clear from his expression that Bennacio and I weren't what he was expecting after being pulled over by the Highway Patrol.

"What's up?" he said.

"Don't be alarmed," Bennacio said. He motioned to me and, as soon as I stepped forward, Bennacio ripped the shotgun out of my hand and pointed at the big guy's nose.

"Sure looks like I should be!" the big guy cried out, instinctively bringing his hands up.

"Step out of the car, please," Bennacio said.

"Sure. You bet. Don't shoot me."

He had some trouble getting his bulk out of the car, but being nervous probably wasn't helping his coordination.

"This is for your trouble," Bennacio said, shoving the check at him. "I place it upon your honor to fill in an amount you feel is reasonable. Come, Kropp," he said, and he tossed the shotgun at me. I caught it and halfheartedly pointed it at the incredulous guy, who didn't know what to look at by that point: Bennacio getting behind the wheel of his Jag, me holding the shotgun, or the blank check in his trembling hand. I walked around him to the passenger side and said, to be helpful, "We left the keys in the ignition"—motioning toward the cop car—"but it probably wouldn't be a good idea to follow us."

I climbed into the car and Bennacio floored the gas before I could even get my seat belt fastened.

"You're awful trusting, Bennacio," I said after a few miles had rolled by and it was clear the guy wasn't going to follow us in the borrowed cop car. "How do you know he won't write himself a check for a million dollars?"

"Most people are honest, Kropp. Most are good and will choose right when given a choice. If we did not believe this, what point would there be in being a knight?"

Then he reached across the seat, grabbed the shotgun out of my lap, and tossed it out the open window.

25

Through the rest of Pennsylvania, up into New York, Massachusetts, onto 95 up the New England coast, into New Hampshire and then crossing the border into Maine, we stopped only for gas (the Jag gulped it) and to pee, and once to pick up a lobster sandwich at the McDonald's drive-thru. I had no idea McDonald's served lobster sandwiches. I kept looking behind us expecting to see a dozen cop cars bearing down on us—or more AODs, maybe on Harleys this time, sacrificing speed for muscle.

Twenty miles from the Canadian border, hitting 115 along State Road 9, I noticed we had the northbound lane practically to ourselves, but the southbound lane was backed up for miles.

"Something's wrong," I said. "Everybody's fleeing Canada." It was hard to imagine, though, Armageddon starting in Canada.

"Most likely the border has been closed."

"What'll we do?"

"We have no choice. We must cross."

I pictured us flying through the barricades at 110 with the Royal Mounted Police racing after us. Right as I was picturing this, the first set of blue-and-reds shot out of the dark behind us. Soon there were three or four sets of them and I could hear the sirens from inside the car. Bennacio responded by speeding up, the needle hovering around 120. We roared past an electronic sign that was flashing: "Border Closed."

"Look, this is bad, Bennacio," I told him. "We gotta ditch the Jag and find a place to cross on foot." It wasn't the brightest suggestion, given we were being chased by half the patrol cars in Maine.

Bennacio didn't answer. He kept our speed up until he saw the battalion of National Guardsmen with their assault rifles manning the crossing. The first line of soldiers had already gone to its knees and had taken aim at us.

He slammed on the brakes and we skidded about fifty feet to a stop. Then he said, "Get out of the car, Alfred. Make sure they can see your hands."

I stepped out of the patrol car, my hands in the air, as somebody screamed into a bullhorn, "STEP OUT OF THE

CAR—NOW! KEEP YOUR HANDS WHERE WE CAN SEE THEM!"

Behind us the cop cars rolled in, lights blazing, and a dozen brown uniforms took positions behind their open doors. I wondered how Bennacio was going to get out of this one.

"ON YOUR STOMACH WITH YOUR HANDS OVER YOUR HEAD, FINGERS LACED!"

Bennacio nodded to me and we lay on the ground, side by side. These last few feet of America were very cold. Somebody came and stood right over us, and I could see my reflection in the bright finish of his black shoe.

"Hi. This is the point where I ask what your business in Canada is tonight," the wearer of the shiny shoe said.

"There is a card in my jacket pocket," Bennacio said. "Before you do anything rash, I suggest you contact the person on that card."

I couldn't see if Mr. Shiny Shoes got the card or not, but he walked away and was gone for some time.

"What's going on, Bennacio?" I whispered.

"I am calling in a favor."

"I'm cold," I said. Bennacio didn't say anything.

Somebody grabbed me by the collar and hauled me up. A guy in a blue Windbreaker, the owner of the polished shoes, handed Bennacio the card and said, "This is your lucky day."

"It isn't luck," Bennacio answered. "It is necessity."

We climbed back into the Jag. The guy in the blue Windbreaker and the very nicely shined shoes waved to the border guard. He hit the code to open the gate. The guy in the Windbreaker stepped back and waved us through.

"Good luck!" he called, as we roared through the gate into Canada.

"Necessity," Bennacio muttered.

26

I had never been to Canada, but I didn't
see much of it because it was dark and Bennacio took sec-
ondary two-lane roads. He drove through the night like the
hounds of hell were after us. I knew Halifax was on the coast
and probably he had a plane waiting there for him, but what
good would it do if all flights were grounded? I tried to sleep,
but you try sleeping in a Jaguar going 120 miles an hour in a
strange country.

We crossed a long bridge at three a.m. and Bennacio told
me we were in Nova Scotia. We may as well have been on
the dark side of the moon for all I could tell. We drove in silence until a faint orange glow appeared on the horizon. At

first I thought it was the sun rising, then remembered it was three a.m.

"We may be too late," Bennacio said.

He slowed down to a leisurely eighty and, coming up on a huge fire, I saw we were at a private airstrip. There was some kind of wreckage burning on the runway.

Bennacio pulled into an access road that led directly to the airstrip. Three guys were standing at the end of it, next to a tan Chevy Suburban, wearing long brown robes like the one Bennacio wore the first time we met.

"I thought you were the last knight," I said.

"I am," he said. "And I believe I have told you, Alfred, that the Sword has many friends."

He stopped the car and we got out. A light, freezing rain was falling. I could hear the ocean and taste the salt on my tongue. Bennacio left the headlights on and we gathered in front of the car. The air seemed to sparkle as the light danced in the tiny droplets of rain.

One of the guys came toward Bennacio. They kissed each other on both cheeks, and then the guy gave him a big hug and looked at me.

"Cabiri, this is Kropp," Bennacio said.

"He is a Friend?" Cabiri asked, studying me.

"A Friend and a Wielder."

"Indeed! Then he is my friend," Cabiri said, and he kissed both my cheeks and wrapped me in the same tight bear hug.

He turned to Bennacio. "We had a little trouble, as you

can see." He nodded toward the burning wreckage. "They came on foot, apparently, and that took us by surprise. We expected an aerial assault. They used this."

He nodded to one of the guys standing behind him. He was toting what looked like an oversized bazooka, but I figured it was probably a rocket launcher.

"Derieux?" Bennacio asked.

"He was inside the plane, Lord Bennacio."

Bennacio closed his eyes. I saw the other two brown-robed guys staring at me and I looked away.

"*Diabli!*" Bennacio muttered. "Did they escape?"

Cabiri smiled grimly. He jerked his head toward the burning plane. "Come, I will show you."

We followed him across the tarmac, past the twisted, burning husk of the plane, where the rain hissed and spat and smoke billowed upward, to the other side of the airstrip. Three men in black robes lay there faceup, staring blankly straight up into the rain. Bennacio pulled the hoods away from their faces and studied each one for a long time. He gestured toward the one lying in the middle, the biggest of the three, with a large, flattened nose and black slits for eyes.

"This is Kaczmarczyk," he said. "The other two I do not recognize."

Cabiri turned his head and spat. "Local fishermen, I suspect, recruited by Kaczmarczyk."

"Perhaps." Bennacio turned from the bodies and stared at the burning plane, and the light of the fire danced in his gray eyes.

"We cannot stay here, Bennacio," Cabiri said. "More will come when Kaczmarczyk fails to report. Many more, I fear, than the four of us can manage." Actually, five of us stood there, but I guess Cabiri wasn't counting me. "Come, my house is not far from here. You may rest and we will decide our course."

"Our pilot Derieux is dead," Bennacio said. "Even if we can find another plane, we have no one to fly it."

Cabiri placed one of his large hands on Bennacio's shoulder. "Come, Lord Bennacio," he said softly. His eyes were filled with tears, though his tone was jovial. "A hot meal, a warm bed, and things will look brighter in the morning."

He glanced at the other two guys. "And there is someone who would very much like to see you."

27

We left the bodies lying there. Bennacio covered the faces of the men he did not recognize, but left Kaczmarczyk's exposed to the rain. I wasn't sure why, but thought maybe he was getting at something symbolical.

We climbed into the Suburban. We left the Jaguar sitting on the runway and nobody said anything about it.

Bennacio, me, and the guy with the bazooka, Jules, sat in the back of the Suburban, with Cabiri and the other brown-robed guy, Milo, up front. Jules had a funny smell, like black liquorish, and a very long nose with a turned-under tip. Milo had long blond hair that he wore in a ponytail, and piercing blue eyes, like Windimar's. Thinking of Windimar reminded me of the painful fact that I wasn't Windimar, but Alfred Kropp, and I had no business hanging with these bazooka-wielding warriors.

We drove in silence for a few minutes, then Cabiri said, "The outsiders stormed Mogart's keep in Játiva yesterday. Of course, they found nothing."

"Where is Mogart?" Bennacio asked.

Cabiri shook his head. "I don't know. We've heard nothing, Lord Bennacio."

His whole attitude toward Bennacio was tender and respectful, like it was a great honor just to be around him. If he had known I was responsible for this whole mess, he probably would have directed Jules to take me out with the bazooka.

"And now there is no way to cross the Atlantic," Bennacio went on.

"They closed the border and yet you crossed. Do not despair, Lord Bennacio. I know you loathe them, but I see no choice now. We must use what tools we have."

Bennacio sighed. "I will consider it."

I wondered who Bennacio loathed.

"Who are the outsiders?" I asked. "OIPEP?"

"OIPEP!" Cabiri sneered, and he made a spitting sound.

"What *is* OIPEP anyway?" I asked. "The best I could come up with was 'Operatives Investigating Powerful Evil Persons.'"

"Ha ha!" Cabiri shouted. "You have found a witty one, Lord Bennacio!"

Nobody said anything for the rest of the drive, which lasted about thirty minutes. We ended up in this little hamlet with Cape Cod–type houses lining these narrow, twisty streets. It might have been Halifax or it might not; I didn't know how big a town Halifax was or how far it was from the airstrip.

We went inside a house painted blue with white shutters. There was a fire snapping and popping in the fireplace and kerosene lamps set on tables, and I wondered why they didn't have electricity. Maybe these servants of the Sword had to operate on a tight budget. But Bennacio handed that guy a blank check from Samson Industries. Maybe the knights had an expense account but the Friends didn't. Or maybe it was a lifestyle choice, like those reenactors you see on TV.

"We are safe here, Lord Bennacio," Cabiri said. "At least for a few hours. Jules, find Lord Bennacio something to eat." He didn't tell Jules to find me something to eat. "Milo, tell her Lord Bennacio has arrived." He smiled at Bennacio. "She has been quite concerned."

Bennacio didn't answer. He sank into the chair closest to the fire and pressed his fingertips against his eyelids. I didn't know what to do with myself, so I sat on a stool next to Bennacio and wished I had some dry socks; the bottoms of my feet were starting to itch. I wondered if it would be rude to take off my shoes.

Cabiri slipped off his brown robe. Underneath he wore a flannel shirt and Wrangler jeans. He had short-cropped, very curly hair, like a poodle. He looked like the guy on the Brawny paper towels.

Jules carried in a tray loaded down with smoked salmon, big chunks of cheese, bundles of fat grapes, and lumps of little black greasy-looking balls on thin crackers that I guessed was caviar. I had never tasted caviar and didn't want to try anything new on an empty stomach, so I helped myself to some salmon and cheese. The grapes were good, with very tight skin, so when I bit into one the juice exploded in my mouth. Jules left and came back with a bottle of wine and some glasses, but I'm not a wine drinker, so I ate a lot of grapes for their juice. Maybe they'd have the cash for electricity, I thought, if they didn't blow it on caviar and expensive French wine. Cabiri was a big guy like me with an appetite to match, and between us the tray didn't stay full for long.

"You must call them," Cabiri told Bennacio.

"The thought galls me," Bennacio answered.

Just then a girl came into the room, and Cabiri got up and Jules got up and so I got up, and all the crumbs in my lap fell on the throw rug. She was tall, almost six feet, barefoot, wearing a sleeveless green dress that trailed the floor. Her auburn hair was pulled back from her face and her pale skin glowed in the firelight. She was the most beautiful girl I had ever seen.

She went directly to Bennacio, who stood up as she came toward him, and she took his hand and kissed it, then pressed it against her cheek. "My lord," she said softly.

He touched her cheek with his free hand and said, "Natalia, you should not be here."

"Nor should you," she said.

He was turned three-quarters from the firelight, so his face was in shadow and I couldn't see his expression when he said, "I have no choice," but he sounded sad, the same way he'd sounded when he said "Our doom is upon us" back in Knoxville.

He turned toward me and said, "This is Alfred Kropp."

"I know who Kropp is," Natalia said, and she didn't look at me. Her voice had a very clear tone, like the ringing of bells in the distance, so even though she spoke softly, you could hear her across the room.

"He saved my life," Bennacio added. I'm not sure why. Maybe to get her to like me. I could see that was going to be a hard sell.

"That you might sacrifice it," she said to Bennacio.

"That I might keep my promise."

I looked at Cabiri, who was studying the way the light played on his wineglass, and at Milo, who was standing by the front door, like a soldier on watch. I didn't know what had happened to Jules. Bennacio and Natalia were talking like they were the only people in the room, and I was very uncomfortable.

"Your promise!" she said. "No, not *your* promise, my lord, but another's, the promise of a myth, made a thousand years ago to one whose bones have long since crumbled to dust. You trust the word of the dead above the vows of the living."

"I trust the purity of my Order."

"Your precious Order is no more, my lord. The knights have departed."

"All but one."

"And soon you too will fall and I will be alone."

"Is this why you came?" Bennacio asked. "To torment me in this way? I cannot abandon my oath for any human being, no matter who she may be. I cannot sacrifice the world for the sake of one person."

"The world is not worth saving, if not for the sake of one person," she said.

He touched her cheek. "I love you before all things, and I would perish rather than see you suffer. But you do not understand what you are asking, Natalia. I cannot turn my back on heaven. I will not damn myself, even for love."

"You're the one who does not understand," she shot back. Then her shoulders slumped and all the fight went out of her. She leaned against him, and he took her in his arms and held her as she cried softly into his shoulder. He murmured her name into her hair as he looked at me. Our eyes met and I looked away. I couldn't take the look in those eyes.

28

"The hour grows late," Cabiri said. "You must decide, Bennacio. We have lost both plane and pilot. You did not hesitate to use the outsiders to cross the border. You *must* call them now."

Before Bennacio could answer, Milo said, "Someone is here."

The window beside him exploded inward, and glass flew across the room. Something landed in the entryway and rolled toward us, bumping against Cabiri's leg before coming to a stop.

It was Jules's head.

"The lights!" Cabiri cried. He and Milo rushed around,

blowing out the kerosene lamps. Bennacio shoved Natalia toward me, picked up a bucket that was sitting by the fireplace, and threw water onto the logs. There was an angry hiss and a plume of white smoke.

"Down the hall, Alfred," Bennacio said. "Last door on the left. Hurry!"

I grabbed Natalia and pulled her down the hall, feeling my way along the wall with my right hand. She wasn't making it any easier in the pitch dark by trying to pull free. She was a tall girl and strong for someone so thin. Behind us, I could hear the sounds of a pretty terrific fight going on, breaking glass, shouting, the clump of feet, and the sharp crack of furniture breaking.

I reached the end of the hall and found the door, pushing Natalia into the room and slamming the door closed behind us. What were we supposed to do now? Duck in the closet? Hide under the bed? A roaring sound moved directly overhead now, the steady *thumpa-thumpa-thumpa* of a helicopter, and then the *pop-pop-pop* of gunfire and men screaming.

I let go of her wrist. "Maybe we should—" I started to say, but she didn't let me finish. Out of the dark a knee landed right in my crotch and I dropped straight down and curled into a ball on the floor. When you take a hit like that, there's nothing you can do but curl up around the pain and hug it till it fades.

"That is for taking the Sword and sentencing him to death," she hissed at me. Through my tears I saw the door open and her shape silhouetted in the lighter dark of the hallway. She held a tapered dagger in her right hand. Then she was gone and my pain and I were alone together.

I grabbed on to the edge of the bed and pulled myself up. I was swaying there by the foot of the bed, the pain keeping tempo with the beat of my heart, when the beam from a large flashlight stabbed into the room. I just rushed the guy without thinking about it, lowering my shoulder and slamming into his chest, forcing him out the doorway and into the hall. He lost the flashlight when I hit him. I started pounding his middle with both fists, till he grabbed my right wrist, twisted my hand behind my back, swung me around, and forced me to the floor, putting his knee in the small of my back and bringing my wrist up so the tips of my fingers were touching my neck. It felt like he was pulling my arm out of its socket. Then I felt something cold press behind my ear.

All of a sudden it was very quiet. The guy holding me down was breathing hard, but that and the slow *whump-whump* of the helicopter blades turning outside were the only things I could hear.

Then I heard Bennacio call out, "No! He is with us!"

The guy got off me and picked up the flashlight. He kicked me onto my back and shone the light right in my eyes.

"Who are you?" he demanded.

"Alfred Kropp!"

"Alfred Kropp! Hey, my mistake, but you bushwhacked me, kid."

A hand came out of the dark and pulled me to my feet. I

could smell his cologne and hear him working on a piece of gum. Bennacio joined us, carrying a kerosene lamp.

The guy with the flashlight pumped my hand twice, very hard. He was wearing Dockers and a polo shirt beneath a blue Windbreaker. He couldn't have been older than twenty-five or thirty. His hair was shoulder-length and slicked back with some kind of gel.

"Mike Arnold," he said. "How ya doin'?" He turned to Bennacio. "Close call, Benny, huh? You can thank me later. Right now we gotta get the heck outta Dodge. There's more baddies on the way."

He herded us down the hall into the main room. Cabiri stood near the fireplace, a couple of black-robed bodies lying at his feet. Another guy in a black robe was sprawled face-down on the kitchen floor, blood pooling under his head. Natalia stood over him, breathing heavily, the dagger glistening in her hand.

"Milo?" Bennacio asked Cabiri, who slowly shook his head and motioned toward the sofa. I didn't want to look at Milo, but I looked anyway and then was sorry I had looked.

"We all here?" Mike Arnold asked. "All accounted for? That's terrific. That's just jim-dandy. Leave the mess; we'll send somebody over to clean up."

"How did you find us?" Bennacio asked him.

"No time for that now. Grab whatever gear you have and let's go." Mike strode to the front door and flung it open. There was a large black helicopter sitting on the street, whipping cold air into the house.

Cabiri stepped up to Bennacio and said softly, as if he didn't want Mike to hear, "Come, Lord Bennacio. The choice has been made for us. Trust this turn of fortune."

"Oh yeah, you gotta trust it when fortune turns," Mike Arnold said, snapping his gum, and I wondered who the heck Mike Arnold was.

29

We piled into the helicopter, which was one of those big military types that sat seven with room for gunners on both sides. I sat next to Bennacio and Natalia in the seat at the back. My butt was hardly on the cushion when we were airborne, dipping hard to the left as we climbed, and I could taste soured cheese as my stomach came up toward my throat. Natalia was still barefoot and I thought her feet must be freezing in the swirling air inside the open hold. Cabiri and Mike Arnold sat across from us, and Mike was smiling at me with very large white teeth that the gum-smacking made easy to notice.

He leaned forward and shouted in my face, "So you're

Alfred Kropp, huh! Hey, what a boner, taking the Sword like that! You're our century's Pandora! You study Greek mythology in school? Pandora's Box? You must be like, 'Holy moley, what the hell was I *thinking*?'" He laughed and his gum went *smack-smack-smack*. He chewed gum like he was angry at it.

He looked at Natalia. "Don't think we've met. Mike Arnold, how ya doin'?"

Natalia just stared at him. He didn't let it faze him, though. He gave her a wink and turned to Bennacio.

"So anyway, you were asking how I found you. Of course, we knew when and where you crossed the border. Then a couple hours ago we got the intel on the little number you guys did on Kaczmarczyk, so it wasn't brain surgery figuring you were probably gone to ground with Cabiri."

"Your arrival was most . . . fortuitous," Bennacio said.

"Like the cavalry, huh?"

"Where are you taking us?" Bennacio asked.

"We're giving you a ride across the pond, Benny. See, there's been a development."

"What development?"

He glanced at me, then said, "That's classified."

"Mogart has contacted you," Bennacio said. It wasn't a question.

"That's classified, Benny. Class-i-fied." He flashed a meaningless smile in my direction.

"You have made an offer to buy the Sword and he has accepted."

196

"I'm beginning to think we have a communication problem here," Mike shouted at him over the roar of the engine. "We've taken full jurisdiction over this little matter and I'm not authorized to tell you anything else!"

Cabiri turned his head and pretended to spit. I had seen him make that gesture once before, and as I stared at Mike Arnold it hit me I was looking at an agent of OIPEP.

We were in the air only about twenty minutes when the helicopter made a wide loop and started to descend. Mike looked at his watch, pulled a gun from his Windbreaker pocket, and held it loosely in his lap. He noticed me staring at it.

"A nine-millimeter Glock! Wanna hold it?" he asked me. I shook my head. He smiled, smacking on the gum. Mike Arnold clearly didn't share Bennacio's opinion that guns were barbaric. I got the feeling Mike Arnold liked guns—a lot.

The morning sun was just visible below the cloud cover that was pulled across the sky as we touched down. It felt cold enough to snow, and the wind was kicking up. We were at another airfield. About a hundred yards away was a military cargo plane parked on the runway, its huge back door open to a blackness like the inside of a gigantic mouth.

I followed Mike and Cabiri out of the helicopter, but Bennacio stayed inside with Natalia. It looked like they were having another argument, and Natalia's eyes were shining with tears. Bennacio tried to get up, but she put a hand on his arm and it was pretty clear to me she was pleading with him not to go. He shook his head and kissed her cheek before joining us in the tornado beneath the helicopter's spinning blades.

"All set then?" Mike asked. "Great!" He started across the tarmac toward the cargo plane, but nobody followed him. Bennacio turned to Cabiri.

"I am coming with you!" Cabiri shouted at him.

"No. You must stay with Natalia. While I live she is in danger. Keep her safe, Cabiri!"

He turned to me. "I will say good-bye to you now, Kropp. Though not himself a knight, Cabiri is a Friend of the Sword and will help you home if that is what you wish."

Deep shadows crept along his mouth and under his deep-set gray eyes. He looked very old, and tired. "My path is dark and only heaven knows its end. Pray for me, Alfred. Good-bye."

He squeezed my shoulder, then turned and walked quickly toward where Mike was waiting by the rear of the cargo plane door. I watched until Bennacio had almost reached the plane, and then I took off after him, yelling, "Bennacio! Bennacio! Wait! Wait for me, Bennacio!

"Bennacio!" I stopped by the gangplank, gasping for air. It was a hard run; I was big and not used to it, and besides, I had just taken a hard one between the thighs. "Take me with you."

"You do not know what you ask," he said.

"I could help. I could . . ." I had no idea what I could do. "I could be your squire or lackey, whatever it's called. Please

198

don't leave me here, Bennacio. I've got to—you gotta give me a chance to make up for what I've done."

He glanced at Mike, who was smiling at me like a preppie Buddha. Then Bennacio said quietly, "And what have you done, Alfred?"

"Took the Sword," I stammered. Again he was like the stern father and I was like the little kid who just got caught with his hand in the cookie jar. "And that got Uncle Farrell killed, and Mr. Samson and all the rest of the Knights, Jules and Milo now, and God knows who else is gonna die just because I didn't want to live in a foster home. So I can't go back now, Bennacio, don'cha understand? I can't go back."

"Maybe that's so," Mike Arnold said. "But you can't come with us. You don't have clearance and I've got no authorization."

I ignored him. "You owe me," I told Bennacio. "I saved your life and you owe me."

"I saved yours," Bennacio reminded me.

"Look, Mr. Samson sent you all the way back here just to tell me what happened," I said. "Why do you think he did that? There's got to be a reason. I don't know what it is, but he thought it was important enough to have you drop everything just to tell me. You know he would have said I could come. You know that, Bennacio."

He didn't say anything. He turned and walked up the ramp into the plane.

"Gee, what a tough break, Al," Mike said. "But you really should count yourself lucky you made it this far."

He hit a button and the ramp started to rise. Something caught his eye over my shoulder and all of a sudden he said, "Great! Company!"

He reached down, grabbed my wrist, and heaved me into the cargo bay. I turned around and saw three dark shapes on the edge of the sky coming in fast, either helicopters or low-flying planes. Mike pushed me out of the way and ran toward the front of the plane, shouting into a walkie-talkie, "This is Mother Goose, we've laid the egg and we have three baby dragons heading for the nest. Repeat, we are still on the nest! Request immediate air support!" He slammed into the cockpit at the front of the plane. The bay door was still closing as the plane lurched forward, throwing me backwards. I would have fallen if Bennacio hadn't caught me. We both peered out the shrinking opening as the black shapes got closer— they looked like the attack helicopters that brought us here. I looked over and saw ours taking off and one of the baby dragons, as Mike called them, peel away from the other two and head after it.

Then the bay door closed and I couldn't see anymore. Bennacio reached around me, swung the locking mechanism down, and said, "Come, then, Alfred." I followed him to a small bench against the hull and we sat down as the plane accelerated for takeoff.

"There's no safety belts!" I yelled at him over the roar of the engines. He ignored me and flipped up the plastic shade of the small window behind us. He craned his neck but snorted with frustration because he couldn't see anything, I guess.

Then we were off the ground and banking sharply to the right. Bennacio had turned from the window and was sitting with his eyes closed. Maybe he had a fear of flying, like me. I looked out the window and saw two helicopters, one chasing the other, but they were identical, so I couldn't tell which was ours and which was theirs. Little explosions of bright light were coming from the chasing helicopter as the other one rose and dipped, banked hard right, then left, trying to avoid the fire. We kept gaining altitude, until they were about the size of my thumbnail below us, and then I saw a fireball and a great cloud of billowing black smoke. I wondered where the other two baby dragons were and if our plane was armored and how, if it wasn't, it ought to be.

I looked at Bennacio and he still had his eyes closed. I looked out the window again and this time, maybe a thousand or so feet beneath us, saw what looked like fighter jets, maybe F-16s or their Canadian equivalents. The jets were chasing down two of the helicopters. I couldn't see the third one, so maybe the one that blew up wasn't the one with Cabiri and Natalia on board. I hoped so. I looked at Bennacio again to tell him what I'd seen, but he had fallen asleep.

30

Bennacio and I were alone in the cargo bay. His eyes were still closed. He must know something I don't, I thought. If it were me, I'd be beside myself with worry. Were Cabiri and Natalia alive? Did they make it? I looked at his thin fingers folded in his lap. He wasn't wearing a wedding ring, but that didn't mean he wasn't married. Still, she seemed awfully young for him. I had the impression that a lot of these Old World types take younger brides, but like most impressions I had, this one didn't come from firsthand experience. Bennacio was a knight, very up on tradition—maybe it was an arranged marriage. But Natalia loved him, you could tell that. If she didn't, she wouldn't have kneed me in the groin.

I rested my head against the hard shell of the plane. Between the droning of the engines and Bennacio's soft snoring beside me, soon I was asleep too.

I dreamed I was on that plateau atop the same slag heap, under the yew tree, and my head was lying in the lap of the Lady in White. She was stroking my forehead and a light, warm breeze stirred the dark ends of her hair. She was singing something, though I couldn't make out the words, or they were in another language. I interrupted her song to ask her where I was.

Do you not know? she asked. *Have you not been here before?*

"Once, but I didn't know what it was then either."

What do you think it is, Alfred?

"Heaven?"

She smiled like I had said something cute.

And what am I?

"An angel?"

I am the one who waits. And this is the place of waiting.

"What are you waiting for?"

You know what I am waiting for.

I would have guessed she was the Lady of the Lake from the Arthur stories—only there wasn't a lake anywhere in this dream—and that she was waiting for us humans to stop mucking around with Excalibur and give it back.

Lying with my head in her lap, I was looking straight up

at the yew tree, and the leaves were fluttering in the wind you couldn't feel, and I noticed something funny about them: The leaves of the tree were multicolored, red and black and white, and then I saw the branches were bare and it wasn't leaves fluttering at all, but the wings of thousands of butterflies beating uselessly in the air, because each butterfly was pinned to the branch by a long silver needle. That kind of freaked me a little, and I started to pull a needle free to let the butterfly go, but the Lady slowly pushed my hand down.

It is not time.

"Time for what?"

She had a sad, faraway look in her eyes, which were as dark as her hair and shone like she was about to cry.

When the master comes, he will free them.

"The master," I said. "Who is the master?"

The one who remembers.

"Remembers what?"

What has been forgotten.

I stared at the butterflies fluttering helplessly above my head and thought that was my problem: I wanted to forget everything. I wanted to forget, but I couldn't.

"What's been forgotten?" I asked.

She leaned over and pressed her cool lips against my forehead. I caught a whiff of jasmine.

When the hour comes, you will remember.

31

I woke up, rubbing the back of my neck. These military cargo planes were not built for comfort. Bennacio was awake, staring out the window.

"You were dreaming of her again, weren't you?" he asked.

"Is she the Lady of the Lake?"

"I do not know. She is important, whoever she is, if only to you."

"It was one of those dreams where you never want to wake up. You don't think she's kind of the ghost of my mother, do you? She's dead, you know."

"I cannot answer that, Kropp."

"Only my mother was never that pretty, even when she was young. I don't think it was heaven. I mean, you don't picture heaven being on top of a slag heap. Where are we?"

"About an hour from our destination, I would guess. You have slept a very long time."

"What is our destination?"

"France."

"I've never been to France," I said. "I don't have a visa or a passport or anything."

"That will not matter."

"Is Mogart in France now?"

He shook his head. "I do not know. It appears Mogart has offered to sell the sword to OIPEP itself. OIPEP operates a safe house in France, where we will wait for Mogart's final instructions on the delivery of the cash."

"Bennacio, it's none of my business, but whose plane is this? Who's that guy Mike?"

"Surely you have guessed the answer by now, Kropp."

He reached into his breast pocket and handed me the same business card he had showed the guard at the border. Mike Arnold's name was on the card. Above the name was the acronym, in bold type, OIPEP. There was an 800 number beneath Mike's name.

"Bennacio, are you ever going to tell me what OIPEP is?"

He smiled at me. "What do you think it is?"

"Mr. Samson said it was some kind of supersecret spy outfit. You don't trust them, do you?"

"I do not trust outsiders to resist the temptation of obtaining the ultimate weapon."

"So that's the deal? Mogart's offering the Sword to OIPEP?"

"Perhaps."

"You seem awful calm about it, Bennacio."

"I am a man of faith, Alfred."

"What's that supposed to mean?"

"There is a purpose to all things."

"Maybe," I said. "But I don't get it."

"Not many do, when the test comes."

"I think I failed that test."

"Do you? Perhaps you have. Yet it is also possible that the true test has not yet come. Who can say? I have given much thought to your words in Halifax. Indeed, Samson did think it important you knew of our fall."

"Maybe he just wanted me to know what a mess I made of everything."

"Have you learned so little of us, Kropp, that you would believe such a thing? This mess, as you say, does not belong to you, any more than it belongs to me. Do not concern yourself so much with guilt and grief, Alfred. No battle was ever won, no great deed ever accomplished, by wallowing in guilt and grief."

He patted my hand and stood up. "Excuse me, I must speak with Mr. Arnold for a moment."

He disappeared into the cockpit. I yawned. I looked out

the little window and saw nothing but a lot of sky, a lot of water, and something glinting in the fading sunlight off our wing. Probably an F-16. I yawned again. I had slept for hours and I still felt sleepy.

Bennacio was gone a long time. When he came back he was smiling.

"What?" I asked.

"She lives," he said simply, and sat down beside me.

"That's great," I said. "I should apologize, Bennacio. I was supposed to keep her in that back room, but she kneed me in the crotch." My face got hot telling him that. Some kind of squire I was turning out to be.

He gave a little wave of his hand. I didn't know what that meant.

I said, "Is she your wife?"

"She is my daughter."

"Oh." I didn't know what else to say, so I added, "She's, um, pretty."

He didn't answer. He was peering out the window again. "It appears we are making our final approach, Kropp. Say nothing of what you know about the Sword to Mike."

"That won't be hard because there's not a lot I know."

"He is our ally in this quest, but we are strange bedfellows."

"How's that?"

"Surely it has occurred to you that evil men are not alone in their desire for the Sword. It is the ultimate weapon. There is no defense against it."

"I was thinking about that," I said. "Mr. Samson told me an army with the Sword at its head would be invincible, but couldn't somebody just drop a nuke on it?"

"It is impervious to any device of man," Bennacio said, "no matter how terrible. I do not know precisely what would happen, Alfred. All I know is the Sword cannot be defeated or destroyed."

"After Uncle Farrell died, I had this dream. Well, more of a nightmare than a dream." I told him about the faceless army and the rider of the black horse, how he slammed the Sword into the smoking ground, how planes fell and tanks blew up, how the soldiers screamed and ran from the blinding light of the Sword.

Bennacio stared at me for a long time after I finished.

"What interesting dreams you have, Alfred Kropp," he said. "Let us pray they are not prophetic."

32

Two cars waited for us on the edge of the private airstrip when we touched down in France. Three men in dark suits and dark sunglasses stood beside two black cars parked by the runway. I looked up as we walked down the stairs and saw the two F-16s scream by overhead.

"You guys must be wiped out," Mike said. "Come on. It isn't far from here, I promise."

He opened the rear door of one of the black cars. I looked at Bennacio. He nodded and I slid in. He sat down beside me and one of the dark-suited guys got behind the wheel. Mike sat beside him up front and we started to drive. The other two guys followed us in the second black car.

Mike opened the glove box and pulled out something black. It looked like a rag.

"Al," he said to me. "I really hate to do this, but it's a secure location, you know?"

He reached over the seat and, before I could put my hands up, he had slipped the cloth over my head. I couldn't see a thing. I started to yank it off, but felt a hand on my arm. Bennacio. He patted me as if to say, *It's going to be all right.*

"Hope you guys are hungry," Mike was saying. "Jeff joined us from Istanbul yesterday and he is one *heck* of a cook. We'll grab some grub, and then you can take a shower and change your clothes. Al, you especially look like somebody's chewed you up and spit you out."

"Where is Mogart?" Bennacio asked.

"No idea, man." He didn't sound too concerned about it, but that may have come from the gum-chewing. "We know where he *isn't,* which is Játiva. Our folks went in yesterday, took out the whole compound, but he and his boys had already cleared out. Found Samson. Or what was left of him. Man, talk about freaky. You guys operate on a whole different level, don't you? What in the dickens was *that* about?"

Bennacio didn't say anything. I wondered what Mike was talking about. What did Mogart do to Samson that was "freaky"?

I was having a hard time breathing inside my hood. It took everything inside me not to pull it off. I wondered what Mike would do if I did. Maybe shoot me. Casually, though, the way he talked and smacked the gum, like it was a summer afternoon and all he was doing was watching a baseball game. My voice was muffled by the cloth when I said, "Samson was Bennacio's captain; you shouldn't talk about him like that."

He ignored me. "We think he may have slipped into Morocco or maybe even Algeria. Anyway, every border in the free world's been locked down, but that's a lot of square footage to cover and not everybody's a friend of truth, justice, and the American way, if you know what I mean. Anyway, yesterday we get the call he's ready to deal. Tells us to sit tight and he'll be back in touch with the final figure and location of the exchange. Don't know where it'll be or what the final price tag is—they don't tell us much at our level, but we've got a pool going if you want in on it. The rumor is— and this is unconfirmed and classified, by the way—the rumor is one hundred billion dollars. That's *billion* with a capital *B,* man. You wanna know my personal opinion? I think he did all this just to make the Forbes list."

I heard a cell phone ringing and then Mike talking quietly. It seemed like we had been driving for a long time, but it was hard to tell with the hood over my face; time passes differently when you can't see. We went fast, then slow, then fast again, like we were hitting highways, then getting off again onto lesser roads. Then the engine revved as we climbed up a steep incline. Once we leveled off, I heard the engine stop, and my door opened. A hand reached in, grabbed my right arm, and pulled me out.

Somebody said, "Watch your head," and guided me by the elbow along a rocky path. The rocks or gravel crunched under my feet and I thought about my dream and scrambling up the slag heap to find the Lady in White with her long black hair and dark eyes staring sadly into space, waiting for the Master to come.

"Step up," the same voice said, and now I was walking on wooden planks. I shivered in the cold. The air around me suddenly got warmer; I was inside. Somebody pulled the hood off. I squinted in the light, though it wasn't really that bright inside.

We were standing in a little entryway to a cabin, or maybe in France you call it a château. Wooden floors, a cathedral ceiling, and a huge fireplace. About a dozen guys milled about and I could smell bacon frying. Suddenly I was the hungriest I had ever been in my life. My knees were actually weak.

"So what would you guys like? Shower first, or breakfast?"

"Alfred needs to eat," Bennacio said.

"All I had was some cheese and grapes," I said to no one in particular. No one in particular seemed to be listening.

33

An agent named Jeff laid out ham and bacon, biscuits, eggs, sugary things somebody said was *beignets* (a kind of French doughnut that I ate six of), a couple of T-bones, coffee, juice, hot tea, and fresh hot chocolate. Mike was a big Cubs fan and he talked with this other guy, Paul, about their chances this year and the problem was their bullpen like it was every other year. Bennacio sat beside me, nibbled on some toast with strawberry jam, sipped coffee, and said nothing.

After breakfast, Mike led us up the stairs to the second floor and showed us the bathrooms where we could wash up. I stripped down and laid my clothes outside the door as Mike suggested, so they could be washed while Bennacio and I took our showers.

I stood for a long time under the hot spray. I think I may have had jet lag, because I kept dropping the soap, and everything seemed to be taking a very long time to accomplish: it seemed washing my hair took at least a couple of hours.

I stood in the shower until my fingertips pruned up; then I dried off and slipped into a white terry-cloth robe that I found hanging on a hook by the shower. The bathroom was very small and I kept knocking into the sink and hitting my elbows on the walls, but I felt better with a full stomach and a clean body. I found a toothbrush and some paste in the medicine cabinet and scrubbed my teeth. Brushing my teeth made me think of my mother, who was a real stickler for oral hygiene—I'd never had a cavity in my life.

I was late getting back downstairs. The meeting had already started without me. Mike, Jeff, and Paul were sitting on the sofa in the great room, with Bennacio sitting by himself in the rough-hewn rocking chair near the fire.

A lady sat next to Mike. She had large lips that looked very red and wet-looking in the firelight. Her platinum-blond hair was pulled into a tight bun on top of her head. She wore a pinstriped business suit and black high heels.

I leaned against the wooden beam in the entryway, feeling kind of silly in my bare feet, my hair still wet. Bennacio was fully dressed. Nobody acknowledged my presence. Mike was talking.

"So it's all set up," he was saying. "Last night I got final approval from headquarters. I can't tell you how much, that's classified, but I will say we think we've topped the highest bid by at least half a billion."

He stopped, almost as if he was waiting for an answer from Bennacio. He didn't get an answer, though. Bennacio said nothing. He was staring at the fire.

Mike pulled a piece of foil from his pocket, carefully wrapped his used gum in it, and slipped it back into his pocket. He popped another piece of gum into his mouth, wrapped up the foil, and just as carefully put the fresh foil into his pocket.

The lady with the shiny blond hair spoke up. She had a British accent. "Honestly, we think that was his plan from the beginning, to sell the Sword to us."

"Really?" Bennacio said. "You presume much."

"Who else could he turn to?" she asked. "We represent the richest countries in the world. And he can trust us. Not even the Dragon wants to see the whole world go up in flames."

"Right, Benny-boy, that's right!" Mike said. "I mean, how's he going to enjoy his money in a nuclear wasteland? He's known from the beginning he *has* to sell it to the good guys."

"I have told you," Bennacio said. "Mogart does not intend to give you the Sword. He will never part with it."

"How come?" Mike was smiling at Bennacio, a hard, unfriendly smile.

"Would you?"

"Hey, come on now, Benny. We're the good guys, remember? We're all on the same side here, right?"

"He will take your money and keep the Sword."

"World domination, huh? King Mogart. Well, we're just gonna have to take our chances on that one, Benny."

"You are a fool," Bennacio said, turning away from the fire and glaring at Mike. "He will betray you."

"That's precisely why we've invited you to the party." Mike turned to the British lady. "Right, Abby?"

Abby said, "We will not make the exchange until you've verified the Sword's authenticity."

"And then OIPEP returns the Sword of Righteousness to us, its friends," Bennacio said. Now he was the one smiling hard and unfriendly.

"I'm gonna be honest with you, Benny. That's not our call," Mike said. "Point of fact you guys didn't do such a hot job of protecting it in the first place."

"We have protected it for a thousand years," Bennacio shot back. "Only by a freakish accident was it lost."

Mike glanced over his shoulder at me, the freakish accident. Then he looked at Bennacio, smiled and shrugged, as if to say, *Look, buddy, you couldn't even protect it from this big loser.*

"Bennacio," Abby said in a kind voice. "We have nothing but admiration for what your Order has accomplished. But perhaps the time has come for the Sword to pass on to different protectors. Why else would Samson involve us?"

"Abby's got her hands around the issue's throat, Benny," Mike said. "There's nobody on the planet better equipped to keep it safe."

Bennacio wasn't buying it. "I will not do this without your assurance the Sword will be returned to me."

"Like I said, Benny, we can't promise that," Mike answered. "I've always been straight with you and I respect the heck out of you and your knightly buds. We wouldn't dream of busting your chops. But I will give you my personal guarantee The Company has no intention of using the Sword for any purpose. We want the same thing you want: to keep it out of the hands of all the baddies and loonies."

"I cannot betray my solemn oath," Bennacio said. "By my life or death I will hold and protect it. I can do no less. If Mogart indeed returns the Sword, you must kill me to keep it from me."

"Nobody wants to do that," Abby said. She didn't say they wouldn't kill Bennacio, though.

"Benny," Mike said. "We're a go whether you come along or not. We're just waiting for the Dragon to get back to us on the time and location for delivery of the Sword. We—I—want you along, of course, and once we get the Sword back, everything's negotiable. Let's take it one step at a time."

Bennacio sighed. Nobody said anything for a long time. Paul picked at a hangnail. Jeff smoothed creases I couldn't see on his pants. Mike smacked his gum. Abby was the only one looking at Bennacio.

Finally, he stirred in his chair and said, "I will come, on one condition."

"You name it."

"The vengeance is mine."

" 'Thus saith the Lord,' " Mike cracked, but nobody laughed.

34

I went back upstairs and found my clothes in the bedroom. Somebody had washed and laid them on the small bed by the window. I pulled back the curtains to look out, but there was nothing to look at: The window was boarded up. *Secure location*. As if I would know where I was in France. The only way I'd know is if I looked out and saw the Eiffel Tower in the backyard.

I dressed and sat on the bed. I didn't know what else to do. I didn't want to go back downstairs. Being around Mike and his gang of spies or whatever they were made me feel kind of twitchy.

There was a soft tap on the door and Bennacio came in. He closed the door and sat down beside me.

"Do you trust them?" I asked.

"Would you?"

I thought about it. "No choice?"

"We must use the tools given us, even those that are double-edged."

"How'd they find out about the Sword in the first place?"

"When the Sword was lost, Samson realized at once we would need their help. I counseled against it, but now I understand the bitter necessity of it, though it cost us our greatest loss since the founding of our Order."

"I thought I caused that."

He frowned at me. "I am not speaking of the Sword."

"They're not going to let you have it, are they?"

"I think not."

"How're you going to stop them?"

"I will do as I always have done: all that I must to protect it."

"Bennacio, you can't kill them."

He sighed. "Long ago, Alfred, I took a solemn oath as binding as gravity. I know of no other way."

"Well, I'm not sure exactly what you're trying to say, Bennacio. Maybe because I've never taken any kind of oath like that. I've never taken any kind of oath period."

He looked at me with those deep-set, intense eyes.

"Why not?"

"I guess I never had the chance."

"All of us have that chance. But we either choose not to or do not recognize it when it comes. On the plane, when I told you I believed all happens for a purpose, you thought of your uncle's death, and you wondered how something so seemingly useless could serve any purpose. In the past, Alfred, men cast about for reasons to believe. Now we find reasons *not* to."

"I'm not following you, Bennacio."

"The human race has grown arrogant, and in its arrogance assumes nothing is beyond the power of its reason. If we see no purpose, it follows there must be no purpose. It is the fallacy of our times."

"Bennacio," I said. "You can't just kill them. For every one of them you kill, they'll send a dozen to come after you. Sooner or later they'll find you, and I don't care how powerful the Sword is, they'll get it from you somehow. And then they'll kill you."

"Perhaps," he answered. "Yet mercy has cost us much. If I had killed you the night you took the Sword, your friends and mine would still be alive and the Sword would still be safe."

"Yeah, but I'd be dead."

He laughed, then patted me on the knee and stood up.

"I think I shall miss you, Alfred Kropp, when this is over."

He left me alone. I sat there for a few minutes, thinking. Mostly I was thinking the last knight was going to buy the farm. Either Mogart would kill him or the agents of OIPEP would.

I was convinced that Mike's plan was to use Bennacio to help get the Sword, and then kill him (and probably me). That's what Natalia meant when she told me I had sentenced Bennacio to death.

Thinking about Natalia made me feel especially rotten, though I'm not sure why. It's not easy being hated by anybody, but it's especially hard when the person who hates you also happens to be the prettiest girl you've ever seen.

35

Later that afternoon I was lying on my bed, thinking, when overhead I heard the slow *thumpa-thumpa* of a helicopter, growing louder as it approached. From downstairs there was clumping and bumping as the spies ran around in a panic, shouting at each other and looking for their guns.

I heard Mike shouting, "Breached! We've been breached!"

I jumped out of bed and ran into the hallway, where I literally bumped into Bennacio. He was wearing his brown robe and carrying his black sword.

"Mogart?" I asked.

He shook his head. "Something worse, I fear."

I tried to imagine something worse than Mogart. I followed Bennacio downstairs into the great room. Jeff and Paul corralled us and told us to stand back. Mike and Abby went to the front door and flung it open. Over their shoulders I could see a black attack helicopter landing on the sloping ground in the front yard. A big man wearing a black sweater jumped out. He reached into the helicopter and helped out a smaller person.

Mike's shoulders relaxed and he stuck the gun under his Windbreaker as the two people walked up the gravel path to the front door.

Abby glared at Bennacio. "Do you have an explanation for this?" she asked.

Mike stepped back, and then Cabiri came into the room, Natalia right behind him. She ignored Mike and Abby and rushed over to Bennacio. As she passed me, I could smell her hair—peaches.

"Hello!" Cabiri called to nobody in particular. "Hello, hello! And how is everyone? How are all my secret-agent friends?"

Mike slammed the door, threw the dead bolt, and whirled on Bennacio.

"You got an explanation for this?" he shouted.

"I've already asked him that, Michael," Abby said coldly.

"Please, do not hold Lord Bennacio responsible," Cabiri

228

said. "This is entirely my doing." He gave an apologetic smile. "*Scusi.*"

"Save your '*scusis,*' pal," Mike shot back, as the *thumpa-thumpas* of the helicopter grew fainter. "How did you find us?"

"Oh," Cabiri said, "how does the fox find the chicken? How does the bird find the worm?" He smiled at Bennacio.

"*You* called them," Mike said, turning to Bennacio.

"How might I call them?" Bennacio asked. "I have no telephone."

"I am a Friend of the Sword," Cabiri said to Mike, his voice losing its jokey edge. "And Friends of the Sword have friends who have friends. Do you think your presence has gone unnoticed in Saint Étienne?"

Mike didn't seem to be listening. He brushed passed Cabiri and bounded up the stairs, dialing his cell phone as he went. A door slammed above us and I could hear Mike's voice as he shouted to someone on the phone, but I couldn't make out the words. Abby sighed.

Cabiri said to Bennacio, "Forgive me, my lord. It was not my decision to come here." He was looking at Natalia.

Natalia was looking at Bennacio.

"I am coming with you," she said, her chin tilted up in defiance.

"You know you cannot," Bennacio answered, but not unkindly.

"And I," Cabiri said.

"No."

"Who then will stand by you when the test comes?" Natalia demanded. "Her?" And she jerked her head toward Abby.

"My name is Abigail," she said. "And you are?"

"Or *him*?" And now Natalia jerked her head toward me.

"Do not underestimate my friend Alfred Kropp," Bennacio said. "There is more to him than meets the eye."

"Then there is much indeed!" Cabiri said heartily, and he slapped me on the back. "For he is substantial!"

Mike came bounding down the stairs then, and jabbed his finger at Cabiri's nose.

"You are interfering with a matter of international security, mister!"

"Perhaps you should shoot me."

"Enough!" Bennacio said, and everybody shut up and stared at him. "They should not have come, but they have and so we must make the best of it. When Mogart calls, Cabiri will stay here with my daughter. I will return for them both once we have the Sword."

That ended the discussion. None of the OIPEP people seemed happy about it, but they couldn't come up with a good argument for sending Cabiri and Natalia away. There was some discussion of sleeping arrangements, since all the bedrooms were taken. Then Jeff volunteered to sleep on the sofa downstairs so Natalia could have his room. Cabiri decided he would bunk with me.

"For you and I are the only Friends here," he told me. "It

will be delightful, Alfred Kropp! Only I must warn you of my snoring and my flatulence."

Bunking with Cabiri didn't turn out to be delightful. He had been telling the truth about his snoring and farting.

Natalia and Bennacio holed up in his room for hours, and I could hear their voices through the walls as they argued. Sometimes I could hear her crying.

When she wasn't in the bedroom, she would be in the great room, sitting in the rocker by the fireplace, staring at the flames, her knees drawn up to her chest, her dark eyes reflecting the firelight. Sometimes she passed close to me coming down the hall or in the kitchen at dinner, and each time she passed I smelled peaches and thought of being a little kid, turning the handle of the ice cream churn while Mom dropped fresh peaches into its belly.

Natalia barely spoke to me, but sometimes I would catch her staring at me and she would look away quickly.

Then one night Cabiri's flatulence chased me from the room (his farts seemed to gather underneath the covers and attack any time I rolled over, fluffing the blankets). I padded downstairs, thinking maybe I'd wake up Jeff for a game of poker or pool. But Jeff wasn't on the sofa; Natalia was, curled up under a blanket, wide-awake, staring at the dying embers in the fireplace.

I stood for a second at the bottom of the stairs. I thought about going into the kitchen for a snack, but that was like covering up for disturbing her and didn't seem cool at all.

"Hi," I finally decided to say.

She didn't answer.

"I, um, I couldn't sleep. Cabiri won't stop farting."

She still didn't say anything.

"Look," I said, taking a step into the room. "About what happened in Halifax . . . it's okay."

She slid her dark eyes in my direction. I felt like a bug on a pin when she looked at me.

"What is okay?" she asked.

"You know, the fact that you kneed me in the groin."

"I should have stabbed you."

"Sure, I understand that." I eased myself into the rocker across from her.

She was looking at the fire again.

"Who are you?" she asked softly.

She whipped her head in my direction, her dark hair flying to her right shoulder.

"Who are you, that you have done this?"

"I was just a kid trying to help out his uncle."

"You are a thief."

"Yeah. As it turned out."

"My father should have killed you when you took the sword. *I* would have killed you."

"Don't you think life's funny that way?" I asked. She stared at me as if I were speaking a language she didn't understand. "I mean, I guess you've noticed, but there isn't a lot to do around here, and I'm not sure how long I've been here, but it seems like it's been a very long time, and all there is to do is eat and sleep and think. And I was thinking, look at how many things had to happen for me to end up here. You know, if only my dad hadn't run off on my mom. If only my mom hadn't died of cancer. If only Uncle Farrell hadn't volunteered to raise me. If only Mr. Samson had hired somebody else to be the night watchman at Samson Towers. Or if Uncle Farrell had just said no to Mogart like he should have. Or if I had said no to Uncle Farrell. I guess I could go on, but you probably get the point. Your father talks a lot about fate and doom, which is something I never really bought into, but now I'm thinking maybe something does guide us or use us for something bigger . . . What do you think?"

"What do I think?" she asked. "I think you are an idiot."

"You wouldn't be the first," I admitted.

"Your sympathy for my father disgusts me."

"Well," I said. "Maybe you shouldn't be so hard on me, Natalia. I know how it feels."

"You know how *what* feels?"

"Losing a parent."

She looked at me for a long time. It was so long, I started to feel very uncomfortable, more uncomfortable than usual.

"And at least there's a chance he won't die," I went on. "My mom didn't even have that."

36

Things changed between Natalia and me after that night. I'm not saying they got much better, but it was like we'd reached some kind of understanding. I still caught her staring at me sometimes, and once or twice I think Mike noticed too. Once at dinner, I looked up from my plate and saw her looking, and then I looked over at Mike and he was looking at her looking at me, and he was smiling.

One morning, after I finished my shower, I passed Bennacio's door and heard Natalia's voice, followed by the low hum of Bennacio's. It sounded like a heated debate was going on; I figured it was about Natalia going with him to the rendezvous with Mogart. I went to my room and closed the door. After a while I heard a door slam and the light tread of Natalia going down the hall.

I went to Bennacio's room and knocked softly on the door. There was no answer. I tried the knob. It was unlocked.

I stepped inside. The light was off, but there was a glow in the room from two candles sitting on the small table pushed against the far wall. Propped up between the candles was a small painting in a gilded frame of a man in a white robe, kind of floating against a black background, with great white fluffy wings outstretched on either side, holding a sword in his right hand.

Kneeling in front of this picture was Bennacio. He didn't lift his head or move when I came in. I felt ashamed, almost as if I had walked in on him naked. The main thing that struck me, though, was how terribly small he seemed, kneeling there in front of that picture, how terribly small and alone.

"Yes, Kropp?" he asked without turning or getting up.

"You should take her with you," I said.

He didn't move.

"Take her with you, Bennacio," I said.

"You do not know what you are asking," he said finally.

"Maybe I don't," I said. "There's a lot I don't get. Most stuff I probably never will, but this one thing I'm pretty sure of, Bennacio."

His shoulders dipped, his head fell to his chest, and when he stood up, for the first time he struck me as an old man, old enough to be a grandfather, even. He turned and looked hard at me.

"What are you so sure of, Kropp?"

"Look, Bennacio, when my mom got sick she would get on me all the time about coming to see her at the hospital. She was all worried about me missing school or sleep or meals, but she was dying. There was no hope for her. But I didn't care. I came every day anyway, for over a month, and I sat there for hours, even when she didn't know I was sitting there." All the memories came rushing back then, of Mom shrunken to the size of a pygmy in that hospital bed, bald from all the chemo, big black circles around her eyes. Her teeth seemed huge against her hollow cheeks and thinned lips. And the way she would whimper, *Please, please, Alfred, make it go away. Make the pain go away.*

"Maybe it was useless my being there. Maybe there was nothing I could do, but where else was I supposed to be? You say you don't have a choice, but you think she does. Well, maybe she doesn't have any more choice than you do. It's kind of hypocritical, if you ask me, saying you don't have a choice but she does."

I don't know if anything I was saying was making any sense. But he listened. He didn't say anything. He just stared at me, but he listened, I think.

"Okay," I said. "That's it. That's about all I had."

I walked out of the room, pulling the door closed behind me. Standing a couple of feet away was Natalia.

I wiped the tears from my cheeks and walked hurriedly past her, muttering as I passed, "There's no such thing as accidents." I don't know why I said that.

37

I went to my room and after a while—I don't know how long, maybe a couple of hours—there was a knock on the door and Bennacio came in, still wearing that brown robe. He was carrying a long box. He sat beside me, setting the box down on the bed behind us.

"Kropp," he said.

"Bennacio," I said.

"I cannot take her."

"Well," I said. "You should."

"One day, perhaps, you will have a child, and you will understand."

"Whatever," I said.

"Do not think too bitterly of me."

"Okay," I said, as if what I thought about Lord Bennacio, Last Knight of the Order of the Sacred Sword, really mattered. Bennacio was giving off some serious sadness sitting there beside me, as if an invisible cloak of sorrow was wrapped around his shoulders.

"That picture in your room," I said. "Is it Saint Michael?"

"The Archangel Michael, yes."

"You know, I was thinking about that. Mr. Samson talked about the master of the Sword and so did the Lady in my dream. Michael is the master of the Sword you're waiting for, isn't he?"

He slowly shook his head and smiled. I didn't know what he meant by that. Was I right or wrong?

"When I was a boy of thirteen," Bennacio said, "my father took me aside and told me that we were of the house of Bedivere. I had heard the story of the Sword, of course, but like you had always thought it merely a legend. My father took me to the head of the Order, Samson's father, who had just moved to America. I saw the Sword and I believed. Upon his deathbed, my father told me of Bedivere's failure."

Bennacio sighed. "Bedivere *was* to cast the Sword into the lake—those were the direct orders from Arthur—but he chose to keep it instead, and our Order was created. Of all the knights, he loved his king the most, and from this love rose the belief that one day another master would return for the Sword."

He sighed again, a longer, sadder sigh. "It is a particular burden, Alfred, to descend from the house of Bedivere. There have always been knights of our Order who saw what he did as a betrayal of his king's trust. Many believed the Sword should be cast back into the waters from which it rose, thus removing any possibility of the Sword being used for ill. By my honor, as the last knight and the last son of Bedivere, if ever I retrieve the Sword, that is what I shall do. I will atone for his sin, though his sin was of the most peculiar kind, born of love."

He picked up the box, laid it on his lap, and opened the lid. Inside, lying on the purple velvet lining, was a sword, thin and black-bladed. It looked like the same kind of sword he used the night I stole Excalibur. He held it up.

"This is the sword of my father. OIPEP recovered it when they stormed Mogart's keep. On the day my father died, I swore upon this sword the ancient oath of our Order."

He turned to me. "It may be my fate to fall to Mogart when the hour comes. If so, will you not make the same oath and take up this sword?"

"Gee, Bennacio," I said. I was shocked. "That's a big honor and I really appreciate your asking me, but I think you've got the wrong guy. Maybe you should ask Mike or Paul or one of those guys . . . Even that Abby woman would be a better choice. I think she might be the toughest one of the lot. Mike's kind of scared of her, you can tell."

"Those people, Kropp? They are arrogant and full of their own wisdom. They are fools."

"Well, some people might say I'm not the ripest apple on the tree, Bennacio. You gotta know your limitations, and what you're asking is way over my head. Basically, I'm a loser."

He stared at me with a stern expression. "What do you mean?" he asked.

"Well, I lost the Sword, for one. But besides that, there's nothing I'm good at. You know how most people have talents? Like some people are good at sports and others good at school—science and math and stuff like that? Well, I'm not very good at anything. I played football, but I wasn't very good at it, and my grades are pretty mediocre. You know, I'm just . . . average."

"Average," he said.

"Yeah. Just your average, um, Kropp. Though I've been screwing up more than usual lately. The idea of me taking up your sword and being some kind of hero—well, that's kind of ridiculous."

He put a hand on my shoulder. "But we fall only that we might rise, Alfred. All of us fall; all of us, as you say, screw up. Falling is not important. It is how we get up after the fall that's important."

He gave my shoulder a little pat. "And as for being a hero—who can say what valor dwells in the soul unless the test comes? A hero lives in every heart, Alfred, waiting for the dragon to come out."

38

Bennacio took my hand and placed it on the flat part of the blade.

"I'll just let you down," I said. I was about to cry. Maybe I should cry, I thought. That'll change his mind about a hero dwelling in my heart.

"Perhaps. Our will often falters. My mind tells me you are a weak young man, timid and unsure, but my heart tells me something altogether different. For all your faults, Alfred, you are without guile, without pretense. The Sword shall never be won or evil defeated through trickery and deceit, as those downstairs believe. Will you not speak the oath now, while there is still hope?"

I looked away. His expression was so desperate, I couldn't look at him. Things really couldn't get any worse, when a knight like Bennacio had to turn to Alfred Kropp to help him.

"Alfred," he said softly. "There is something else. Something you do not know that might help you make your decision."

I turned back. "What?"

"You asked if I had finished Windimar's training. It was indeed I who finished it, which is not uncommon, as I've said. Samson too completed a certain knight's training, when that knight pledged himself to the Order upon their first meeting in France. You can guess who that certain knight was."

He waited patiently for my Kropp mind to grasp what he was saying.

"Mogart?"

"Yes, Mogart was Samson's squire, and more. Samson named him his heir."

My Kropp mind couldn't get a grip on that one. "So why did Mogart turn on him?"

His dark eyes glittered beneath his shaggy eyebrows, the same way they had about a lifetime ago in the halls of Samson Towers.

"Have you not wondered, Alfred, more than once, why your name was the code to unlocking the secret chamber beneath Samson's desk? Have you not wondered why, at the most desperate hour, Samson ordered me to return to

America to find you? Have you never wondered why Samson hired Farrell Kropp, an underskilled mechanic, to be the night watchman at Samson Towers? Two years ago, Bernard Samson discovered he had another heir, a true heir, and he wanted to make sure his son was taken care of until he came of age and could be brought into his full inheritance as a Knight of the Order."

"Uncle Farrell was Bernard Samson's son? Wouldn't that make me his . . ." I tried to figure it out. "Grandnephew or something?"

"Alfred, Bernard Samson was *your* father."

I stared at him for a long time. "I don't understand, Bennacio."

"Sixteen years ago, the man you know as Bernard Samson fell in love with a woman he met on a business trip. A business trip to Salina, Ohio, Alfred. That woman's name was Annabelle Kropp."

I was slowly shaking my head. Even though it was larger than average, it wasn't big enough to hold what he was telling me.

"Samson did not wish to expel Mogart from the Order. In many ways, Mogart was the best of us: intrepid, clever; with sword and lance he had no equal. But Mogart wanted more than to be a mere knight like the rest of us. He desired Samson's place. But when *you* were born, he could not have it."

"Oh, great. This is just great, Bennacio. Now that's my fault too?"

"It is no one's fault, Alfred. It is merely a fact. You are

the last in the line of Lancelot, the greatest knight who ever lived."

I didn't know what to say. Of all the things that had happened to me since my mother died, this was probably the weirdest—and the worst.

"You're just making this up to get me to take this stupid vow or oath or whatever it is. I'm not his . . . He's not my father . . ."

I couldn't go on and Bennacio didn't make me. He sat very still while I cried.

"Why did he leave my mom?" I finally made myself ask.

"So as not to endanger her—or you."

"That didn't work out too well, did it?"

"Not all good intentions do."

"I still don't believe it."

"As with the angels, Alfred, that hardly matters."

I looked down and saw the sword across my lap.

"Why didn't you tell me, Bennacio? Why did you wait till now to tell me?"

"I was hoping I wouldn't have to."

Bennacio whispered, "Speak the words now, Alfred Kropp. Speak, son of my captain, heir to Lancelot. 'I, Alfred Kropp, swear in the name of the Archangel Michael, my guardian and protector, that I will sacrifice my life in defense of the Sword of Righteousness, and that by my life or my death, I shall defend it against the agents of darkness.'"

I repeated the words, and in the silence that followed,

waited for some heroic valor to swell my breast. I didn't feel anything except a little sick to my stomach.

Bennacio smiled, patted my shoulder again, and placed the sword back into its box.

Then from downstairs came the sound of Mike's cell phone ringing. I knew it was Mike's because the ringer played "Take Me Out to the Ballgame."

"Ah," he said. "At last. The call comes. Perhaps a good sign."

"Am I a knight now?"

"There are no knights left, save one, and his reckoning is soon upon him."

39

Mike knocked loudly on the door and stuck his head in. He was smacking gum and smiling.

"Great news, cowboys. We're a go. Let's load 'em up and move 'em out!"

He clapped his hands and clumped down the hall in those big hiking boots he wore.

"You want me to take up your sword," I told him. "But I don't even know how to use a sword."

"There is no time to teach you, Kropp. However, I suspect the day will not be lost or won through swordsmanship."

We went downstairs. Jeff had laid out sandwiches. He said Mike had given orders to eat before we left.

"Where are we going?" I asked Mike.

"That's classified."

Bennacio and I took our sandwiches into the great room and ate by the fire. Abby was standing off by herself, talking quietly on a cell phone and checking her watch. Cabiri was there, and Natalia, of course, but neither of them ate anything. Cabiri was very quiet too, not his usual jokey self, and Natalia looked like she was about to cry.

Everybody gathered by the front door.

"Okay, here's the game plan," Mike announced. "Jeff, Paul, Bennacio, and *moi* head for the rendezvous point. Everybody else hangs here until we get back." He was kind of smirking in Abby's direction.

"I am going with Bennacio," Cabiri said.

"No can do, pal," Mike said cheerfully. His mood was a lot better now that the game was finally on. "You don't have clearance."

"I do not need your clearance," Cabiri said. "I found you once . . ."

"You try to leave this château and I'll have you shot in the back of the head," Mike said with a smile. "I've already given the order."

Cabiri turned his head and made a spitting motion.

"Cabiri," Bennacio said. There was a faraway-ness in his voice and eyes, as if he were already at the rendezvous point, the Sword of Kings within his grasp. "Stay."

"Jeez, this is heartwarming," Mike said. "Parting, the

sweet sorrow thing and all that, but we're on a tight schedule here and we've got to get shaking."

He opened the door and waved at Bennacio. I stepped forward with him.

"You're staying here, Al," Mike said.

"Kropp is coming," Bennacio said. "He is my second."

"Your second *what*?" Mike asked.

"He will take up my sword should I fall."

"No offense, Benny," Mike said. "But if it were me, I'd take Cabiri here."

"But I have no clearance," Cabiri said sarcastically.

"Look, Ben," Mike said in a tone usually reserved for a little kid. "The kid can't come."

"Michael!" It was Abby. "We don't have time for this. Let him take the boy."

Mike's mouth moved a little, but no sound came out. His face grew red.

"Headquarters is going to hear about this in my report," he said.

"Headquarters is going to hear about many things," Abby shot back.

Then she nodded to Jeff, who stuffed my head into that black sack again.

As we were going through the door I heard Bennacio say, "No, I shall lead him." I felt a hand leave my elbow and another take its place.

Bennacio helped me into the backseat of the car and

closed the door. After a second it opened again. I heard Cabiri saying, "No, no, no, Natalia . . ."

And I smelled peaches.

"Good-bye, Kropp," her voice whispered. "Protect my father."

The hood lifted over my right cheek, and I felt something warm and moist press against my chin. From the front seat, Mike let out a whistle and a loud whoop.

" 'Love is in the air!' " he sang.

Then my door slammed closed and the gravel crunched beneath the tires as we started down the mountain.

I figured we had been driving for an hour at least before we finally stopped. I could hear the sound of a jet engine warming up. The hood was lifted and I was blinking in the blinding light, getting a sinking feeling when I saw the plane about a hundred feet away. Mike turned to me.

"It's not too late, Alfred. We can have another plane here in ten minutes."

I looked at Bennacio, who had come to stand beside me.

"That's okay," I said. "I'm coming."

We walked up the stairs and took our seats. I took the aisle because I didn't want to look out the window. Mike put on a big pair of headphones. He said something into the microphone and the plane began to taxi toward the runway.

"Well, here we go!" Mike said. His cheeks were flushed. "This reminds me of the time the US Defense Department called us in to help with their little containment problem in Area Fifty-one! Whew, what a mess! But 'nuff said—that's classified!" He was shouting now as the plane began to accelerate, pushing me back in my chair as I fumbled for the safety belt: I had forgotten to fasten it. "Or the time we were lost for six days in the Bermuda Triangle! Talk about some funky vibes! Saw things in that operation that would turn your hair white!" He laughed in Bennacio's face. "But yours already is, so what the hey!"

Bennacio didn't say anything, but he had a disgusted look on his face. I was pretty sure he was going to kill Mike before all this was over. I wondered if Mike knew that and had similar plans for Bennacio. I felt almost sorry for Mike; he didn't know who he was screwing around with.

Mike explained that we would proceed immediately to the rendezvous point, where we would exchange the cash ransom for the Sword.

He wouldn't tell us exactly where the rendezvous point was, but he did say we would be met by some agents of OIPEP, or "The Company." OIPEP agents never called OIPEP "OIPEP." Maybe it was *Officers Investigating Perpetrators of Evil Pranks.*

"Let us do the talking," Mike said. "All you got to do, Benny, is hang back and wait. I'll let you know when to step up and authenticate we've got the real McCoy."

"And then?" Bennacio asked quietly.

"And then he's all yours. Have fun with your vengeance."

"And the Sword?"

"Let's take it one step at a time, Benny. Let's get it back first, okay? Then you and my superiors can talk."

Bennacio nodded, but I could tell he wasn't happy about it. My stomach was knotting up. I reached for the airsick bag.

After we touched down, I waited for the hood, but Mike just stood at the plane door and smiled at me, smacking his gum, and jerked his head toward the door. The sun had set and a cold, dense fog had rolled in. I wondered what the date was; I had lost track.

Mike led us to a pair of Bentleys parked on the tarmac. Bennacio had to reposition his sword so he could sit. He leaned his head back and closed his eyes. After a minute his lips began to move as if he was saying a prayer. It probably *was* a prayer.

We turned off the main road onto a narrow lane that weaved through a forest. The headlights barely penetrated the fog, and I worried we'd run into a tree before we could even get there. Our driver was driving way too fast for the fog, but I had heard Europeans always drive too fast.

After another fifteen minutes or so the trees opened up and we were driving through a rolling countryside. In the distance, I could see floodlights shining on black shapes pointing like thick fingers at the night sky. I had seen this place before, and it wasn't until the car began to slow down that I realized that Mogart had chosen Stonehenge as the place where the fate of the world would be decided.

40

We parked about a hundred yards away from the lighted circle of stones. Huge spotlights had been set up just outside the circle, and the fog separated each beam as it shone into the center. The air was so cold, I could see my breath. Men in dark suits waited for us just outside the outer ring. One of them came over and said to Mike in an English accent, "No sign of our quarry yet, Mike. We've established the perimeter; he won't get within ten kilometers without us spotting him."

Mike nodded and clapped the Brit on the back, but Bennacio said calmly, "No, he is already here."

"I'm afraid that's quite imposs—" the British agent began,

then stopped, because just then a group of robed men stepped from behind one of the larger stones ringing the center. Six of them, in black robes, with a tall man in the middle, wearing a white robe with the hood thrown back.

Mogart.

We stepped into the circle on the opposite side. The guys from OIPEP stood in front of me and Bennacio, seven in all, not counting us two. An even match, except Mogart had the Sword that no army or combination of armies could resist. Mike took one step toward Mogart and raised his hand.

"You're very punctual, Monsieur Mogart! That sort of thing impresses the living daylights out of me!"

"And you are late, Mr. Arnold," Mogart answered. "I see you have brought some unexpected guests. How good it is to see you again, my brother knight."

He bowed at Bennacio, and then looked at me. "And you, Mr. Kropp! How extraordinary that you are here! Please accept my gratitude for delivering the Sword!"

"You can go to hell," I muttered under my breath. Bennacio touched me on the arm as if to say, *Be still.*

"Well," Mike said. "Now that we've dispensed with the pleasantries, do you think we could talk a little business?"

"You Americans," Mogart laughed. "Always so abrupt."

Mike motioned to Paul, who reached into his coat and pulled out a long white envelope. Mike tossed it toward Mogart. It landed about three feet away and one of Mogart's men snatched it off the ground and handed it to Mogart.

"That is the location and the account number," Mike

called over. "Deliver the item and we'll give you the access code."

Mogart peeked inside the envelope, a sly smile playing on the corners of his lips. He handed the envelope to the guy on his right and nodded to the one on his left. This guy walked into the circle holding something long and narrow wrapped in a golden cloth that shimmered in the glare of the floodlights. He laid it on the ground in the center of the ring and stepped back to rejoin Mogart.

"Okay, Benny," Mike breathed. "You're on."

Bennacio walked slowly past Mike. I started to follow him and he whispered to me, "No, Alfred. Only if I call."

He walked alone into the center of the ring of stones and knelt beside the bundle lying on the ground, the cloth glittering and sparkling as he unfolded it. He made some motion with his right hand. It was hard to see from where I was, but it looked something like the sign of the cross.

I don't know everything that happened next, because a lot happened all at once, though it seemed to go in slow motion, like a car wreck. All of a sudden black-robed figures were flying from everywhere, swarming toward Bennacio, swords raised high over their heads. Paul yelled something beside me; I turned, and there was a swirl of black robes and the flash of a long black blade before it sank into Paul's back. There was the pop of small-arms fire on the other side of me. A head flew past my nose. It was Jeff's.

A figure in a black robe twirled past me: One of the British agents had him in a headlock, but he shuffled backwards and slammed the agent into one of the stones, breaking his grip, before turning to sink his sword into him to the hilt.

That's when somebody forced me to the ground, hissing in my ear, "Get down!" A gun went off right next to my ear and my whole head hurt from the explosion. A body fell right on top of me. I rolled him off and saw the bullet hole through the center of his forehead.

I looked to my right and there was Mike, a gun in his hand, lying flat on his belly and staring into the middle of the circle. His left hand was on the small of my back, I guess to remind me to stay down.

I looked around and saw nobody left standing except Mogart and Bennacio. Around Bennacio lay four or five of the black-robed AODs, most of them without their heads, some with their legs still jerking. I could see a thin line of blood trickling down the side of Bennacio's face where one of the AODs must have smacked him as he knelt beside the Sword.

I looked for the Sword in Bennacio's hand, but it wasn't there. Mogart was holding the Sword.

Neither of them moved or said anything for a long time. They just looked at each other, standing about six feet apart, both taking in big gulps of air and breathing out in little jets of steam.

Finally, Bennacio said, "Surrender the Sword, Mogart." He sounded very calm. "Surrender it now and I will show mercy toward you."

"Oh yes, how I long for mercy from *you*," Mogart sneered. "Sir Bennacio! Gentle Bennacio! The kindest and bravest of knights! The last knight!" The mocking expression disappeared and a shadow fell over his face. "*I* am the last knight, Bennacio. I am the heir to Lancelot, the master of the Sword!"

I leaned over and whispered into Mike's ear. "Shoot him."

Mike shook his head. I could have grabbed the gun from him and fired, but I had never fired a gun in my life. I was afraid of guns, to tell you the truth. Mike was slowly chewing his gum, working it so hard, his jaw clicked as he gnawed.

Bennacio drew his black sword from the folds of his brown robe and held it by his side, casually, like a man carrying an umbrella.

"You always had poor taste in friends," Mogart said. "Cowards and fools. But what an admirable choice in your squire, Lord Bennacio! A fat, bumbling simpleton with hardly the intellectual wherewithal to tie his own shoes. You have outdone yourself, Bennacio."

"The Sword belongs to neither of us, Mogart." Bennacio used the same tone he had used with me sometimes, like a patient father talking to a thick-headed kid. "In your heart, unless it is totally corrupted, you know this. You may betray your sacred vow, but you cannot change the truth. You lay claim to something that is not meant for you. Abandon this madness that you might yet live."

"Wise words coming from the man whose sole purpose is to kill me."

"I wish harm to no man, Mogart. I shall ask you just once more. Relinquish the Sword that you might live. Answer now, yes or no."

Bennacio raised his sword, holding it with both hands, the hilt at chest level, the blade right in front of his face, about two inches from his sharp nose. Mogart smiled and raised Excalibur, holding it with both hands like Bennacio, so they mirrored each other, Bennacio with his brown robe and black sword, Mogart in his white robe and the much longer and wider Sword of Kings.

"Here is my answer," Mogart said softly, and launched himself at Bennacio.

41

Bennacio's blade was a black blur, its shiny surface sparking now and then in the glare of the floodlights. As he spun and turned and sidestepped around the circle, his brown robe fluttered and snapped. Bennacio was taller than Mogart, and he was faster. They held their swords with both hands as they fought, and each time Excalibur struck Bennacio's sword, I saw black flecks and sparks shooting off against the charcoal-colored backdrop of the great stones.

The blades whined and whistled as they cut through the cold air, and I don't know if it was the ringing in my ears from the gunshots, but there was a faint sound like a choir singing, and I remembered Bennacio telling me of the angels lamenting the last time he and Mogart met.

I remembered how it felt when I used the Sword, how it seemed a part of me or more like I was part of it. I remembered Bennacio telling me how it could not be defeated or destroyed, and then I realized what Bennacio had known all along: There was no winning against the Sword. Bennacio didn't have a prayer, and that made my chest hurt, because Bennacio didn't have a prayer—*and he prayed anyway*. He couldn't win, *but he fought anyway*.

Mogart was getting impatient. He must have thought Bennacio should be dead already. His blows came faster and Bennacio's parries a little slower, until Mogart swung the Sword high and brought it down in a sweeping arc straight at Bennacio's head. Bennacio raised his sword to block the downward blow and, when Excalibur struck, Bennacio's sword flew from his hands and skittered away into the shadows. The force of the blow knocked him to his knees.

Then he did a strange thing, a horrible thing, the strangest, most horrible thing I've ever seen anybody do: Bennacio raised his head and brought his arms straight out from his sides, very slowly, palms turned upward. He was offering himself!

Mogart hesitated, the tip of the Sword poised a few inches from Bennacio's heaving chest.

"No," I whispered.

Then Mogart slammed the Sword into the last knight's chest and Bennacio fell over without a sound, his eyes still open.

42

Somebody was screaming loud enough to drown out the high-pitched singing or ringing or whatever it was going on inside my head, and it took me a second to realize the screaming person was me.

The next thing I knew, I was running across the circle of stones, straight for Mogart, with Mike yelling after me, "Kropp! Kropp! Kropp!"

When I was about twenty feet away, Mogart pulled the Sword from Bennacio's chest, and the last knight fell to his side, eyes wide open staring right at me as I ran.

At ten feet, Mogart began to turn toward me.

At five, he was raising the tip of the Sword, its blade still glistening with Bennacio's blood.

At two, he actually started to smile.

I didn't let him finish that smile. I smashed my forearm into his face and he staggered backward. My forward momentum carried me right into him and we fell into the grass. I landed on top, knocking the wind out of him. He started to bring the Sword up, but I slapped my hand down hard on his wrist. When his hand struck the ground, I pulled the Sword out of his hand and stood up.

I backpedaled, gasping for air, my breath fogging and swirling. Mogart slowly sat up, gulping air.

A voice behind me said, "Alfred."

I turned, the Sword rising without me thinking about it. Mike was walking toward me, smiling widely, still holding the gun in his right hand, the left outstretched.

"Awesome, man! Simply awesome," Mike said. "You wanna come work for us?"

"It's the football," I gasped. "Finally paid off."

"Mr. Kropp," Mogart said. "I beg you to reconsider."

I took a couple of steps backward, so I could keep both of them in sight. Mogart was smiling now.

"It is not yours to take," Mogart said.

"It isn't yours either," I said. My voice sounded very small and quivery to me.

"Actually, it's mine," Mike said. "I mean, it's the property of my employer. Anyway, we bought it fair and square. Alfred, I'm gonna give Monsieur Mogart here the access code to the Swiss bank account so he can have his money and then you, me, and the Sword are outta here. How's that sound?"

"Not very good, Mike," I said, and then I ran.

43

Of course it was dark and foggy and I was
in a strange country, but as I stumbled along I thought I'd try
to make it to the forest we had driven through. The back of
my neck tingled and my hair stood up, waiting for Mike's
bullet. He wouldn't have hesitated to kill Mogart for the
Sword and I didn't think he'd hesitate to kill me for it either.

I'm not a fast runner to begin with, and hefting the
Sword didn't make me any faster. The long wet grass pulled
at my feet and I might have just gone in circles in the dark,
but the floodlights helped; I kept looking over my shoulder
and they kept getting smaller as I ran. I listened for the sound
of Mogart's army coming after me, but there was no sound

at all except my huffing and puffing and the *swish-swish* of the grass rubbing against the soles of my shoes as I ran.

I stumbled onto the edge of the paved road. If this was the same road we drove in on, then following it would take me back into the woods. I still couldn't hear any sound of pursuit and I was too tired to run any more, so I started walking. Fog and sweat flattened my hair and I kept having to wipe the moisture off my face. My shirt clung to my chest and I shivered. I could feel a bad cold coming on. For some reason, the scar on my thumb was throbbing to beat the band. Maybe because the Sword was near it.

I was still walking with no woods in sight, just rolling hills that disappeared into the fog, when I heard the car coming up the road behind me.

I ran to the side of the road and threw myself onto the ground, making myself as flat as a fat, bumbling simpleton can get. But I didn't get flat enough, because the car stopped and a voice called out softly, "Alfred! Alfred Kropp, get over here!"

I lifted my head. Mike was sitting behind the wheel, smiling, smacking, waving his hand urgently at me.

"Come on! We don't have much time . . ."

He was probably right about that and I didn't have much of a choice. I scrambled up the embankment to the car and dived into the backseat. Mike hit the gas and the Bentley's back wheels spun out, screeching on the wet pavement like a wounded animal.

"Boy Howdy!" Mike yelled. "That was close, huh? Took

heavy casualties, but we kinda expected that goin' in, right? The main thing is we got the Sword. Got the Sword and saved the world, not bad for a night's work, huh?"

I leaned back, the Sword against my chest, still breathing heavily.

Mike said, "Pretty quick thinking back there, Al. You and Benny plan it that way, or was it all your idea?"

I didn't say anything. That didn't seem to matter to Mike. He kept talking.

"Darn it, dropped my cell back there in the fight. Well, everybody's on standby anyway. Me and Jeff have been together since Cairo—that wacky death-cult thing in the Valley of Kings. But, oh, jeez, enough about *that,* that's all classified. Anyway, I'm gonna miss that son of a gun and what a dingy-darn shame about Benny, huh? Heck of a guy. *Heck* of a guy. If I had my cell I'd call in a couple of Stealths and knock the living you-know-what out of that medieval madman, take out those thousand-year-old rocks with him. Small price to pay, don't ya think?"

"Did you kill him?" I asked.

He laughed. "What do you think, Al?"

"I don't think you did." I sat up and pressed the tip of the blade against Mike's neck.

He didn't react, except his hands tightened slightly on the wheel.

"Stop the car, Mike."

"Hey, Al. Ally boy. What the heck are you doing?"

"Stop the car, Mike."

He slowed down and pulled to the side of the road.

"Okay, now what? Talk to me, Al. What's this all about?"

I wasn't sure. I was making this up as I went along. "Give me your gun. No, Mike, with your left hand. Keep the right on the wheel. Slowly, Mike." I took the gun from over his left shoulder and slipped it under my belt.

"Okay," I said. "Now put your left hand back on the wheel."

"Al, I'm one of the good guys, remember?" His voice was calm enough, but he was working the gum hard. "Look, nobody's sorrier about Benny than me. That was a damn shame, but you were there, you saw—what did you want me to do about it?"

"You set him up."

"Ah, come on, Al!"

"You planned it from the beginning. Mogart didn't want just the money. He wanted Bennacio too."

Mike didn't have anything to say to that. He was watching me in the rearview mirror. I knew I was right when he didn't say anything.

"And you set up Mr. Samson and the rest of the knights in Spain. You tipped off Mogart they were coming."

He shook his head, smiling now. "Why would I do that, Alfred?"

"Because you both knew the same thing: As long as the knights lived, they were the only hope of ever keeping the

Sword safe. You both needed them out of the way. So you made them part of the deal."

"Man, that's a pretty interesting theory, Al."

"Mr. Samson trusted you to do the right thing," I said. "He didn't have to tell you about the Sword and you double-crossed him. Bennacio knew you were double-crossing us tonight, but he didn't see how he had a choice. He took a vow, see . . . he gave his word . . ."

"Look, Al, no offense, I know you mean well and every-thing, but you're in this thing way over your head. Put down the Sword, pal. We'll talk about this on the plane, okay? Don't you want to go home?"

"I don't have a home anymore."

"Really?" He whistled. "That's gotta be tough. I'm truly sorry to hear that, Al. Well, we could take you anywhere you want to go. Natalia is still at the château. You wanna see her? You got kind of a thing for her, don't you?"

I didn't say anything, but I could feel my face get hot. Mike Arnold noticed me blushing and smiled.

"Get out of the car," I said.

"Al . . ."

I pushed on his neck with the tip of the Sword.

"Okay, I'm getting out."

He opened his door and stepped onto the road. I got out and pointed the gun at his head.

"Get down on your stomach and fold your hands on the back of your head."

"You're making a huge mistake here, Al. A heck of a boner . . ."

"Lay down, Mike. I'll shoot if you don't."

"You think so? I'm sorry, Al, but I really don't think you can."

He took a step toward me and the gun went off. We both jumped. Neither of us was expecting that. I couldn't even remember pulling the trigger.

"All righty then," Mike said softly. He lay down.

"Hands on the back of your head," I told him.

He laced his fingers behind his head.

"Where do you think you're gonna go, Alfred? You can't get out of the country, and what are you goin' to do with the Sword? Take over the world? Donate it to the Smithsonian? You're not thinking this through, kid."

"Good-bye, Mike," I said, and I climbed into the car and drove off. I kept looking in the rearview mirror, but I never saw Mike get up.

44

The steering wheel was on the wrong side and I had trouble keeping the car on the road; the right wheels kept dropping off the road until I remembered I was supposed to be driving on the left side. That made it a little better, but it still felt funny. I knew I needed to ditch the car as soon as possible: A Bentley's a little too conspicuous for a getaway car.

I drove aimlessly through the English countryside, not even knowing what direction I was heading. I kept going until I came to a road that looked bigger and kept taking bigger roads until I came to a highway or whatever they're called in

England, and after a few miles passed a sign that read: "London 40 miles."

The traffic began to pick up as I got closer to the city. I drove with both hands on the wheel, my knuckles bone white, the Sword lying on the seat beside me. I couldn't stop yawning, and all I wanted to do was pull to the side of the road and go to sleep, but I kept driving.

The sun was rising by the time I reached the outskirts of London. I was definitely not driving into the heart of the city in a hot Bentley, so I pulled into the first hotel I saw in a place called Slough. I took off my jacket and wrapped the Sword in it, but that left the butt of the gun sticking up from my waistband in full view. I worried what to do about this and if the clerk would wonder why this fifteen-year-old kid was checking in without any bags or parents, and why I had a jacket in the shape of a large sword. But some things you can't do anything about, so I pushed the gun all the way down, into my underwear. The cold metal of the barrel pressed against my groin.

The hotel looked old, as if it had been something else before it was a hotel, maybe a nobleman's country estate. The lobby was very small, and just felt old compared to the American hotels I had been in. The clerk didn't say anything about my sword-shaped jacket. He put me in a room on the third floor, and told me I'd have to take the stairs because there was no lift. He asked how long I'd be staying. I told him I was taking a walking tour of England and I'd leave when I was tired of walking. He didn't ask anything else. He didn't smile once, and I thought maybe he had bad teeth. I had read somewhere that's a problem in England.

In the stairwell, I took the gun out of my underwear and kind of tucked it under my arm. The hall was narrow and there were water stains on the baseboard. The paint job and carpet looked at least ten years old and smelled of mold. My room was at the end of the hall, next to the bathroom.

My bed was narrow, about six feet long, and shook a little when I sat on it. I was afraid it was going to break. I thought about calling the front desk and asking if they had rooms with bigger beds. I put the gun on the bedside table and laid the Sword down on the bed beside me. I took off my shoes, peeled off my wet socks, and lay down.

What was I going to do with the Sword now? Mike had a good point. They'd lock down the whole country and go door-to-door if they had to. They'd find the Bentley parked in the hotel parking lot, and I hadn't even used a fake name to check in.

I expected a knock on the door any second, but they probably wouldn't knock, just burst in with guns blazing, because after all, I had the Sword of Kings and might use it to take over the world.

I yawned. I needed sleep, but my instincts told me sleep should probably be the last thing on my to-do list. I pushed myself off the bed. On the wall next to the TV was a mirror. I looked at myself and decided I probably should take a shower, but that would mean leaving the room, and I didn't want to take the Sword with me into the shower or leave it in the room. I looked in the mirror and thought about Mogart calling me fat. I wasn't fat; I was just big. I had always been big and blocky, like one of those blocks at Stonehenge, wide and rectangular, the most boring shape next to a square there is.

I sat back on the bed and tried to figure out my next move. I couldn't stay here long—no more than a few hours. I should shower and brush my teeth and go, except I didn't have a toothbrush. I didn't have anything except the most powerful weapon on earth. I could declare myself the Emperor Kropp, King Alfred the First, Lord of the Earth, but right then all I wanted was a toothbrush.

If I made myself king, I could summon all the world's leaders to Slough and declare world peace. I could demand all the tanks and bombs and guns be melted down and turned into playground equipment. I could tell all the rich countries to feed the poor ones and outlaw war and tell them from now on every penny they used to spend on weapons they now had to spend on finding cures for diseases and making cars that burn clean fuel. I could demand the end to every evil under the sun. No more war or disease or famine. I could fulfill what Bennacio said was the reason the archangel gave the Sword to Arthur: I could unite mankind. I could finish what Arthur started. It might not bring Bennacio back, or Samson and the knights, or Uncle Farrell, or anyone who was lost because of me, but it might make up for what I had done. It might even make Natalia not hate me anymore.

Maybe my destiny was to be the sword-wielding savior

of the world, and wouldn't that just make Amy Pouchard regret not giving me her cell phone number! I had a vision of myself on a great throne, with a great big golden crown on my great big head.

The cold I had felt coming on was now fully on: My head hurt, my nose was running, and my forehead was hot. I lay on the bed and told myself in a minute I would get up and take a cool shower to bring my fever down and be ready to think more clearly. It's pretty sad when you reach the point of scheduling your clear thinking.

"That's it. You've figured it all out, Kropp," I told myself. I was pretty feverish by this point. "The Knights of the Sacred Order kept the Sword hidden for a thousand years, waiting for Alfred Kropp to come along and save the world. Right! It never occurred to any of them, from Bedivere on down, that maybe one of *them* could take up the Sword and bring peace to this rotten world. They were waiting for *you*, Mr. big-headed high school dropout, to take care of things."

I touched the cold metal of the blade—after a thousand years, how smooth and perfect it was! Just touching it made me happy and sad at the same time.

Eventually, I fell asleep, and I was back in the dream of the dark rider on the terrible battlefield, the Sword in the rider's hand. Just as he was about to slam the blade into the ground and blow away his enemies, he lifted his head and I could see his face. It was *my* face. Not Kropp the Benign . . . but Kropp the Conqueror, Kropp the Terrible.

When I opened my eyes again the room was dark and the

phone was ringing. I turned on the table lamp and wondered how long I had been asleep. I stared at the phone on the bedside table and wondered who was calling. Maybe the front desk, to tell me some guys in black robes were waiting for me down in the lobby.

I picked up the receiver. "Hello?"

"Bonjour, Mr. Kropp."

I picked up Mike's gun from the bedside table and held it in my lap.

"Mr. Mogart."

"Are you watching television?"

"Excuse me?"

"Is there a television in your room? If so, I suggest you turn it to channel one."

"Right now?"

"Immediately."

"I'm gonna have to put the phone down."

"That's quite all right."

I set the phone down and turned on the TV. The BBC news had just started. About five minutes into the show, they ran a story about the American attorney general's news conference that afternoon. He was announcing an update to the FBI's most wanted list. Before they flashed the photograph on the screen, I knew what I would see.

It was my picture.

The attorney general was saying I was an international fugitive with ties to terrorists and was responsible for the deaths of sixteen British and American personnel in an attempt to destroy one of England's most famous national treasures. Then he announced the Justice Department was offering a six-million-dollar reward for information leading to my capture and conviction.

The big-headed loser was finally tops in something: I was the most-wanted fugitive in the entire world, but all I could think of was how difficult it would be now to assemble my summit of world leaders and declare the founding of the Kingdom of Kropptopia.

I turned the set off and went back to the phone.

"I'm back," I said.

"Congratulations, Mr. Kropp. You are a celebrity. Perhaps you will even make the cover of *People* magazine."

"How—how did you find me, Mr. Mogart?"

I walked over to the window as I talked. I pulled back the curtain, expecting to see a SWAT team or their British counterparts storming the building. But all I could see was the empty parking lot and some woods. To my left, the dirty yellow lights of London glowed on the horizon.

"A fifteen-year-old boy—and not a particularly clever boy at that—alone in a strange country, afraid and without friends, driving a car equipped with a Global Positioning System—how difficult do you think that really is?"

"I guess not too difficult," I said.

I sat back down on the bed.

"I know what you want, Mr. Mogart. But, see, if I give it to you it's going to mean the end of the world. I'm only fifteen, like you said, and it's really important to me that the world sticks around for a while, at least until I'm forty. Maybe fifty, even."

"Ah, but you are missing the point, Alfred," Mogart said. It was the first time he had called me by my first name. "Whether you live to fifty is of little importance to me. I want only one thing, so you see we are both equally disadvantaged. You have something I want and I have something you want."

"What?" I asked, since I couldn't think of a single thing I had left that mattered. Everybody who mattered to me was dead. But that wasn't true and the funny thing was that, of the two of us, Mogart was the only one who knew it.

"Kropp."

It took a second for it to sink in that the voice on the other end wasn't Mogart's. It wasn't even a man's voice.

"Kropp," she whispered again.

"Natalia?"

I heard a little screech, then silence, and Mogart's voice came back.

"Understand, Mr. Kropp, that I care not for what I have, as you care not for what you have. I would sacrifice my life for what you possess, as you would sacrifice yours for what I possess. To my mind, there is only one way to satiate our particular desires. Are you following me, Mr. Kropp?"

"Wouldn't it have been easier just to come here and take it from me?" My voice was shaking badly.

"Why should I come there for it, Mr. Kropp, when you are bringing it to me?"

Just then I heard a sharp rap on the door. I jumped and gave a little yelp.

Mogart said, "Someone is at your door. Open it."

"I have a gun," I said. "I'll use it."

"Do so and she dies."

The rapping on the door continued.

"Who's at my door?" I asked.

"Answer it and find out. I'll wait."

I walked to the door and called out, "Who is it?"

"Your escort, Mr. Kropp," came a voice from the other side. I unlocked the door and shuffled backwards, lifting the gun, so when he walked into the room it was pointed right at his nose.

"Don't even think about going toward that bed," I told him.

He nodded. He was a big man, about my size. He wore a long gray cape over his shoulders, fastened by a dragon-shaped pin just below his Adam's apple. Under the cape, he was dressed in an expensive tailored suit. His long hair was greased and combed back from his face.

"Stand right there," I added, backing toward the bed, keeping the gun on him. He nodded again. "Don't make any sudden moves!" I said sharply to him. He nodded a third time. I picked up the receiver with my left hand and brought it to my ear.

"Mr. Kropp," Mogart said softly. "I believe I told you some time ago that the will of most men is weak. Thus nations crumble and decay, great enterprises are lost, needless suffering and humiliation ensue. I believe I also told you—in fact, demonstrated to you in the most graphic way—what would happen if your will opposed mine. You will accompany my associate to our little meeting or the girl will die."

My knees completely gave out then and I sat on the bed. The gun dropped to my side. I had made a vow and if I kept that vow, Natalia would die. I felt so miserable at that point, I almost picked up the Sword and handed it to the escort, who was still standing by the door, smiling at me.

Mogart's voice lost all its playfulness and it got hard. "Listen carefully, Kropp. You are not adept at what you're attempting to do. You are a boy playing a man's game. You might be enjoying this make-believe game of being a hero, but truly you are fortunate that I found you first."

"I don't know what you're talking about!" I screamed into the phone. "I never wanted to be a hero! I never wanted any of this!"

"They are coming, Mr. Kropp. Remember the report you just saw on television? The OIPEPs are coming for you and they *will* find you. And when they find you, they will take the Sword and I will kill the girl. You will have lost both. You have no choice now but to bring it to me."

"But if I bring it to you, you'll kill her anyway."

"You wound my feelings, Mr. Kropp."

"You'll kill her, because the last time I gave you the Sword you killed Uncle Farrell, and you didn't need to kill Uncle Farrell."

He sighed. "No. I should not have killed your uncle. I should have killed *you*."

"You're gonna do that too," I said into the phone.

"Then your answer is no?"

"You already know what my answer's going to be."

"Just so," Mogart said.

45

I hung up the phone. Mogart's associate was still standing by the door, smiling at me.

"Come," he said. "The master is expecting us."

"I've got the Sword now," I said. "Doesn't that make me the master?"

"Do you claim it?" he asked mockingly.

I looked at it on the bed beside me. "No. But that's the point, I think. Nobody can. You could wait a thousand years, ten thousand even, but nobody can really claim it. I think that's where your boss has got it all wrong and why the knights kept it hidden all those years, maybe even why

Arthur had to die. It's not something you can own." He wasn't getting it. I asked, "Where are we going?"

"Did the master not tell you? To Dundagel, now called Tintagel."

"Oh. What's in Tintagel?"

"Camelot is in Tintagel, and the caves of Merlin."

"Sure," I said. "That would make sense."

Then I picked up the gun and shot him in the left kneecap.

He yelled and pitched forward onto the floor, wrapping his arms around his knee. I grabbed Excalibur from the bed beside me.

"In the name of Saint Michael!" I yelled, and brought the Sword, flat side down, toward his head. He didn't even see it coming. I hit him in the head with the broad part of the blade and he went still.

I knelt beside him and pressed my fingertips against his wrist. He wasn't dead. I remembered what Bennacio had told me after he dispatched those two thralls in the forest back in America: *You would not pity them if you knew them as I do.*

"Well, Bennacio," I murmured as I unhooked the dragon pin to remove the gray cloak. "I know what they did to my father. And I know what they did to you and to the rest of the knights, but at some point somebody's gotta say enough. At some point all the blood and guts have to dry up."

Underneath the cloak the escort had concealed one of those black-bladed swords. I searched his pockets and found a set of car keys.

I hooked the black sword around my waist and twisted the belt around so it hung on my right side. I slipped Excalibur into the other side of my belt, to hang on my left side. I threw the gray cape around my shoulders and hooked the dragon pin, then looked at myself in the mirror. Sir Alfred of the Castle Screws-up-a-lot.

I stepped over the escort, opened the door, looked both ways before going into the hall, and closed the door behind me.

I took the back stairs to the main floor, praying there was a back door to the place. The Sword pooched out of the cloak on the left side, and its shape was kind of obvious.

The stairs ended just to the right of a glass door that opened onto the parking lot. I slipped outside and walked around, looking for the escort's wheels. There was a black Lamborghini Murciélago parked in the handicapped space right by the door. I knew it was the right car before I even tried the key. These guys liked their cars.

I couldn't sit with both swords jutting out, so I pulled them from my belt and laid both in the small backseat, throwing the gray cloak over them. I cruised the lot once before leaving, to see if any spooks or other black robes were hanging around, but saw nothing suspicious.

I had no idea where Tintagel was, so I pulled into the first gas station I saw, though apparently it isn't called gas in England; it's called petrol. The clerk gave me a funny look when I walked through the door in my gray cloak with the dragon-shaped pin.

"And what are you supposed to be?" he asked.

"The heir to Lancelot, the greatest knight who ever lived."

One of his eyebrows went up and I said, "Yeah, it's a stretch. I've been having a heck of a time with it."

"If you're Lancelot, I'd hate to see Guinevere."

"I didn't say I *was* Lancelot. I'm *descended* from Lancelot."

"Oh, right. And I'm the Queen of bloody Sheba."

I told the clerk I needed a map of England and asked him where Tintagel was.

"Tintagel? That's in Cornwall."

"About how far is it?"

"Around two hundred miles."

He spread the map open on the counter and showed me where Tintagel was, on the southwest coast.

"Now here is Tintagel Head," he said, pointing out a spot on the map right by the Atlantic Ocean. "Lots of Yanks go there. Spectacular view, sits on a cliff with a three-hundred-foot drop to the sea."

"Is there a castle there?"

"Some ruins, yes. Not much to look at. King Arthur's castle is the legend, but you know that already, of course, being the descendent of Lancelot. Did you know he wasn't British? He was French."

"Was he? Well . . . *très magnifique.* Nothing but ruins there, you said?"

"Above, yes. Now, in the cliffs directly below is a cave they say was the sanctuary of Merlin, the king's wizard.

290

Some say when the tide is out and the wind begins to blow from the sea, you can hear the ghost of Merlin wailing for the kingdom that was lost—if you believe such things."

"Oh," I said. "You bet I do, mister."

"Of course, sir knight," he said. "You would."

46

So I drove to Tintagel at ninety miles per hour, expecting any minute to hit a roadblock or to see a helicopter gunship swoop out of the night sky and take out my tires. But nothing like that happened. I tried to think. I really needed a plan. In fact, this was probably my last chance to come up with one, but all I felt was naked, like I was caught up in a tornado, every scrap of clothing torn away, naked in the screeching wind with nothing to hold on to.

After an hour and a half I could smell the sea. I slowed down because the road signs were different and I couldn't read them very well going that fast. I bore off the main highway at the turnoff for Tintagel and followed the signs toward

Tintagel Head. I rolled down the window and could hear the ocean as well as smell it.

I came to a roadblock, just a couple of sawhorses painted red and placed in the middle of the lane. A sign beside them read: "Site Closed for Archeological Dig." I backed the Lamborghini up about fifty feet and floored the gas. One of the sawhorses sprung into the air and smashed into the windshield, making a series of intricately laced cracks, like a spiderweb.

I cut the headlights and crawled along the lane, expecting any second for men in black robes to jump out of the dark onto the hood of the car. The road ended about fifty yards from the cliff's edge. I turned off the engine and got out.

A cold, icy wind was blowing in from the sea. I stood for a second in the biting wind and my eyes were watering up pretty bad, the tears running straight back across my temples and into my hair. I should put the swords in my belt and march off to my doom like Bennacio—and the world's doom, since losing the Sword now left nobody to get it back, if you didn't count OIPEP. But I wasn't sure about which side OIPEP was on. Mike Arnold was kind of a jerk and I wasn't sure about Abigail either, except she seemed nice and didn't like Mike, which was a point in her favor.

But instead of grabbing the swords, I got back in the car again. I asked myself, "Okay, Kropp, which is it, Natalia or the Sword?" and that made me get out again and throw the car keys as far as I could into the darkness.

I put the swords back in my belt, the black one on the

right, Excalibur on the left. I threw the cloak over my shoulders. I patted my pockets, checking for the gun, and then remembered I had left it lying on the bed in the hotel room. Over my head, all right. Not very adept for sure.

I could see some squat, dark shapes silhouetted against the moonless sky, blocking out some of the stars. I hiked toward them, and I didn't see any sign of activity, just a bunch of whitish-looking blocks jutting out of the ground like gigantic discarded teeth. I couldn't quite imagine this as a gleaming white castle by the sea.

I noticed a path made of large white stones leading away from the ruins toward the edge of the cliff. I couldn't find any rope or handrails, nothing to hang on to as you descended. I skittered and slid on the wet stones as I crawled down sideways. Droplets of rain and sea spray clung to my cloak.

I stopped at the bottom of the path, wondering where Mogart's gang was. You'd think they'd be all over me by now.

About thirty yards away a light glowed from an opening in the cliff face. Merlin's cave.

I eased along the path, hugging the base of the cliff wall. The stones beneath my feet were smooth and wet, worn from centuries of the sea's coming and going. I let out my breath as I reached the edge of the opening. I could hear men talking quietly inside the cave, their voices echoing against the cave's walls. There was another sound too, a kind of high-pitched whistling that I guessed was the wind moving through cracks in the cliff. The cries of Merlin.

I didn't really have a plan. I'd never stormed a bad guy's

hideout before, and all I knew about it came from movies and books—and those weren't real. I stood to the right of the jagged cave opening, my back pressed against the cliff wall. Directly across from me was another, slightly shorter cliff that formed the other wall of the inlet, so I couldn't see the ocean. I could hear it, though, and taste the salt on my tongue. You'd think carrying the greatest weapon mankind had ever known would have given me some courage, but all I felt was insignificant.

I took a deep breath and said aloud, "I'm going to die."

Then I turned and stepped into the opening.

47

Two men sat by a small fire about twenty
feet inside the cave. They stared at me for a second; then one
of them stood up. He was wearing a black robe and held a
thin black sword just like the one tucked into the right side
of my belt.

"Where is the boy?" he snapped at me. "Where is the
Sword?" He must have thought I was the escort.

"We're both right here," I said, and drew out Excalibur.

It took him a second to get it, and then he came at me
with a loud cry.

He fell at my feet. I looked down at him, startled,

because he'd just dropped there; he hadn't even had a chance to raise his sword.

I stepped over him, fighting the feeling that I was going to throw up. I looked toward the second guy, who turned on his heel and made for the back of the cave, slipping on the wet rocks as he tried to run. He wasn't wearing a black robe, but a blue and gray Windbreaker, a pair of Dockers, New Balance running shoes, and a Chicago Cubs baseball cap.

I caught him at the back of the cave—it wasn't very deep, maybe fifty or sixty feet—spun him around, and held him against the wall with my left forearm while I pressed the tip of the Sword against his Adam's apple.

"Hey, Mike," I said.

"Hi, Al." He was smacking him gum and smiling, showing his large white teeth.

"Where's Mogart?"

"Dunno."

I pressed the tip of the Sword harder against his flesh. His eyes grew wide and he said, "Look, I swear, kid, you just killed the one guy who knows where he is. He was going to take us to him once you got here with the escort. I swear to God I don't know!"

"You gave him Natalia."

He didn't say anything. He was smiling, but his eyes were cold.

I said, "Tell me where she is."

"Even if I did know, what're you gonna do, Al? Give him the Sword? He'll kill her anyway. And if you try to take him, he'll kill her before you can kill him. Don't you see you can't win? Time to cut your losses. You gotta step back and take a look at the big picture. We're talkin' the fate of the whole ding-dong world here, Al! You're going to sacrifice humanity for the sake of one person? I mean, let's be reasonable here!"

"Okay, Mike, I'll be reasonable. I'll make a deal with you. You bring me to Mogart and when it's over I'll give you the Sword."

He stared at me and slowed some on the gum.

I said, "That's why you're here, isn't it? Give me Mogart and it's yours."

Mike thought about it. "How do I know you won't double-cross me?"

"I guess you don't. But like Mr. Mogart told me, you don't have a choice."

I stepped back, but kept the Sword pointed toward his neck. "Give me your gun."

He reached into the pocket of his Windbreaker and held out the gun, his finger hooked around the trigger guard. I took it from him and slipped it into my pocket.

"Anything else?" he asked. He acted like he was trying hard not to laugh.

"No," I said. Then I thought of something. "Yes. What does OIPEP stand for?"

"'Only Idiots Pursue Extraordinary Persons.'" He laughed in spite of himself and smacked his gum. "Okay? Are we done now?"

"One more thing," I said. I held out my hand. "The gum."

He started to laugh again but saw I was dead serious. He took out the gum and dropped it into my hand. When he did that, about half his personality evaporated. I tossed it into the shadows.

He turned to his left and I followed him along the back wall of the cave. The walls were smooth and slightly concave. He stopped at a fissure in the wall near the south corner. It was barely the width of one person, running from the floor to the ceiling.

"You first," I said.

As we slipped into the opening, the sea sound became softer, and the drip of water and the wailing of Merlin a little louder. The floor here was rough, littered with stones and angled downward slightly. The path twisted right, then back left, then dropped steeply, and I had to press my free hand against the jagged wall to keep my balance. We eased our way down very slowly. Loose rocks and jutting outcrops as sharp as knives slowed our way down.

Gradually the walls drew back and the floor leveled and became smooth. A circle of light glowed in the distance. When we were about a hundred yards from the opening, Mike turned and whispered urgently, "Al, you gotta give my gun back."

"Why?"

"He's gonna think I've stiffed him. You've seen what he does to people who stiff him."

I thought about it. "Okay," I said. I took the gun from

my pocket and hit him in the head as hard as I could with the grip.

He fell straight down. I slipped the gun back into my pocket, stepped over him, and walked the final hundred yards to the portal, alone.

48

I stood at the entrance to a huge cavern whose walls and ceiling were lost in vast, arching shadows. The floor was as smooth and as dark as a frozen pond. My footfalls echoed against the unseen walls as I walked slowly across the floor. There was no other sound and nobody in sight. I walked holding the Sword in front of me, thinking maybe there was another passage somewhere and I'd knocked out Mike too soon. Then I heard Mogart's voice. It seemed to come from everywhere and nowhere.

"Mr. Kropp. You never cease to surprise me."

I stopped. I slowly pulled the gun out of my pocket and

held it loosely in my left hand, more to comfort myself than anything else.

"To have come this far, with so little experience and even less intelligence . . . I salute you, sir."

"Where's Natalia?" My voice sounded small and tinny, almost like a little kid's.

"Here."

His voice sounded right by my ear. I whirled around and saw them coming toward me, Natalia in front of him. He held the back of her neck with his left hand. In his right he held a tapered dagger.

They stopped about twenty feet away and Mogart smiled.

"I'm glad to see you have taken care of Mr. Arnold," he said, nodding toward the gun. "I never cared for that man."

Natalia's eyes were dry, but very red; she must have been crying. Her dark hair was tangled around her face and there was a large bruise near the hairline.

"I'm sorry," I told her. "Are you okay?"

She nodded, cutting her eyes at Mogart. I said, "I brought the Sword, Mr. Mogart. Let her go."

"First the gun, yes? It's hardly necessary, Mr. Kropp, and you might make a terrible mistake. You might strike the wrong person."

I thought about it. If I refused, he might stab Natalia before I had a chance to get off a shot, a shot that would probably miss. But I'd still have the Sword and he knew if he killed her there'd be no reason for me to let him live. But that didn't really matter to me, since Natalia would be dead.

I threw the gun and it slid across the smooth floor into the shadows.

"Very good," Mogart said. "Now, the Sword, please."

"Let her go first."

He laughed. "My, how bold we've become! But boldness, Mr. Kropp, can never be a substitute for intelligence."

The dagger pressed into Natalia's side. Her eyes went wide and she cried out, "Kropp!"

Mogart said, "Decide now, Alfred Kropp. Throw down the Sword or watch her die."

Natalia was just one person and, like Mike said, what was one person when the whole world was at stake? If I refused to give him the Sword he'd kill Natalia; if I gave him the Sword he would probably kill her anyway and my sacred vow—and the only vow I ever made—would be broken.

I knew whatever decision I made would probably turn out to be wrong, as wrong as every decision I had made since this whole thing started. I kept screwing up and then just kept coming back for more. Maybe to fix it I needed to decide what the best thing to do was, and then do the opposite.

Looking at Mogart, I realized the plain truth was that he wasn't my greatest enemy. My greatest enemy was the fifteen-year-old homeless loser holding the Sword of Kings.

"Choose, Mr. Kropp," Mogart said softly.

I chose.

I tossed the Sword toward him. It clattered to the ground about halfway between us. I expected him to throw Natalia to the floor and dive on the Sword, but he didn't move. He wasn't even looking at the Sword; he was looking at me and I got that sinking feeling I had in Uncle Farrell's apartment, right before Mogart rammed the Sword into his body.

"Don't, Mr. Mogart," I pleaded. "You don't need to do that now. Don't hurt her, please."

"Oh, Mr. Kropp," Mogart answered. "After all that has happened, have you learned so little?"

And with that he plunged the dagger into Natalia's side.

49

She fell without a sound. I froze for a second, watching her fall, before lunging for the Sword, but I was too late. Mogart dived on it first, rolling out of the way as I launched myself at him.

I scrambled to my feet and pulled the black sword from my belt, meaning to switch it to my right hand, but Mogart was on me too fast, the Sword of Kings whistling toward my head.

I lifted my blade just in time and then cried out when Excalibur smashed against it with a ringing crash. The force of it almost snapped my wrist. I stepped back, flailing my sword in the air as Mogart, almost leisurely, took swings at me. He smiled, enjoying himself, and he was saying things like, "Good, Mr. Kropp! Excellent! Fine parry, sir! On the balls of your feet, step lightly and keep your sword up!"

He kept advancing and I kept backing up. He came from the right, then the left, then the right again, very fast, and finally the force of a blow slung my arm away so hard, I heard the joint in my shoulder pop.

His free hand caught the wrist of my blade hand, and his grip was cold and hard. I felt the tip of Excalibur pressing under my chin. Mogart brought his face very close to mine and he whispered, "There is one thing that has always troubled me about you, Alfred Kropp: Why do you persist? I kill your uncle, and you join Bennacio. I kill Bennacio, and you strike out on your own. I kill Natalia, and still you fight. So tell me, boy, tell me why you persist."

"I . . . I made a vow . . ." I stammered.

He cocked his head to one side, and his eyes twinkled as he started to smile.

"A vow! Alfred Kropp has made a vow!" He laughed harshly. "To Lord Bennacio, no doubt."

"No," I answered. "To heaven."

And I brought my knee up into his crotch as hard as I could. I ripped my blade arm free and stepped back as he went down to the stone floor. This was it! Go, Kropp, while he's down—take him out with your sword! But something stopped me. Instead of killing him, I just stood there, gulping air, waiting for him to stand up.

"It isn't yours, Mr. Mogart," I said. "Don't you see? It isn't anybody's."

Mogart stood up, his face distorted by pain and something else, not anger exactly, but something like anger and sadness mixed together, like a pouty little boy who's just learned he can't have his favorite candy.

"Who are you?" he gasped. "Who are you, Alfred Kropp? How is it that I find you at every turn, like a fat stone in my path, blocking my way?" With each question, he took a step toward me. And with each step he took forward, I took one backward.

"Why did Bennacio come to you after Samson's fall?" Step. "And bring you here?" Step. "Why did he demand the vow of you?" Step. *"Who are you, Alfred Kropp?"*

"I'm Bernard Samson's son and the heir to Lancelot."

He stopped. He looked as if I had slapped him. Then all the pain and sadness drained out of his face and left nothing but anger.

He launched himself at me with a terrible roar. I raised my black sword just in time to block the downward arc of Excalibur, and the impact made my ears ring with pain. Mogart's eyes glittered with rage as he swung at me, so fast, Excalibur was just a silvery blur.

As Mogart swung furiously at me, I backed up until I ran out of room and smacked into the wall behind me. Now I was left with two choices: Stand up and fight, or give up and die.

I was moving on just instinct, holding the sword in both

hands as Mogart's shoulders dipped and hunched and swiveled, and the sound of our swords meeting was an awful screech of metal striking metal. I could feel the jagged teeth of the wall behind me cutting through the gray cloak, taking nibbles from my back.

I screamed Bennacio's name as loud as I could. This only made Mogart angrier, and he slammed his left hand against my right shoulder. The force of the blow jarred the sword from my hand, and the blade clattered to the floor.

Mogart pressed his forearm against my neck, and as I struggled to breathe against the pressure, I knew the fight was over.

"The heir to Samson!" he hissed into my face. I felt the tip of Excalibur pressing into my stomach, penetrating the cloak and tearing slowly into the shirt under it. "The heir to Lancelot! The reason for my exile! How things have come full circle, Alfred Kropp!"

"Please," I whispered. "Please, Mr. Mogart . . ." I wasn't sure exactly what I was begging him to do. Or not do.

"Did noble Bennacio tell you how your father met his fate? Did anyone tell you, Alfred Kropp, how Daddy died?"

I felt the steel tip pierce my skin, and the sickening warmth of my own blood trickle down my stomach.

"Please," I whispered. "Please."

"I tortured him. I cut him a thousand times, until upon his knees he begged me to finish it, to end his miserable life. Just as you are begging now."

His arm moved forward. The blade sank deeper into my

body, maybe four or five inches, and I could taste blood in my mouth.

"And when he had no more breath for begging, I lopped off his miserable head."

His right arm jerked forward, harder this time, and now my mouth was full of my own blood.

His face was fading and his voice was growing fainter.

"And then I took Bernard Samson's head and mounted it on a steel pike. I placed his head at the entrance to my keep, where the carrion fed upon it, where the crows feasted on his eyes and tongue. And so you see we have indeed come full circle, Mr. Kropp. The time has come for our parting. The time has come for you to leave me and join your father."

And with that he slammed the Sword all the way into my body, up to the hilt, and I heard the cloak rip as the tip passed out through my back and bit into the stone wall behind me as easily as if the rock were sand.

Mogart let go and backed away. His smile came back.

"Now," he said. "*Die,* Alfred Kropp."

I'll never be sure, but I think when he said that, I did.

50

I saw some things after I died.

First, I was floating near the cave's roof, looking down at
myself impaled against the wall. Mogart had both hands
wrapped around the hilt of the Sword, pulling with all his
strength, his face contorted with the effort. His roars of rage
and frustration echoed against the walls of the cavern.

He pulled and pulled, but he couldn't pull the Sword
from the stone.

He staggered backwards, then turned and found the two-
foot dagger he had dropped when he dived for the Sword. I
guess he was going to cut my body away from the Sword

because you can't get much leverage against a human body—it's too soft—and then that faded.

There was silence, and then the sound the wind makes whispering through leaves.

Suddenly, I was sitting beside Mom's bed in the hospital and she was saying, *Take it away. Please take the pain away.*

I couldn't take that, so I turned away and Uncle Farrell was on the sofa and the Sword was in his gut, and I watched as he pulled it out and held it toward me. *Take it, Al. Take it away.*

I turned away from Uncle Farrell, and Bernard Samson, my father, was beside me, saying, *They are part of an ancient and secret Order, bound by a sacred vow to keep safe the Sword until its Master comes to claim it.*

I turned again, and saw Bennacio. I heard us speak, but it was more like I was remembering hearing us speak.

Who is the master if Arthur's dead?

The master is the one who claims it.

And who would that be?

The master of the Sword.

Then Bennacio turned away and I was sad to see him turn away, because I think I missed him most of all.

Then I saw the Lady in White sitting beneath the yew tree, and I felt no wind, but her dark hair was flowing behind her and the folds of her white robe were rippling like waves.

She didn't look at me as I stopped under the tree beside her. Her cheeks were wet.

"Am I dead?" I asked.

Do you wish to be?

"I think so. I'm awfully tired." More than anything, I wanted to lie down with my head in her lap and feel her stroke my brow.

A tear rolled down her cheek and I said, "Please don't. It's not like I didn't try. From the beginning I did what anybody asked. Uncle Farrell asked me to help him get the Sword, and I did. Bennacio asked me to help him get it back, and I did. Mogart asked me to bring it to him, and I did. But every time I did what they asked, somebody got killed. Uncle Farrell, Bennacio, and now Natalia. So, you see, Lady, there's nobody left now. Nobody left for to me help and nobody left to die because I tried. There's no reason for me to go back."

I turned away because I couldn't bear to see her cry. She was still there, only I couldn't see her, but I could see the memory of her and the memory of the yew and the long grasses and the glittering shards like teeth in the slag heap below. And, over my head, the butterflies.

The hour has come. Do you remember, now, Alfred Kropp, what has been forgotten?

Then there was nothing. Even the blackness wasn't black, because my memory of *black* was gone. No light, no sound, no sensation or memory—there wasn't even any *me* anymore. Alfred Kropp was gone.

And when the last of me was gone, I remembered what I had forgotten.

I reached into the yew tree and pulled a silver pin from the body of a butterfly. Freed, it burst into flight, black and red and gold against the bright blue sky, soaring higher and higher, until it was gone.

Darkness came back, but this time only because my eyes were closed.

So I opened them.

I was back in Merlin's cave, with the silver Sword of Kings jutting from my stomach.

And I knew, I finally knew, who the master of the Sword was.

51

Mogart came toward me, the black dagger in his hand, but he stopped when he heard the sound of my voice.

"The master . . ." I gasped. "The master of the Sword is . . . the one . . ." I coughed and blood filled my mouth and ran down my chin. "The one . . . *who claims it.*"

I brought my hands up and wrapped my fingers around the hilt. Behind me, metal screeched against the rock as I pulled the Sword from my body. Mogart was opening his mouth to either scream or say something, I'll never know, because I was free of the Sword now—or it was free of me—and, free, I swung the Sword around in one gigantic arc, my own blood flying from the blade, and I cut off his god-damned head.

I dropped to the cold stone floor. I realized I might die again, but I had already died once and I wasn't worried about it anymore, at least not once I finished what I had started.

I started to crawl toward Natalia, but my arms gave out and I flopped onto my belly on the cold stone. I let go of the Sword; I needed both my hands to push myself along the floor.

There was a soft white glow surrounding her and through my tears, in the trick of the light, I thought I saw a shadow hovering over her and the shape of wings.

My head felt hollow and black stars began to bloom before my eyes. I would never make it to her in time, but I told myself I could go one more inch. One more inch, Kropp, I told myself. One more inch. And after that inch, another inch.

My teeth chattered and I was very cold, colder than I ever remember being. The soft light around her burned my eyes to look at, so I closed my eyes and felt something warm around me, as if someone had wrapped me in a blanket.

There was a rushing sound and I thought of a great river running to the sea. Hundreds of years, thousands, whole centuries passed, and I still didn't know how close I was or if I was even close at all.

Then I breathed in the scent of peaches.

I opened my eyes and saw the face of the most beautiful girl I had ever seen.

I whispered in her ear, "By the power of the Sword, Natalia . . . in the name of the Archangel Michael . . ."

Dipping my fingers into the wound in my stomach, I brought the blood to her side where Mogart had stabbed her.

I bathed her wound in my blood, whispering in her ear, "See, I remembered. I remembered what I had forgotten. I was going to stay dead, mostly because I was just so darned tired, but then I remembered what I'd forgotten, which is *the power to heal as well as to rend . . .* so get up, Natalia, get up, because I am the master now and you have to do what I say."

I smoothed her hair and stroked her forehead with my other hand. "Live," I said. "Live."

And after what seemed a very long time, her eyes opened, she took a deep breath, and I knew I had saved her.

52

I guess after all that, I would have bled to death beside her, but Mike came to and found us inside the cave. Soon we were loaded onto stretchers and men carried us up the path to the top of the cliff, where a helicopter was waiting. We were flown to a hospital in London.

After a couple of weeks I was able to sit up and eat some solid food, though hospital food in the best of circumstances isn't that good, and this was England, after all, so the food was really lousy.

They did two operations on me to remove part of my lower intestines and fix up my left lung, which Mogart had torn with his final thrust. After another couple of weeks I could walk around, and sometimes Natalia would walk with me in the hallway. We didn't talk much on these walks, though she did thank me for saving her life. Once I asked her if she believed in angels.

"As a little girl I thought I had a guardian angel."

"That doesn't count," I told her. "Little kids believe in Santa Claus too. Your father said the angels live whether we believe in them or not."

She looked away then. I could have kicked myself for mentioning her father. For once she was actually talking to me as if I were a halfway normal person.

"I guess it would be tough for you to forgive me," I said. "I can't seem to, no matter how hard I try."

"You should have left me to die," she said. "It would be better. Why didn't you leave me to die?" She began to cry.

I had apologized, but that only made it worse for her. I was beginning to think that was my special gift: taking something bad and making it worse. I tried to hold her hand while she cried, but she turned away from me. I could save her life but not her broken heart.

After Natalia left, I felt really bad, the worst I'd felt since this whole thing with the Sword started. You would think the prospect of saving six billion lives might make me feel better, but it didn't. I could save the world, but it wouldn't bring Uncle Farrell back. It wouldn't bring my father back.

Or Bennacio. I kept seeing him fall, the way he raised his arms and just let Mogart run him through. Why hadn't Bennacio fought? He could have lunged forward and tackled

Mogart by the knees. Why had he just given up like that? How was that keeping his precious vow? I was pretty sore at him for that. If he hadn't quit, I wouldn't have ended up with the Sword, he would be alive, and Natalia's heart would not be broken.

A shadow fell into the room but I hardly noticed it. I just wanted it all to go away. The hospital, London, my memories, me.

The shadow came closer and I heard her ask softly, "Alfred, why are you crying?"

I said, "It works on everybody but me, Natalia. I can heal everybody but myself."

She sat in the wooden chair beside the bed. She had changed into a long red cloak over a gray dress with one of those soft, high collars, and her earrings were fat diamonds about the size of green olives. Her reddish gold hair was loose and flowed over her shoulders. She looked like some medieval princess, beautiful and terrifying at the same time. Seeing her dressed like that, I realized Natalia was leaving.

"You are forgetting something," she said.

"I can't forget anything," I said. "That's the problem."

"You are forgetting you saved the world."

I didn't say anything. I wondered why she had come back, but at the same time I knew why, though I couldn't put it into words.

Then she did. "I'm leaving, Alfred."

"When?"

"Tonight."

"Don't."

"I must." She drew a deep breath. She was sitting very straight in the chair.

"But before I go," she went on, "I wanted to pay homage to the master."

She looked down at my snotty face.

"I'm not the master of anything," I said.

"Alfred," she answered softly. "Like my father, I have waited a very long time for your coming. My father would tell me stories of our ancestor Bedivere, how he betrayed the king by refusing his command to return the Sword to the waters from which it rose. I would spend hours imagining what the master would be like. Tall, handsome, brave, honest, chaste, modest, the knight of all knights—in short, everything that I believed my father to be." She looked sideways at me, clearly not the guy she had pictured as the master of the Sword. "In fact, when I was still very young I told him that *he* might be the master, that perhaps it was his destiny to claim the Sword as his own, a fitting end to Bedivere's shame."

"What did he say?"

"He told me of the prophecy Merlin made before he departed the world of men, that the master would not come until the last male heir to the house of Bedivere had perished. My father believed that prophecy, Alfred. He believed it because he believed in the justice of it. It was the price we would pay for Bedivere's failure, our atonement for his sin."

I thought of Bennacio kneeling before Mogart, and I understood then why he had spread his arms in that way, as if saying, *Here I am. Here I am.*

"Oh, jeez," I said. "Like I didn't feel bad enough, Natalia. What am I supposed to do, huh? What do you want me to do? I was just, you know, helping out my uncle. I didn't know my father and I sure didn't know I had stolen the Sword of Kings for a black knight or an agent of darkness or whatever he was. I mean, what rational person believes in all this stuff, Merlin and King Arthur and magic swords and angels and prophecies—who believes in that kind of stuff these days? I don't know what you want from me, Natalia. Can you tell me what I'm supposed to do? Somebody better tell me and they better do it quick, because I'm just about at the end of my rope here."

She came to the bed, and her hair fell over my face. She whispered, "He is at peace, Alfred. His dream is fulfilled, and he is at peace. Now you be at peace."

Then she kissed me on the forehead, and her hair was like the walls of a cathedral around me, a sanctuary, and she murmured into my ear, "Be at peace, Master Alfred."

53

One afternoon, about a week before I was to be discharged, the door opened and a dark-suited man came into the room. Tall and stoop-shouldered, with a hound-dog face and very long earlobes, he reminded me of a sad-eyed Basset. He closed the door behind him as I pushed myself up in the bed, thinking, What now?

He didn't say a word; he barely looked at me. He crossed the room and peeked through the curtains, then strode to the bathroom and looked in there. Then he opened the door and spoke softly to someone in the hallway. He stepped back and a woman came in next, dressed in a tailored pinstriped business suit with shiny black heels that made a clicking sound on the linoleum as she walked. Her bright blond hair was pulled into a tight bun on her head. She carried a bundle wrapped in white satin.

"Abigail?" I said.

"Alfred." She smiled, and I was impressed by the excellent condition of her teeth. "How good of you to remember."

She handed the bundle over to the hound-dog man and sat down beside my bed.

"How are you feeling?" she asked.

"Pretty lousy," I said. "Physically I'm doing okay; it's the other departments that are bothering me."

"You have been through a great deal," she said.

There was an uncomfortable silence. I blurted out, "I don't have it."

"Don't have what, dear?"

"You know what. I don't have it. And I don't know where it is, though I have a guess."

"And where would that be?"

I bit my lip. Her smile didn't leave her face and her blue eyes were glittering brightly.

"You don't trust me," she said calmly. "I don't blame you, Alfred. We've done little to earn your trust. At any rate, you don't need to tell me. I believe I already know. The gift has been returned to its giver." I didn't say anything and she lowered her voice. "The master claims the Sword and, in claiming it, understands that it can never be claimed."

She was just beaming by this point. "We tore that cave apart, Alfred, and dragged the inlet. The Sword is gone, which is both a great loss and a great boon. Its time on earth has passed, and now there is one less piece of wonder in our world. Perhaps it is the price we must pay for our . . . growing up."

I stared at her. "Who *are* you, anyway?"

"I thought you knew, dear."

"All I know is you guys double-crossed Mr. Samson and his knights, and you double-crossed Bennacio and you double-crossed his daughter and nearly got her killed, and *did* get me killed and—"

"OIPEP didn't double-cross them, Alfred, Mike Arnold did." She made a little sour face, as if just saying the name bothered her. "You of all people can understand the effect the Sword can have on the minds of . . . weaker men. Mike was seduced by it from the beginning. Without our knowledge he contacted the Dragon and gave away Samson's plans to storm his castle in Spain, and he did agree to sacrifice Bennacio in order to gain the Sword. He also told Mogart where he might find Natalia—all without our knowledge. He was what you might call a 'rogue agent,' and he has been terminated."

"You killed Mike Arnold?"

She smiled. "He is no longer with The Company."

"The Company," I said. "What is The Company? What is OIPEP and why does it care so much about the Sword?"

"It cares because its purpose is to care."

I stared at her for a second, and then I said, because I had learned some things along the way, "That was my fault. I asked two questions, which allowed you to choose which one to answer."

She laughed one of those gentle trills you associate with very cultivated people or people from England.

"Our organization dedicates itself to the research and preservation of the world's great mysteries," she said.

"Really? And all this time I thought you were some kind of supersecret spy outfit dedicated to killing people you don't like."

"We are not spies, Alfred. Not in the sense you mean. We are clandestine in that few know of our existence; and we do have certain . . . technologies that have yet to be officially acknowledged, but we are more likely to wear pocket protectors and carry laptops than body armor and guns. OIPEP has more scientists, historians, and theoreticians than field operatives like Mike Arnold. The head of my department is a doctor of thaumatology. And I hold a doctorate in eschatology."

"What's that?" I asked. She was being very Bennacian: The more she explained, the more confused I got.

"Eschatology is the study of final things. Death. The afterlife. The end of the world."

"Oh. Gotcha."

"And thaumatology is the study of miracles. So you see, it was only natural that Samson should involve us once the Sword was lost."

She motioned to the large man with the dog face and the big flappy hands, and he brought her the long object wrapped in satin. She laid it on my lap.

"What's this?" I asked. But I figured it out before she could answer. I pulled on a corner of the cloth and the black blade tumbled out.

"Bennacio's sword," she said. "We recovered it at Stonehenge and thought you might like to have it."

I stared at the sword. "Thank you," I whispered.

Abigail said, "There is one other thing before I go, Alfred. I must say The Company is quite impressed."

"Impressed by what?" I asked.

"With you," she said. "It is nothing less than extraordinary."

"What is?"

"That you not only survived your ordeal, but accomplished what we, with all the resources at our disposal, could not."

"Well," I said. "The whole thing was basically my fault, so I kind of thought it was the right thing to do."

"Don't be so hard on yourself. You're very young. You have no idea how rare that is."

"Youth?"

"Doing the right thing. Not only doing the right thing, but understanding what the right thing is."

"Oh," I said. "You bet." Though I wasn't completely sure what she was getting at or why we were having a philosophical conversation.

"We will be keeping an eye on you, Alfred Kropp," she said.

"You will?" That didn't sound good.

"We are very interested in your . . . development."

A shiver went down my spine. "Look, Abby . . . Abigail . . . ma'am . . . I don't have any intention of getting involved in anything like the Sword again, so if you're worried—"

She raised her hand to shut me up. "We're not worried at all. In fact, I wanted to give you this, in the event you decide you want to know more about The Company. We are always looking for fresh talent—for the extraordinary, if you will."

She dropped a business card in my lap, shot up from the chair, nodded to hound-dog man by the door, and left me alone. I picked up the card and read it:

OFFICE OF INTERDIMENSIONAL PARADOXES
&
EXTRAORDINARY PHENOMENA
(OIPEP)

Abigail Smith, MD, PhD, JD, MBA
Special Agent-in-Charge
Field Operations Division

Washington • London • Paris • Tokyo
Brussels • Rome • Moscow • Sydney

54

My foster parents, the Tuttles, arrived in London the next day to take me back to America. I had no idea they were coming. They just showed up in the doorway and Horace Tuttle shouted, "Alfred Kropp, you big-headed pain in the rump! What in heaven's name are you doing in London, England?"

"If you ever run away like that again, we'll have to let you go, Alfred," Betty Tuttle told me tearfully.

"Might do that anyway," Horace puffed. "You have a lot of explaining to do, young man!"

"Actually," I told them, "I saved the world from total annihilation."

"Of course you did!" Horace shouted. "And I'm Tarzan, Lord of the Apes!"

"Now, Horace," Betty said. "You know what the social worker told us: Alfred is a *troubled youth*."

"We all have troubles," Horace grumbled.

"I'm sure Alfred has every intention of getting back into school and living up to his potential as a solid citizen and contributing member of his community," Betty said. She patted my arm. "Don't you, dear?"

"That's right," I said. "You bet."

"Well, I didn't fly all the way across the Atlantic to this God-forsaken foreign English country to chitchat," Horace said. "Where're your things, Alfred? We're leaving."

"I don't have anything," I said. "Except this."

I showed them Bennacio's black sword. Horace tried to grab the sword and I told him not to touch it; the blade was very sharp. I also didn't want him touching it because the thought of Horace Tuttle touching the blade of the Last Knight of the Order of the Sacred Sword made my stomach heave.

"We'll never get this through Customs," he said.

"Then I'm not going," I told them. "I won't leave without it."

And I didn't either. I stuck the sword in Horace's bag and, when the screeners went nuts over it, I showed the supervisor Abigail Smith's card. A call was made and in five minutes we were cleared through Customs.

55

So that's how I ended up back in Knox-
ville, Tennessee, after saving the world and everybody in it,
including the Tuttles.

After a week, I was back in school, but my picture had
been flashed around the globe after the Stonehenge incident
and now I was something of a celebrity. I don't know what
calls were made or who said what to whom, but I was back
in school like nothing had happened. There was a rumor that
I was an international terrorist because that's what they
called me on television, but I guess some people just can't
grasp nuances.

Amy Pouchard pulled me aside after math class on my first day back. She was working a piece of gum really hard, which reminded me of Mike Arnold, and suddenly I didn't like Amy Pouchard as much as I thought I did.

"You disappeared, blew up something, and now you're back," she said.

"I didn't blow up anything," I told her. "I did kill somebody, though."

Her eyes got wide. "Get out!"

"But he kind of had it coming."

"Was he a terrorist or something?"

"No, but you might call him an agent of darkness."

"Whoa. That's too cool!" She touched my forearm with her hand. Her hand was very cold, and I wondered if she had a circulation problem. "You shot him?"

"I beheaded him."

Her mouth opened a little and I could see the knobby bright green of her gum between her tongue and her teeth.

"Kropp! You! Kropp!"

It was Barry Lancaster, pushing people out of the way in the crowded hall to get to me.

"Are you still his girlfriend?" I asked Amy Pouchard.

"Sort of. Not really. I mean, he's never beheaded anybody or anything like that. Do you want my cell phone number?"

Barry had reached me by that point. He shoved me hard in the right shoulder and said, "What are you doing here, Kropp? Aren't you supposed to be in jail or something?"

"Actually," I said, "I'm supposed to be in social studies."

"But instead you're talking to my girlfriend. Pretty stupid, Kropp."

"She's not your girlfriend, Barry."

"Like you would know."

He shoved me again.

"Don't shove me, Barry."

"Yeah? Who's gonna stop me, Kropp?"

He shoved me again.

"Barry," Amy Pouchard said. "Cut it out."

A crowd had gathered by that point. The bell rang but nobody paid attention.

"Maybe this is the point I should tell you that the last guy who shoved me around like this got his head chopped off," I told Barry.

"You're so full of it," he snarled, and then he launched himself at me.

He really didn't have a chance. I sidestepped to the right and landed a haymaker to the side of his blond head as he flew past. Barry went down and he stayed down, and I guess if I had been Barry, I might have kicked him in the ribs. But I wasn't Barry Lancaster. I was Alfred Kropp, not exactly a knight bound by the code of chivalry, but I was the descendant of the greatest knight who had ever lived. Plus I guess dying gives you some perspective on what's worth fighting about.

I held out my hand.

"This is nuts, Barry," I said. "We're both gonna get expelled."

"That was just a lucky punch," he gasped, and he slapped my hand away.

"The odds are against that," I answered. "I've never had too much luck."

I pulled him to his feet and he spat, "You're a freak."

But he didn't shove me again or try to punch me, and after that nobody teased me about my size or the remark about my IQ. People left me alone. Even my teachers kept their distance and went out of their way to give me a break. Of course, it got all around school that I had admitted to killing someone, and the rumor about me being a terrorist persisted.

I spent most afternoons in the Old City, walking aimlessly or sitting in the Ye Olde Coffee Shop, where I had met Bennacio. I always took the last stool at the end of the counter and sipped lattes, staring at the people walking past the big window. Sometimes I took out the card Abigail Smith had given me in London and stared at it. Most of the time, though, I just stared out the window. And I always dreaded going home to the Tuttles.

Sitting in the coffee shop made me feel close to Bennacio, the nearest thing to a father I ever had, and sometimes I would hear his voice in my head: *Do not concern yourself so much with guilt and grief, Alfred. No battle was ever won, no great deed ever accomplished by wallowing in guilt and grief.*

I began to understand I had claimed more than the Sword of Kings in Merlin's cave. I had claimed something even more powerful and scary.

I had claimed who I was.

One afternoon, after I finished my coffee, I looked at my watch and realized it was almost six o'clock. Dinner would be over by the time I got to the Tuttles', and Betty would fuss at me and wonder where I wandered off to every afternoon instead of coming home and studying like a good boy. Horace would stomp and shout, and the thin walls of the little house would shake. I would eat the leftovers and retreat to the little room I shared with Lester and Dexter. The next morning I would go to school and that would be my life, the life of Alfred Kropp, Heir to Lancelot, Son of the Sacred Order, Master of the Sword of Kings, and Adventurer Extraordinaire.

I left the coffee house and turned on Central to Jackson, but instead of walking toward the bus stop I went straight to the pay phone half a block down and dialed the 800 number scrawled on the back of the card.

"This is Alfred Kropp, Abby . . . Abigail . . . Ms. Smith, *Doctor* Smith, ma'am," I said. "I was wondering about what you said. About, um, needing fresh talent . . ."

ACKNOWLEDGMENTS

From the beginning, my wife has been there, through the long dry season of the repetitious rejection letters, the unreturned phone calls, the cold silence that dragged on for months—hiding rejected manuscripts under the bed and rescuing them from the trash, encouraging, pleading, cajoling, helping me fight the inner demons and, when my strength gave out, fighting them herself, in battles that should never be fought alone.

My failings belong to no one but me. All success, however, I owe to her. She was there before the agents and book deals and television appearances, behind the door long before Hollywood—or anyone—came knocking. God willing, she will be behind that same door, by my side, long after the world has passed me by.

Though no poor words of mine can begin to express it, thank you, my love.

STEALING EXCALIBUR WAS JUST THE BEGINNING . . .

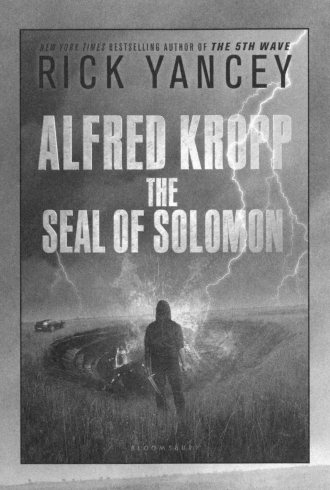

Things have just started to settle down for Alfred, when he's suddenly kidnapped and forced to face a terrible threat—the Seal of Solomon. For millennia, the fallen angels of heaven were controlled by the ring. Now the ring has been taken, and all hell is breaking loose . . .

Read on for a sneak peek at Alfred's next thrilling adventure, *The Seal of Solomon*.

Every summer when I was a little kid, my mother threw me into our old Corolla and drove us down to Destin, a beach town in the Florida Panhandle. I loved those trips. We stopped at roadside restaurants to eat, greasy spoons with the vertical coolers that held the pies and cakes, and little one-story motels two blocks from the beach, like the Seabreeze Motor Court or the Conchshell Conclave.

The Seabreeze was my favorite, mostly because the beds had this vibrator built in: you dropped a quarter into the timer and the bed would vibrate for five minutes. Two quarters got you twelve minutes. As soon as we hit the door, I flopped on one of those beds, feeding it quarters. Mom wouldn't let me use the vibrating function at night, though. She thought the vibration while I slept would give me vertigo or bad dreams, or maybe both.

I woke with the name *Destin* on my lips. I could hear the

low, deep-throated hum of engines, one of those sounds that seem to come from everywhere and nowhere.

I started to notice other things too, things that came in flashes as I slowly woke up.

Crisp white sheets. The smell of lavender. Gray walls lined with rivets; even the floor was riveted. A round door with a ship's wheel for a handle. A porthole on the wall opposite the bed, nothing beyond the glass but darkness.

"Destin," I whispered again in the semidarkness of the little cabin.

Mom in her jean shorts and halter top, sunglasses covering almost her entire face, tiny beads of sweat on her forehead, a paperback novel resting on her stomach, calling to me, *Don't go out too far, Alfred! Don't go out too far!* Because I can't swim. She knew I wouldn't go far: there were scary things in the ocean, jellyfish and the sharp spines of dead horseshoe crabs and busted aluminum beer cans and sharks, of course. Swimming in the ocean is a little crazy when you think about it. The ocean is nature untamed, just like the woods, and who in their right mind would strip to their shorts and go running through the woods?

I remember wearing old bathing trunks with a starfish on the butt, faded from a bright yellow to a kind of dingy white, and a wide white stripe of sunscreen on my nose. I waded knee-deep in the languid surf of the gulf, kicking up little underwater puffs of sand, never worrying where she was, because I was sure she would always watch over me.

The wheel spun counterclockwise and the round door swung open. A big man dressed in black, with enormous ears and a face that reminded me of a bloodhound, stepped inside and looked down at me beneath the lavender-smelling sheets.

"Hi," I said. "I'm Alfred Kropp."

"I know who you are," he said.

"I know who you are too," I said. "Well, not your name, but I remember you. You came to my hospital room in London. Where's Abigail . . . I mean, Dr. Smith?"

As if on cue, Abigail Smith, Special Agent-in-Charge, Field Operations Division, of the Office of Interdimensional Paradoxes and Extraordinary Phenomena, stepped into the cabin and swung the door shut behind her.

"Hello, Alfred," she said.

She looked just like I remembered, her bright blond hair in a tight bun. But this time her three-inch heels were replaced with black lace-up boots and she wore a black turtleneck and pants.

"Where am I?" I asked.

"Aboard the jetfoil *Pandora*, somewhere off the coast of Oman," she answered.

"Oh." I had no idea where Oman was. "Why?"

"There has been a . . . development that has necessitated your extraction from the civilian interface," the dog-face man intoned.

"Huh?"

"What Operative Nine means is you were kidnapped for your own good, Alfred."

"Operative Nine?"

"Yes," she said, nodding toward Mr. Dog-Face. "Op Nine for short."

"What's his real name?"

"Whatever it needs to be," Op Nine said.

Abby said, "Only the director knows his real name."

"How come?"

"The nature of his work."

"And that is?"

"Classified," he said.

"That's pretty clunky, though, Operative Nine," I said. "Why don't you just use a code name like 'Bob'?"

" 'Bob' would be more an alias than a code name, don't you think?" Abigail was smiling.

"What's going on?" I asked, struggling to sit up, but my head was throbbing and the room was spinning, and I decided sitting up wasn't such a good idea at that moment.

"We don't know the answer to that question," Abby said. "It seems an odd turn of events, given what we know about Mike Arnold's plans."

"Maybe that's something you could share with me," I said. "Mike's plans."

"After he was terminated, Michael Arnold stole two very valuable items from the OIPEP vaults. We are on our way to intercept him before he can put them to use."

"What did he take?" I asked, and waited for the usual answer: *That's classified.*

Op Nine glanced at Abby, who gave him a sharp nod. He looked at me. His eyes were very dark, almost black.

"The Seals of Solomon," he said in that deep, undertaker-like voice. If he was waiting for some sign of recognition from me, he was going to be waiting for a long time. I just stared back.

"You have heard of King Solomon," he said.

"From the Bible, right?"

"Yes. In the days of his reign, Solomon possessed two items of great power, immeasurable gifts from heaven. The Great Seal and the Lesser Seal, also called the Holy Vessel.

These two charges he jealously guarded until his death three thousand years ago. The Great Seal was lost in antiquity, but the Lesser Seal was recovered from its hiding place in Babylon by an archeological expedition in 1924—"

Abby cut off the lecture. "The Greater Seal, or Seal of Solomon, is a ring, Alfred. The Company recovered it in the 1950s from a now-defunct apocalyptic death cult in the Sudan—"

"Wait a minute," I said. "Did you say the Seal of Solomon is a *ring*? Like a wear-on-your-finger-type ring?"

"Precisely.

"Have you paged Elijah Wood? I think I saw this movie."

She smiled. "The ring to which you refer is a product of art, a fiction. The Great Seal of Solomon is an artifact of history. It belongs to our world, not an imaginary one. Most significantly, Solomon's ring is not the creation of evil. Of course, in the wrong hands it could be used to that purpose, and that is precisely why we recovered it and kept it safe for the past fifty-five years—"

"Until Mike stole it."

"We have since launched a complete overhaul of our security protocols."

"Boy, that's a comfort. So Mike stole these two things from you guys . . . and then comes to Knoxville to kill me. Why?"

They looked at each other.

"We don't know," Abigail said. "We were hoping you might."

"Me? OIPEP's looking to me for answers? We're in bigger trouble than I thought. What about Ashley?"

Op Nine frowned. "What about her?"

"Why was she spying on me?"

Again they looked at each other.

"The Company often assigns operatives to keep tabs on Special Subjects."

" 'Special Subjects'? I'm a Special Subject?"

"How could the last son of Lancelot *not* be a Special Subject?" Abby asked tenderly. "Mike's entrance into your particular interface took all of us by surprise. Fortunately, Ashley was watching your house when Mike made his move."

"So you knock me out and bring me to this boat off the coast of Oman—where is that, Africa or something?—to do . . . what?"

"Intercept Michael Arnold before he can use the ring to open the Lesser Seal."

"Lesser Seal . . ."

"The Holy Vessel," Op Nine said.

"Why don't you want the Holy Vessel opened?"

For the third time they exchanged a glance. I was like the little kid in the room while the parents danced around the facts-of-life lecture.

"The ring, the Great Seal," Op Nine said slowly, "is the key. Without it, the wearer cannot control the . . . agents confined within the Vessel. Indeed, without the ring, the Lesser Seal cannot even be broken. One without the other is useless. With both . . ." He took a deep breath. "Catastrophe."

The door swung open and a guy in a black jumpsuit like Ashley's stepped in, carrying a tray with orange juice and two slices of toast.

"Ah," Op Nine said. "The food is here." He seemed relieved.

"Not much of it, though," I said, trying again to sit up.

Op Nine bent to help me. The room whirled around my head. I wondered why I felt so light-headed and weak. What was in that shot Ashley gave me on the chopper—and why had she given me a shot in the first place?

I drank the tall glass of orange juice down in three gulps. The toast was cut into quarters and that's how I ate it, stuffing a whole quarter in my mouth and barely chewing before I swallowed.

"Okay," I said. "Let me see if I have all this. After you guys fired Mike for trying to take Excalibur, he breaks into your vaults and steals the two Seals of Solomon. I'm still not clear on what they are or what they do, but anyway, after that you assigned Agent Ashley to keep tabs on me because now I'm a person of special interest or something. Mike shows up, kidnaps me, takes me up into the mountains to kill me—only Mike knows why—and Ashley rescues me in the nick of time. Now we're on a boat on our way to . . . where?"

"The nexus," Op Nine said.

"The what?"

"The center. The place of opening."

"Right. Gotcha. And the plan is to stop Mike before he can pull off this opening."

"Correct."

"Or else . . . ?"

"Catastrophe."

A bell went off, a blaring sound that seemed to come from everywhere and nowhere. Op Nine checked his watch.

"It's time for the briefing," he said to Abigail.

She nodded, then turned to me and gave my shoulder a little pat.

"We have to go, Alfred."

"When are you taking me home?"

They both looked away.

"You're not taking me home, are you?" I asked.

"You'll be safe here, Alfred," Abby said.

"I'd rather go home and take my chances."

Abby was looking at Op Nine. She pursed her fat red lips and for some reason I thought of goldfish, those big koi you see sometimes in little ponds outside Japanese restaurants.

He said, "Perhaps we will discuss it, once the Seals have been recovered."

They left, slamming the big round metal door closed behind them. The wheel turned and I heard a clanking sound, like a dead bolt sliding home. It hit me then that I had traded one kidnapper for another. OIPEP might not want to kill me like Mike did, but I was at their mercy just the same.

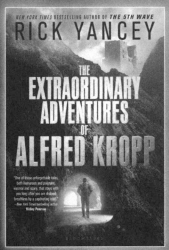
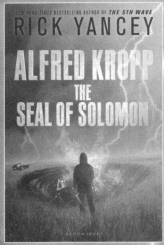
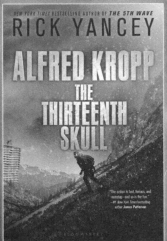

ALFRED MEETS ARTHUR:
THE REAL LEGEND OF KING ARTHUR AND THE KNIGHTS OF THE ROUND TABLE

King Arthur: Man or Myth?

"You're talking about King Arthur, right?"
"Yes, King Arthur."
"That's just a legend, a story, Mr. Samson."
"I don't have the time to convince you of anything, Alfred. You held it tonight. In your inexperienced hands, the Sword bested three of the finest swordsmen in the world." (pg. 77)

Despite watching the movie *Excalibur* about fifty times, Alfred Kropp doesn't 100-percent buy into the whole King Arthur thing until he's cruising down the highway in a silver Mercedes with Bennacio, the last descendent of the Knights of the Round Table. Alfred isn't alone. For centuries, people have questioned whether King Arthur was, in fact, a real person.

The first significant reference of King Arthur and his exploits appeared in a twelfth-century text called *The History of the Kings of Britain*. But what isn't agreed upon is whether the author, Geoffrey of Monmouth, made up Arthur or not.

Three hundred years after the book's publication—long after Geoffrey had taken the secret with him to the grave—historical debate ignited, and the flames have been burning ever since. During the Renaissance, Tudor monarchs vigorously defended Arthur's authenticity—and even justified their rights to the throne by claiming to be his descendents. Apparently, the Tudor mentality prevailed. Today it is generally assumed that there was an actual person at the heart of the legends, and, after reading *The Extraordinary Adventures of Alfred Kropp,* you might, too!

Two Awkward Youths,
Both Destined for Greatness

Arthur was this kind of goofy kid, actually, a squire to his brother Kay, toting around his sword and taking care of Kay's horse and his armor, kind of his lackey, not even a knight. Nobody believed this kid could actually pull the Sword from the Stone until Arthur did it and told them, "If you would be knights and follow a king, then follow me!" (pg. 88)

So let's assume Arthur was a real guy. Like Alfred Kropp, Arthur didn't discover who his real father was until *after* his father's death. Legend claims that Arthur was the illegitimate son of Uther Pendragon, king of Britain during the late fifth century. Since Arthur was born out of wedlock, King Uther could not raise him as a prince in the castle. Instead, the king's magician, Merlin, stole away with the newborn heir under the cover of night to the countryside estate of Sir Ector, an English nobleman. Until Arthur was a teenager, he had no knowledge of his royal lineage.

When Arthur was fifteen, King Uther died. No one but Merlin knew the king had a son, and there was much debate over who should inherit the throne. One day a mysterious stone with a huge sword stuck in its middle appeared in the churchyard of St. Paul's Cathedral in London. It was said that whoever pulled the sword from the stone was the rightful king of Britain. Men from far and wide tried in vain, but not even the strongest knight could make the sword budge. You can imagine the amazement when the least likely candidate succeeded: a scrawny teenage boy from the countryside, named Arthur.

So you see, sometimes heroes appear in strange packages. Remind you of anyone?

The Master of the Sword Is the One Who Claims It

"The sword is in this world, Alfred, but it is not of this world. Forged before the foundations of the earth, not by mortal hands, it is the True Sword, Alfred, the Sword of Kings. In another time it was known as Caliburn. You may know it by its other name, the sword Excalibur." (pg. 77)

Many people in England didn't think a fifteen-year-old kid like Arthur should (or could) be king. Luckily, Merlin was on Arthur's side. He led Arthur to a magical lake where an enchantress living beneath the surface of the water gave Arthur a gift of great power: the sword Excalibur.

Excalibur was kept in a magic scabbard that protected the wearer from hurting himself. Whoever used Excalibur in a fight always defeated his opponent. This is why our hero, Alfred Kropp, was able to use Excalibur as if he'd been sword-fighting his whole life, and why the descendents of King Arthur's knights were willing to give up their lives to protect the artifact.

With such a powerful weapon at his side, Arthur was able to secure his kingdom and set up his royal palace at Camelot. Arthur also married a princess named Guinevere. As a wedding gift, Guinevere's father presented Arthur with a large round table. Only the twelve bravest knights in the country were allowed to sit at this table. Because it was round, the positions of all the seats, including Arthur's, were equal, and he gained the reputation of being a fair and noble king.

Every Story Needs a Villain

"Samson too completed a certain knight's training, when that knight pledged himself to the Order upon their first meeting in France. You can guess who that certain knight was."

He waited patiently for my Kropp mind to grasp what he was saying.

"Mogart?"

"Yes, Mogart was Samson's squire, and more. Samson named him his heir."

My Kropp mind couldn't get a grip on that one. *"So why did Mogart turn on him?"* (pg. 244)

Sir Lancelot was the bravest of Arthur's knights, and it wasn't long before he and Queen Guinevere fell in love and began an affair that would end in disaster. Trouble arose when Mordred, King Arthur's evil nephew, discovered the infidelity. Mordred saw the affair between the king's best knight and the king's wife as the perfect opportunity to create discord in Arthur's Camelot. When Mordred happily revealed the news to Arthur, Lancelot and Guinevere fled to France and Arthur followed them across the English Channel.

King Arthur left Mordred in charge while he was away. As Arthur had no children, Mordred would inherit the kingdom when Arthur died; but he did not want to wait. Instead, Mordred told everyone King Arthur had been killed while fighting in France and made himself king of Britain. But Arthur would not take defeat lying down. He raised an army and returned to Britain to squelch the insurrection. The mighty armies of Arthur and Mordred fought at the climactic Battle of Camlann.

The Final Act?

Bennacio whispered, "Speak the words now, Alfred Kropp. Speak, son of my captain, heir to Lancelot. 'I, Alfred Kropp, swear in the name of the Archangel Michael, my guardian and protector, that I will sacrifice my life in defense of the Sword of Righteousness, and that by my life or my death, I shall defend it against the agents of darkness.'" (pg. 246)

The battle was so brutal, only a few people were still alive by its end, including King Arthur and Mordred. Grueling man-to-man combat ensued. Arthur killed Mordred, but Arthur was very badly injured himself. Knowing he was going to die, Arthur gave Excalibur to Sir Bedivere and asked him to return it to the magical lake. Bedivere pretended to do what he was told, but he hid Excalibur under a bush instead. Arthur knew he had disobeyed and told him to go and do the job properly. The traditional legend says that Bedivere then threw the sword into the lake and saw the hand of the Lady of the Lake come out of the water to catch it. But as you'll learn in *The Extraordinary Adventures of Alfred Kropp*, the story doesn't end there . . .

Bennacio sighed. "Bedivere was to cast the Sword into the lake—those were the direct orders from Arthur—but he chose to keep it instead, and our Order was created. Of all the knights, he loved his king the most, and from this love rose the belief that one day another master would return for the Sword." (pg. 240)

To learn more about the legend of King Arthur,
visit these cool sites:

www.arthurian-legend.com

www.britannia.com/history/h12.html

www.kingarthursknights.com

A Note on the Author

It was, perhaps, inevitable that Rick Yancey would chronicle Alfred's quest. Writing and Arthurian legend have been his passion and fascination since he was a teenager. Rick wrote his first book when he was fourteen—roughly Alfred's age. Around the same time, he saw the movie *Excalibur* and has been captivated by the story (and swordplay) ever since.

"I've wanted to write a great adventure story that combined my love for swords with the Arthur stories," he said. "It's also an incredibly romantic legend, set in a time that I think we all idealize and in some way long for."

As a boy, reading was Rick's favorite subject in school—math his least favorite. The books he enjoyed most were *Charlie and the Chocolate Factory*—he loved the humor; *The Hobbit*—for its whimsy and adventure; *The Borrowers*; and *A Wrinkle in Time*.

Rick lives in Florida with his wife, three sons, and their two dogs, Maddie and Casey. Maddie is a little dog and Casey is a big dog. But Maddie is definitely in charge! He wrote most of his novel while sitting in his car during his sons' soccer and karate practices.

www.rickyancey.com
www.facebook.com/AuthorRickYancey
@RickYancey